PRAISE FOR GHOST EMPEROR

"*Ghost Emperor* is the kind of story that reminds us why we tell stories in the first place — to wrestle with ambition, mortality, and the cost of legacy. McDaniel captures the collapse of an empire with a filmmaker's eye and a historian's precision. Every scene feels lived-in, every choice haunted by consequence. It's a masterpiece of scope and restraint — intimate and immense all at once."

—**JUDD PAYNE**, President of Intelligent Design Agency (IDEA);
Film and Television Producer at The Hideaway Entertainment
(*Cherry, Bernie, Mile 22, Southland Tales*)

"*Ghost Emperor* reads like an excavation of memory and power — a story that feels both ancient and unnervingly modern. McDaniel doesn't just reconstruct history; he animates it with the precision of a filmmaker and the soul of a philosopher. The world and story ecologies he builds are vivid, brutal, and beautiful — a mirror held up to every age that rises and falls on ambition."

— **OLIVIER PRON,** Award-winning Visual Futurist,
Concept Artist, and Art Director.
(*Doctor Strange, Jupiter Ascending, Harry Potter, Guardians of the Galaxy*)

GHOST EMPEROR

SCAN THE QR CODE BELOW TO JOIN THE SUBSTACK
FOR *GHOST EMPEROR* AND THE *ASHES OF EMPIRE* SAGA.YOU'LL
GET ACCESS TO EARLY CHAPTERS OF SEQUELS, BEHIND-THE-SCENES
RESEARCH, MAPS, AUDIO DROPS, AND RELEASE UPDATES.

YOU'LL ALSO GET EARLY ACCESS TO EVERY NEW
PREMIUM PULP FICTION TITLE.

NO SPAM. UNSUBSCRIBE ANYTIME.

IF THE CODE WON'T SCAN, PLEASE VISIT:
WWW.CITIZENONE.WORLD/PREMIUMPULP

GHOST EMPEROR

VOLUME ONE IN THE EPIC SAGA

ASHES OF EMPIRE

BY

DOUGLAS STUART MCDANIEL

This is a work of historical fiction grounded in extensive research. While inspired by real events, places, and historical figures, the narrative reimagines them through the author's interpretation. Timelines have been compressed, details adjusted, and dialogue recreated to serve the integrity of the story. Some names, identifying features, and locations have been altered to enhance the narrative and deepen the worldbuilding. Unusually for a novel, an appendix and bibliography are included for readers who wish to explore the historical record behind the fiction.

Premium Pulp Fiction Books
www.citizenone.world

SAVANNAH | OCEAN SPRINGS | BARCELONA

This work is being published and distributed under the Premium Pulp Fiction imprint.

For ordering information or special discounts for bulk purchases, please contact Premium Pulp Fiction at: 1305 Barnard St #805 Savannah, GA 31401-6746.

Cover design and interior composition by Premium Pulp Fiction with creative direction by the author.

Publisher's Cataloging-in-Publication data is available.

Print ISBN: 979-8-9935850-0-0

eBook ISBN: 979-8-9935850-1-7

Printed in the United States of America on acid-free paper

25 26 27 28 29 30 31 32   10 9 8 7 6 5 4 3 2 1

First Edition

AUTHOR'S NOTE

I first imagined this novel while wandering the scorched sandstone canyons of Wadi Rum in the Hashemite Kingdom of Jordan, where films like *Rogue One: A Star Wars Story, Dune,* and *Lawrence of Arabia* were shot. That spark deepened as I toured the carved silences of the ancient Nabataean city of Petra, a central character in *Indiana Jones and the Last Crusade* (1989). My story ecologies thickened amid the wind-hewn tombs of Mada'in Salih, or Hegra, near Al-Ula in northwestern Saudi Arabia.

In these remote desert regions—beneath red cliffs and stone-cut Nabataean tombs—I learned of half-forgotten Greek campaigns: brutal encounters not long after Alexander the Great's death, when the empire he built began to rot from within. There, amid myth-soaked landscapes, the outlines of *Ashes of Empire* began to form.

Few have heard these stories: the Greek general Antigonus I and his son Demetrius launched an invasion into Nabataean territory around 312 BCE, hoping to seize the spice routes and dominate Arabia's frontier. What they found instead was resistance. The Nabataeans, masters of desert warfare, met them with eight thousand camel cavalry—an act of tactical brilliance that shattered the Greek columns in the rock-cut passes near Sela. Dozens of officers were killed, entire regiments lost to ambush, thirst, and hubris.

It was an omen—one of many foretelling the chaos to come. That obscure footnote lit the spark for *Ashes of Empire: Volume One, Ghost Emperor.*

I wanted to write something no one else had attempted: a prestige historical epic that treated the Wars of the Diadochi as myth-soaked political horror—a dark inheritance where the body of a god becomes the crown, and every loyalty hides a blade.

Think *Game of Thrones*—but without dragons, because it was real. As saturated with cult, blood ritual, and fractured mythology as *Vikings*, yet grounded in a moment more ruthless than any fantasy dared invent. *Succession* played out on the ruins of empire: poisoned funerals, cult assassins, cities devouring their own kings. That's the world I found in the wake of Alexander—and no one had rendered it with the visceral, cinematic weight it deserved.

So I did. What follows is history carried in blood—betrayal, ambition, grief, and spectacle. The end of one world—and the desperate invention of the next.

—The Author

For my daughter, Jolene—

You've shown me time and time again that consciousness isn't just internal—it's shared. It moves across time and space, between people, through grief, forgiveness, and personal transformation. It shapes how we show up, how we listen and respond, who we allow ourselves to become, and how we build vastly uncertain futures together.

Your presence has changed the way I see, think, and build worlds old and new. This book carries that vision forward.

Love,
Dad

CONTENTS

PROLOGUE

BEFORE THE WARS OF THE DIADOCHI, there was a funeral—of sorts. Not a quiet one. Not a sacred rite. But the beginning of something far more violent—something that would echo for generations.

Alexander, conqueror of the known western world, had died without naming an heir. No declaration. No final command. Only silence—and a body too sacred, too dangerous, too charged with prophecy to rest.

And so the question became not who would rule, but who would carry the corpse.

Perdiccas, closest to the throne, stepped forward first. With Roxana, the widow-queen, at his side, and Eumenes—Alexander's loyal secretary—he claimed the regency. He spoke of stability, of holding the empire together. But Babylon was already fracturing. The air thick with incense and ambition, the palace halls crowded with men who had once called each other brothers, now whispering and drawing up lists.

Ptolemy, ever smiling, offered his support for the funeral procession. His allegiance was spoken plainly. His intent was not. Gold moved quietly into the hands of bodyguards; the route shifted west, then south. He waited.

Olympias, the grieving mother of Alexander, far away in Epiros, lit candles in the temples and sent killers disguised as priests. She called it purification.

Others called it madness. Either way, blood answered.

And then there was Cassander—watchful, silent, calculating. Not a general, but the son of one. Raised in the shadows of power, he poisoned slowly—not just men, but memory itself. He erased loyalists, rewrote decrees, and prepared to outlive them all.

The body moved. Not toward peace, but toward Egypt.

The procession meant to honor the dead became a campaign. What should have been sacred turned brutal. Perdiccas marched south toward the Nile, determined to reclaim what had been stolen. But betrayal traveled with him.

He would not return.

When the fires died down and the dust settled, Alexander's body had vanished from the world stage—not buried, not burned, but installed—half relic, half threat—inside a new kingdom built on lies.

And still, Roxana watched and waited, her son yet unborn. Alexander's son. She had already removed her rival, already whispered stories of divinity into any ear that would listen.

The wars would go on. They would wear many masks—honor, vengeance, legacy. But it began here: with a corpse no one could bury, generals who could not grieve, and a widow who would not break.

The first betrayal was the funeral.

And the body became the crown.

PART 1

THE BODY OF THE KING

THE DEATH THAT UNMADE AN EMPIRE.

ROXANA

CHAPTER 1

THE HEART OF THE EMPIRE

BABYLON, JUNE 323 BCE. The flies came first—before the generals, before the widow, before the priests with their copper bowls and bull's blood. They came for the wet skin of a god as it cooled in the heat, crawling over nostrils, lips, and half-lidded eyes.

Alexander had been dead less than a day, and already the body was under siege. Some whispered the skin stayed warm too long. Others claimed the lips twitched once, as if about to speak.

Myth arrived first.

The Old Palace of Nebuchadnezzar II had been built for spectacle. Its walls, glazed in lapis and firebrick, still bore the striding lions of Babylon—enamel cracked but unyielding. It had echoed with god-king boasts and priestly processions, conquest lacquered into myth.

Here, empires had once paraded as divine.

Now the wind carried a stranger heat. Guards reported hissing in the corridors at night—something dry and serpentine beneath the flagstones. Not voices, just movement, a whisper like scales on stone. The corpse of the empire still radiated heat.

The throne room, once gilded with tribute from Phoenicia, Egypt, and the Levant, had dimmed beneath layers of occupation. Greek tents stitched with Macedonian sigils choked the courtyards. The Hanging Gardens slumped into war camps. Elephants shat where scribes once knelt. Even the sacred Ishtar Gate bore the scuff of iron boots and foreign tongues.

Alexander had taken Babylon without siege.

Now his body lay at its core—arranged on the lion-headed couch, limbs washed in resin, mouth filled with salt and cedar. The boy-king who broke the world had become its most contested artifact.

This was no burial. This was the opening act.

Factions whispered: Macedon, Siwa, a tomb buried somewhere in Egyptian sands. The body hadn't cooled, yet already they plotted its path. In Babylon, nothing stayed still—not even death.

The body was the last true crown. Every man and woman in that palace knew it. Soon the greatest funeral in history would ignite the next campaign. The Wars of the Diadochi would not begin on a battlefield, but here—in a city swollen with ambition and rot.

A maze of courtyards and vaulted halls, the palace stood on bricks baked from Euphrates clay and glazed in lapis, cobalt, and ash. Yellow enamel lions still bared chipped teeth along the outer wall. Columns shaped like bundled reeds rose four men high, painted with saffron and malachite, their capitals curled like lotus blooms.

Two centuries earlier, this place had belonged to a god-king who crushed Jerusalem and dreamed in ziggurats. Now it belonged to no one. Babylonian servants still swept the floors and lit the braziers, but the soul of the palace had been overwritten. Alexander had stabled his elephants in its courtyards, planted Macedonian cypress where sacred palms once stood, and ransacked the archives for omens and rebel names.

Now the empire's lion lay dead inside its lion-hearted walls. His body rested on a lion-headed couch. Naked, as was ritual—but nothing else followed the old rites. Guards paced behind bronze-framed drapes, kopides drawn. Persian elders whispered in Aramaic at the base of the platform. Horses stamped restlessly in the courtyard. No incense burned. No priests invoked the dead.

This chamber had become a vault of silence.

Once, this was where priests read dreams aloud to trembling kings. Now the plaster peeled, gilt flaked, and reed mats covered cracked marble. Flies nested in forgotten censers. The air reeked of conquest gone stagnant.

Alexander's body, framed by murals of Ishtar and Marduk locked in embrace, looked smaller beneath the weight of stillness. Even the gods on the walls seemed weary of it all.

Roxana stood at the threshold, hands stained with myrrh and ash. Slim, dark-haired, wolf-eyed—she had once moved like an omen. Her voice was cooled wine. Now her frame had rounded with pregnancy, once heralded as prophecy, now treated as provocation.

She hadn't changed since the hour he died. Her Indo-Bactrian silk dress, storm-colored and soaked with heat, clung like parchment.

"He saw the child in a dream," she said, her voice carrying into the chamber. "A lion cub, gold-maned and blood-mouthed, nursing from the sun. It will be a boy. He will be king."

It wasn't a request. It was a warning.

Perdiccas stood closest to the body—towering, broad, a Thracian jaw shaped by campaigns, carved from bronze. No helmet, no crest. Just the red scarf Alexander had given him at Arbela, now sun-faded and browning at the edges.

He had shown no tears. He had folded his grief into silence.

"You speak of crowns," he said quietly, "while every sword here still searches for its master."

Roxana turned her head—slowly, like a wheel of fate shifting. "Then pick one up."

His mouth twitched. A flicker. She had chosen him—or believed she had. That might prove useful.

The air thickened: spoiled blood, burnt oils, judgment disguised as summer. Babylon's heat didn't scorch. It fermented. Sandals slapped stone. Parchment rustled.

Eumenes entered—pale and breathless, fine-boned, fingers stained with ink, wrapped in a scholar's belt and a frayed Macedonian chlamys. The last loyalist with a pen.

"There will be a council," he said. "Tonight."

"Let them gather," Perdiccas replied. "They don't choose."

Eumenes pressed his lips together—silence measured like a physician's pulse.

"They think they do," he said.

He didn't need to say more. Perdiccas had seen it—the doubt behind his eyes, the belief in the unborn child. That belief made him valuable—or volatile.

Outside, the palace began to hum—too many voices, too much heat.

The warlords had arrived.

Antigonus, with oaken limbs and an oil-black beard, moved like a siege tower. His missing eye, replaced with a marble orb beneath a leather patch, gave him the look of a maimed god. He spoke for the old Macedonian guard— Philip's iron men, uninterested in sharing what they bled to build.

Seleucus followed, narrow as a spearhead, his eyes already mapping the division of continents. A commander of the Shield-Bearers and former satrap of Babylon, he wielded numbers like blades—temple inventories, grain flows, marching orders. He didn't crave a throne; he sought a blueprint—with his name etched across it.

Nearchus, bronzed and perfumed, drifted between them—a naval poet, more coral than steel. He carried sea myths like weapons: omens in foam, monsters in delta tides. He wore stories like armor and gold rings like badges. His charm could steer a room, but his soldiers numbered fewer than the rumors.

And behind them, silent as mildew—Cassander.

Pale. Cold. The son of Antipater. Raised on scrolls, trained in poison and protocol. Where others ruled by command, he ruled by removal. His skin never colored in sun. His meals were taken alone. His voice never rose. Rumors clung to him like perfume—of eunuchs who died in their sleep, of tablets switched in libraries, of orders written in invisible ink.

He did not arrive to mourn. He came to audit the corpse.

Roxana moved to the bier and placed her hand on Alexander's brow. It was no longer warm. Oils clung to her fingertips, mixed with sweat already congealing.

The room hushed.

"His heart didn't rupture. The gods didn't strike him," she said. "Someone did."

Eumenes looked up. Something brittle cracked behind his stare.

"Have the somatophylakes changed the watch?" Perdiccas asked.

"Ptolemy sent two officers," Eumenes said. "Claims they're here to protect the body."

Perdiccas narrowed his eyes.

Ptolemy—smooth-faced, honey-voiced, laughing at things that should have silenced him. He had drunk beside Alexander on the Indus. Now he sent proxies with flattery and claims.

He didn't need an army. Just timing—and a cart strong enough to carry godflesh.

Perdiccas touched the red scarf at his wrist. The fabric had thinned. Memory frayed faster than blood.

"Triple the watch," he said. "Get the names of every man Ptolemy sent. If one of them breathes wrong, bury his tongue in the bricks."

Eumenes nodded and disappeared into the corridor.

Perdiccas stood alone for a breath, his thumb on the fraying silk. He wasn't sure if it was habit or ritual. Either way, it felt like oath.

He turned back. Roxana was still kneeling, whispering to the corpse. Her palm pressed to Alexander's chest, as if she could stop the empire from bleeding out through his ribs.

He watched her—and in the silence, allowed one cruel wish: that the child never draw breath.

Outside, dusk tore open. In the shadows, someone wrote: a priest, a scribe, a spy. One version for Macedon, another for Babylon—each a different lie.

And then, the first jackal laughed.

ALEXANDER III

CHAPTER 2

COUNCIL OF JACKALS

BABYLON, LATE JUNE 323 BCE. The Hall of the Lions had not seen mourning in centuries. Now it bore witness to something worse: ambition dressed as reverence.

The goat at Esagila had refused food. Doves flailed in temple shadows. The sun rose blood-orange over the Euphrates, as if the gods themselves had turned away from what was about to unfold.

Built by Nebuchadnezzar II to awe emissaries of distant empires, the audience hall stretched two hundred cubits long—its walls lined with marble lions carved from the same stone that adorned Persepolis. Once inlaid with lapis, their gouged eyes now stared darkly, hollow witnesses to the war council beneath them.

Alexander's generals stood beneath a ceiling of cedar and ash, the Babylonian heat collecting above them in heavy spirals of incense and sweat. The doors had been sealed at dawn. The air had not shifted since.

At the far end of the hall, beneath a velvet arch draped in imperial purple, lay the king. Shrouded. Unburied. Untouched by time, and yet claimed by it.

The body was the crown now. And no one dared to wear it.

Alexander had lingered eleven days. He did not die the death of a demigod on horseback, but as a man unmade from within. A banquet. A fever. Pain so sharp he bent double. Then silence. Some believed his mind remained clear, even as his body betrayed him—locked inside his flesh, helpless to speak.

Some claimed the corpse would never rot. That his skin stayed warm, his form untouched by decay. Later chroniclers would call it divinity.

The men in that room saw something stranger: the stillness before rot learns its name.

Theories were offered like prayers—malaria, poison, divine punishment. Each reflected more on the speaker than on the truth.

Thirty pitched battles, half a dozen attempts on his life, deserts crossed, rivers nearly drowned in. Arrows to the chest. Fever won where iron failed.

And yet, even fever didn't come fast. It crept. A few days after the feast, his skin flamed. His gut twisted. His hands shook. Then his voice fell to whispers and vanished.

He lay silent in the palace built by a man whose name still burned on bricks: Nebuchadnezzar. A king who once claimed to dream through lions' eyes and command angels with fire. Now his palace held a man mistaken for a god.

The walls remembered: lapis chipped by Persian chisels, cedar beams blackened by conquest. Nebuchadnezzar had ruled Babylon with brutality and grandeur—burning cities, planting gardens, branding his name into ziggurats and sky. He would not have allowed this.

But the palace had changed. It was now a trap. A tribunal. A tomb in waiting.

Every echo came back sharper. Even the silence cut.

Nebuchadnezzar would have laughed at the Macedonian—a foreigner, young and burning with borrowed myth. He would have warned the generals gathered here: visions are not inherited; they are remade or lost.

And still they gathered—a priesthood without faith—staring not at the dead man but at what remained: the map, the seal, the body.

Too sacred to burn. Too dangerous to bury. Too powerful to be left in Babylon.

Some believed Alexander could still hear them. That he watched, mute and trapped, as the thing he'd built began to collapse into memory, myth, and maneuver.

They called it council. But already, it was theft.

Outside, the courtyards boiled in sunlight. The Euphrates ran thick and slow. Somewhere nearby, incense was lit again—a losing battle against the scent of imperial rot.

The gods were gone. The ghosts had learned arithmetic.

Perdiccas stood with one hand on the hilt of his kopis, the other gripping a scroll begun but never finished. No name. No seal. Just a sentence blurred in wine or blood. That single fragment, too, had become a battlefield.

Eumenes was beside him. Foreign-born, ink-stained. Loyal—but not trusted. He said little. But already, he was memorizing every word he heard.

Roxana sat near the bier, silent beneath her veil. Her body heavy with the future.

She closed her eyes and saw what Alexander had seen in fever: a lion cub, blood on its mouth, nursing from the sun.

The child would rule. Or the child would die.

Across the bier, Ptolemy turned a fig slowly in his hand, its skin softening in the heat. He was not praying. He was measuring—weight, timing, risk. Always calculating the Nile before the tides turned.

Cassander stepped forward with the poise of a man who had practiced this moment many times. "You hold a shroud," he said, voice even, "but I see a crown." He twisted the serpent ring on his finger—not out of nervous habit, but ritual. His eyes searched the faces around him, as if looking for the precise moment the old world would yield to the new. He had once watched his father fall from grace. He would not repeat the lesson.

Antigonus, broad-shouldered and iron-throated, waited until the murmurs subsided before speaking. His bronze eye patch glinted beneath the cedar beams. "Partition the empire," he warned, "and you unmake it." The words hung heavy, but even he could see the fractures already spreading. There would be no center to hold.

A single fly landed on Alexander's upper lip. No one moved to brush it away. Whether out of reverence or fear, the gesture was withheld. The gods no longer dwelled here—only echoes and intentions.

Peithon arrived late, his cloak clotted with dust from Media's high roads. Nearchus leaned in to whisper, his words lost beneath the creak of sandal leather and shifting weapons. Leonnatus stood nearby, his expression a mask of fury, half lit by torchlight. Arrhidaeus, the half-brother, trembled at the edge of it all—a man born too close to the throne to be safe, and too slow-witted to wield it.

Beyond the pillars, where the sun had begun to drop behind the walls of Babylon, a thin chain of couriers moved through the crowd. They passed nothing that bore a seal or signature. No scrolls. Only coin. Agreements forged in silence and sealed in private.

This was no council. It was a quiet coup unfolding in plain sight.

When the smoke cleared and the ink dried, the verdict became fact: Perdiccas would rule as regent. Roxana and her unborn child would remain under guarded hospitality. The body of Alexander—the last true constant in the room—would be removed from Babylon under escort, its final destination yet to be named.

THE VOICE BENEATH THE SHROUD
ALEXANDER, IN HIS FINAL HOURS

They think I sleep. That I drift between fever and shadow.
But I hear them. Every whisper. Every lie.
Perdiccas prays with one hand, draws blades with the other.
Ptolemy smiles like a brother,
but he's already measuring the Nile.
Cassander—coiled, clever—has the eyes of a child who
watched his father fail and swore never to beg.
Even Roxana watches like a queen already widowed, her
hand resting where the heir might be.

Or might not.
They do not ask what I wanted.
So I will tell you.
I did not bleed into the sand to see my world
split like meat on a butcher's slab.
I did not ride through fire and ice to give satrapies to
vultures.
I wanted a son. A crown he could inherit unbroken.
Or if not, then unity—one regent, one throne, until the line
could be secured.
Not this. Never this.
The scroll was not finished. I know. But the shape of my will
was clear:
Hold the center. Keep Babylon. Keep the dream whole.
The world is not meant to be ruled in fragments.
They think I do not see them circling.
But I see.
I remember every oath sworn in the dust of Persia, in the
snows of Bactria, in the blood of India.
They swore to follow me to the ends of the earth.
And now they cannot even follow me into death.
So I listen.
Breathe what breath remains.
And wait for the one who will take my body and not betray
my name.
Let them squabble. Let them lie. Let them think me deaf.
I will rise again in legend, if not in flesh.
And when they bury me—if they ever do—
I will not be still.

STATEIRA

CHAPTER 3

THE WIDOW AND HER WOMB

THE WIFE OF A GOD WAS NOT SUPPOSED TO GRIEVE. It had been a mere eight years since Alexander was declared divine in the Egyptian tradition. At the Oracle of Siwa, in the shifting sands west of Memphis, the priests had named him pharaoh, son of Amun, cloaking a Macedonian conqueror in the skin of an Egyptian deity. From that moment in 331 BCE, divinity followed him like a dust cloud. Not just symbolic—it was strategy. Propaganda. A new kind of empire needed a new kind of ruler. One who could straddle pantheons, outlive mortality, and walk unchallenged between Babylon's ziggurats and Zeus's mountaintops.

But Roxana had not been with him in Egypt.

They were not yet married. She would not meet him for another four years, not until 327 BCE, after the brutal siege of a rock fortress in Sogdiana—the highlands of the eastern satrapies of the Achaemenid Empire, where the mountains of Central Asia knot together in snow and stone. She had been the daughter of Oxyartes, offered up in surrender. Some said Alexander married her for politics. Others said it was lust, or love, or something stranger—a moment of softness in the blood-drenched campaign eastward.

They had married in the spring, in a Persian ceremony—solemn, symbolic, and deliberate. Not Macedonian. Not Greek. There was no feast of wine and wrestling, no public acclaim from the phalanx. Instead, there were fire altars, veiled witnesses, incense and silence. The ritual followed the rites of Zoroastrian betrothal, binding not just man to woman, but conqueror to dynasty. Alexander wanted to show the eastern satraps that he was no mere invader. He meant to rule as a Persian king. To claim legitimacy not by right of conquest alone, but by blood and marriage.

The Macedonian soldiers grumbled. She was too foreign, they said. Too cunning. Too much like a queen.

But Alexander had already begun the transformation—from king of Macedon to heir of Cyrus, pharaoh of Egypt, son of Amun, Lord of Asia. Roxana, to him, was not just a bride. She was a key.

Roxana followed him from there—into India, into the monsoons, into the desert crossing that nearly broke the army. She bore no children during those years. There were miscarriages. Fevers. Whispers. But her place beside him remained.

When they returned to Persia, he took another wife—Stateira, daughter of Darius, another defeated king. It was theater. A double wedding in Susa, one for each half of the world. Roxana said nothing. She bowed. She drank. She smiled.

Alexander's affections, by then, were already scattered. There was Barsine, his Persian mistress, older and favored, who had borne him a son—Heracles—unacknowledged and exiled to Pergamon. There was Bagoas, the eunuch, beautiful and theatrical. There were men he trusted more than his wives. But above all, there had been Hephaestion.

His shadow had been with them always.

Hephaestion was not just a general. He was Alexander's mirror, his anchor, his lifelong companion—his beloved. Roxana had never seen him weep, not even when his men were dying by the hundreds in the Gedrosian desert. But when Hephaestion died in Ecbatana, something in Alexander broke. He stopped eating. He killed the doctor. He demanded temples across the empire honor Hephaestion as a divine hero. For days, the palace stank of unwashed bodies and funeral resin. Roxana had watched it all from behind a silk curtain, her own grief—quieter, sharper—pushed aside.

It had taken Hephaestion's death to teach Alexander how to mourn. And now it was Roxana's turn. But she was not permitted the luxury.

Because still, she had carried the crown. She alone had traveled with him. She had slept in his tent, learned his temper, mimicked his silences. And now she carried his child.

Not just the heir of a king, but the unborn son of a god.

And gods do not leave widows. They leave cults. Temples. Dynasties.

Roxana, caught in the hollow between blood and myth, understood this better than anyone. She had not just buried a husband—she had been sealed in his tomb. Her breath was still moving, but her fate, like his, was already hardened into marble.

That was why she knew she must act. That was why only one cup would be poisoned.

That was why she stood alone, hours later, before his body, still not embalmed, and whispered her final line.

But the end had begun long before that afternoon.

Roxana moved like smoke through the marble colonnades of the palace—watched, whispered about, obeyed. She said little. She demanded less. But her presence carried weight, the way a knife does even when unsheathed. Her belly was round now, taut with what might be an heir, or might be a grave. Her future, like the child's, was sealed in silence. No seat in council. No seal to press. No sword at her side. Only the rumor of a child and the shadow of a throne.

She had been born in the mountains, beneath cold stars—not the soft, storybook ridges of Macedon, but the jagged spine of the Hindu Kush, where the air split like glass and every breath was a blade. Her cradle had been a goatskin laid on stone. Her lullabies were wind howling through pine and war drums echoing across the passes.

In those high valleys, blood settled fast in snow. The old tribes did not crown kings; they proved them. She had seen men feast on horseflesh and drink the blood of rivals from their cupped hands while the elders watched in silence.

Women there were not soft. They were traded, hidden, praised, or broken—but never pitied. She had been taught not to cry when taken. Not to scream when bartered. Only to wait. And to remember.

Babylon called her queen. But she had come from something older than queenship. Something that wore no silk and did not beg for survival.

In Babylon, everything was softer. Perfume and petals. The laughter of eunuchs. The rustle of silks. But the game was the same. You killed, or you were forgotten.

Stateira, daughter of Darius, had arrived with her father's empire at her back. She was taller. Paler. Her Persian robes bore the gold-threaded seal of the Achaemenid line, and her belly, too, had begun to swell.

At first, there was a shared performance. She kissed Roxana on both cheeks. She brought a circlet of pearls threaded on lion-hair, a gift said to ward off envy. She poured mint sherbet for them both and praised the child forming in Roxana's womb.

"Sisters in sorrow," she had said. "And now sisters in power."

But her eyes never softened.

In the days that followed, that mask of grace began to slip—just enough to show the blade beneath. Stateira began to wear white: the color of mourning, yes, but also of divinity. She sat slightly higher on the cushions during formal gatherings. She spoke of her unborn child's noble blood, always within earshot of servants. She prayed audibly in Persian and Old Elamite—languages Roxana had never learned. She hung a small oil-lamp beside her chamber door that bore the likeness of Ahura Mazda.

But it was Stateira's sister, Drypetis, who drew the sharpest shadows.

Where Stateira moved with silk and ceremony, Drypetis was unguarded—like a blade without its sheath. She had not been wed to Alexander, and that galled her. She made no secret of it.

"She marries a mountain girl and a widow's daughter, and leaves me for the feasts?" she spat one morning, while watching Roxana from the bathhouse window. "A pretty shepherd's daughter raised on goat's milk and witch-prayers."

That line spread fast.

Roxana said nothing. She never replied to dogs.

But Drypetis's voice carried, always. Loud enough for priests, for servants, for generals' wives who whispered and watched.

"She'll name the bastard Cyrus," Drypetis sneered. "As if that'll change what's between her legs."

In the inner garden, they crossed paths again.

Stateira plucked a date from a tree and offered it to Roxana.

"It is sweet," she said. "But the seed is bitter."

Roxana took it in silence and tossed it into the fishpond.

"I prefer pomegranate," she said. "The fruit of the underworld."

The priest-mothers watched them carefully that day.

*****

Later that evening, in the weaving room, Stateira traced her hand along a bolt of Macedonian wool dyed with Tyrian purple.

"Alexander told me once that Babylon was too soft. That he would remake it in stone and fire," she said.

Roxana nodded slowly. "And yet he died here. Softened."

"Men like Alexander do not die," Stateira replied. "They become legend. The question is—who carries the story?"

Another day. Another room.

In the sunlit apodyterion beside the palace baths, Stateira arrived with two attendants and lingered long at the threshold while Roxana soaked her feet in rosewater. The air was heavy with jasmine and heat. A myrrh-scented breeze passed through the latticed window.

"The child I carry," Stateira said without preamble, "is the blood of Cyrus. Darius. Achaemenes himself."

Roxana didn't look up. "And Alexander?"

"He married me to wed an empire."

"Then perhaps it is the empire who'll raise your son."

That earned a flicker of fury, quickly masked.

"One of us will be Queen Regent," Stateira whispered. "The other will be a footnote."

"You aren't even Persian," Stateira said. "You came down from your eastern mountains barefoot, smelling of goats and blood smoke, and now you think this court belongs to you?"

Roxana smiled, slow and unblinking.

"I came down," she said, "because I was not meant to stay forgotten."

That night, Roxana watched a line of ants carry a dead beetle across her chamber floor. She made no move to stop them.

The omens multiplied.

A slave girl miscarried in the bath and bled down the drains for three days. A hawk landed on the women's roof and would not fly away. The myrrh tree dropped blossoms before the moon had turned. A harp-string snapped while Stateira sang a hymn to Anahita. One of the palace hounds drowned itself in a lily basin.

The old myths stirred again in whispers. Ereshkigal was watching.

They said the Queen of the Underworld did not speak, only waited. That she had seven gates beneath the world, and each required a sacrifice. A ring. A veil. A name. Roxana did not yet know what she would leave behind—but the first gate had opened. She could feel it. The air tasted of copper. The shadows dragged longer.

Roxana sent no reply. She waited.

That evening, Drypetis appeared in Roxana's antechamber, unannounced.

"Poison doesn't always work," she said, arms crossed. "My sister has a strong stomach. And a stronger memory."

"Then she should remember to watch her hands," Roxana said calmly, not looking up. "She's begun to shake."

Drypetis leaned in. "If she dies, you'll hang. And I'll make sure your bastard hangs with you."

"If she dies," Roxana whispered, "you'll be next."

Drypetis stepped back. Her sandals made no sound as she vanished through the curtain.

Then, on the seventh day, she wrote her invitation in cinnamon ink.

They would share sherbet beneath the myrrh trees. The sun had begun to rot the figs on the vine. The wind carried a hint of copper and damp earth.

The attendants were dismissed. A silver tray was placed between them. Two cups. Rosewater and crushed melon. Saffron for the color of joy.

They drank. Slowly. Watching one another. A game of mirrors, patience, and war.

Stateira was the first to speak.

"You think the world will kneel to a mountain girl with a bastard in her belly?" Her tone was honeyed, but there was iron underneath. "You think they will forget who my father was?"

Roxana blinked, slow. "Your father lost an empire."

"And you think you've won it?"

A pause. A breath.

"I carry the son of Amun," Roxana said, softly.

Stateira laughed. "So does every third whore in the harbor."

They drank again. The cups were nearly empty.

A bee hovered briefly over Stateira's hand, then landed on her sleeve and died there, legs twitching. She did not notice.

Roxana placed her cup on the tray and rose to her feet. Her voice was level.

"Drink deep, sister. It is a bitter world."

Only one would rise.

*****

Drypetis found her sister's body just after moonrise.

She screamed—not in grief, but fury. A long, feral sound that split the quiet of the women's quarters like a torn veil. The priest-mothers had already begun their preparations. They did not stop her.

That night, Roxana stood alone on the high terrace of the eastern wall, watching the Euphrates glitter like a vein of silver below.

"You think this ends you?" came the voice behind her.

Drypetis. Breathless. Hair wild. A blade in her fist—a thin bronze thing, half ceremonial, half madness.

"You bitch," she hissed. "You barren mountain bitch. You killed her."

Roxana did not move.

"She was carrying the true blood. And you—you carry dirt and whispers."

DRYPETIS

A pause. The sound of sandals scraping stone.

"Alexander loved her," Drypetis said. "Not you. You were just the first whore in the tent."

Roxana turned, slowly. Her eyes held no rage. Only stillness.

"Then follow her."

In a single movement, she stepped forward, caught Drypetis's wrist, and pivoted.

She screamed as she went over the parapet, arms flailing, mouth open. Her body struck stone below. The sound was not sharp. It was a wet, final thing.

Roxana watched the place where she'd fallen.

"Say nothing," she told the slave girl who had followed Drypetis there, wide-eyed and shaking.

The girl nodded.

The priestesses came for Drypetis just before dawn.

No torches. No procession. Only bare feet wrapped in lambskin, lips marked in ochre, and silence as heavy as a tomb. They did not wear the same veil as they had for Stateira. This one was thicker, older, woven from black goat's wool—the mourning cloth reserved for deaths that came too soon, or too violently.

They did not flinch at the body. They did not ask how it had fallen. One muttered a low incantation, words cracked and half-swallowed, drawn from the ziggurat rites of Ereshkigal—the goddess of sealed mouths and shadowed gates. Another pressed a dried pomegranate husk between Drypetis's lips, where coin or oil should have gone. There would be no shrine. No offerings. No name spoken aloud.

She would be buried in secret. As if she had never stood beside her sister. As if she had never spoken at all.

The priest-mothers knew what had happened. They always did.

The oldest among them—her skin seamed like bark, her presence too still to be human—waited for Roxana in the inner garden later that day. The fig trees were shedding early. Myrrh blossoms drifted on the wind, curling like ash.

She was called Enheduanna, named for a poet long turned to dust. She carried no symbols, no staff. Only a clay bowl, already filled with dark wine, which she offered without ceremony.

Roxana drank.

Enheduanna knelt beside her in the dirt, brushing her fingers through the fallen petals as if they were bones.

"Twin stars fall in opposite directions," she murmured. "But the night does not end."

Roxana said nothing. She did not blink.

"You have chosen silence," Enheduanna continued. "That is wise. The gods favor silence over cleverness. They always have."

In the soil between them, she drew a circle with one finger, then added two smaller orbs within it—three points held in quiet tension.

"One womb now holds three fates," she said. "The living. The dead. And the one still listening."

She traced a circle in the dust, then paused, her hand hovering.

"The first has been named. The second, buried. And the third"—her fingers shifted toward Roxana's belly—"must descend. There is no other way now."

Roxana said nothing, but she remembered the story: how Ishtar, goddess of love and war, stripped herself bare to enter the underworld, and how the world wilted in her absence.

Then she rose and left her alone with the dust.

*****

That evening, the wind changed. The air thickened with cinnamon smoke and the bitter sting of coal ash. On the roof of the women's quarters, a hawk circled three times—then vanished into cloud. In the garden below, the pomegranates split open on their branches, bleeding dark seeds into the soil.

The moon had already risen when Stateira's body was removed. Not in daylight. Not by servants. Not with mourning songs.

Again, the priest-mothers came—faces veiled in black linen, hair dusted with blue ash.Hours later she stood before his body. It had not yet been embalmed. Heat had begun to burgeon in the room—sour and heavy. The flies had returned.

She spoke then—not to the corpse, nor to gods, but into the pressure between grief and power. There was leverage there. She felt it press in.

But this ending had not begun today.

It had begun in whispers, in stares, in choices made behind fans and perfume.

It had begun the moment someone called her queen—and meant it with fear.

Roxana moved through the palace like a ghost through flame—unstoppable, watched. Her silence unnerved more than any proclamation. The marble halls, once built for kings, now echoed with softer sounds: rustling veils, hushed steps, rumors that multiplied like flies on a corpse.

Her body changed. Her gait slowed. She slept with one hand curled over her belly—uncertain whether she guarded life or a claim. The child was both legacy and liability. His breath—if it came—might one day ignite a throne or topple it.

She had no seat at council. No ring to press into wax. No men-at-arms sworn to her. She had only the child, and the child had no name.

The rest—the knives, the poisons, the veils—would come soon enough.

CHAPTER 4

EMBALMER'S GOSPEL

BABYLON—MORTUARY QUARTER. The corpse was still warm when the priests began to fight.

The Egyptians had arrived before dawn, their sandals powdered with fine white grit of desert travel. Two delegations arrived—one by river, the other by road—dispatched from Alexandria as soon as news reached Memphis that the king was dying. The overland group moved fast, skirting the edge of the Syro-Arabian desert and tracing the old northern passes.

Their camels bore packs of natron, resin, and linen pre-soaked in aromatic oils. The river delegation, slower, poled against the Euphrates current with crates of obsidian knives, sacks of ebony, and scrolls sealed in wax.

These were not allies. They represented rival schools—one trained in the rites of Anubis at Saqqara, the other raised in the House of Life near Heliopolis, where embalming was both sacred and surgical. Each believed they were summoned in solitude. Neither had expected to find the other.

The Saqqara priests wore ochre-dyed linen, stained with bloodroot and saffron. The hems of their robes bore embroidered jackal paws and the Eye of Horus. Their hands were tinted stained yellow from repeated anointings with myrrh. The Heliopolitan delegation carried themselves differently—their indigo sashes threaded with silver, each priest bearing the Djed pillar—symbol of Osiris—inked across the throat in temporary tattoo. Bronze idols wrapped in cedar-lined felt boxes dangled hung from their belts: Thoth in baboon form, a crocodile Sobek, Imhotep gripping a scalpel.

Nes-Serqet led them, a high lector priest with skin darkened by years in the sun and cheekbones sharp as flint. His voice carried half a dozen funerary dialects' weight. Behind him trailed a disciplined procession of scribes, assistant embalmers, and knife bearers, some robed in Saqqara ochre, others in the deep blue of Heliopolis. They moved with purpose, murmuring in hieratic verse, heads bowed not in deference, but calculation disguised as prayer.

A third figure trailed them—hooded, silent, and unnamed. He spoke to no one and lingered near the court's outer colonnade. His presence would be remembered, but never explained.

The Egyptians came prepared. They brought hooked knives of volcanic glass, clay urns of natron sealed with pitch, palm wine and date oil in amphorae, scarabs etched with funerary spells, and soot-black canopic jars carved from sycamore. Their linen bandages were resin-soaked, sun-dried strips of desert cloth. The smell arrived with them—thick with frankincense and myrrh, layered over burnt honey, coal ash, and something vaguely animal.

They entered the mortuary quarter without announcement. Their silence was not pious—it was scrutiny. They walked barefoot up the ziggurat steps and passed the soot-stained altars of Marduk without acknowledgment.

The Babylonians were already inside, seated cross-legged in layers of gauze dyed with acacia ash and crushed reed. They had prepared the chamber using the oldest rites of the land. Resin smoke spiraled from copper bowls. They invoked the *Seven—Anu, Enlil, Enki, Ninhursag, Nanna, Utu, Inanna.* Their oils pressed from Tigris seed, their sigils in lapis and hematite traced over brow and chest.

They declared that silence must be preserved: no blades, no foreign salts, no desecration of the god-body.

The Egyptians ignored them.

Then Ptolemy entered.

He pushed past the gate before the guards could raise their spears, his cloak trailing like wings, his boots crushing scattered offerings—charcoal, broken incense shells, an overturned vial of cedar oil. His hands smelled of ink and iron. His eyes did not blink.

Rumor reached him at dawn—organs bartered like coin, hearts turned in palm like gambler's tokens. Enough.

"Begin again," he said to Nes-Serqet, his voice flat and unmistakably final.

*****

The room stilled. Even the flames in the braziers seemed to falter. Ptolemy walked the perimeter of the bier like a commander inspecting a siege line. Babylonian priests glared in offense, Egyptian hands hovered over their instruments, uncertain whether they had been honored or dismissed.

"This is not a shrine," he said. "It is a vault. Treat it accordingly."

Nes-Serqet tilted his head, slow and deliberate. "We were told the general's final wishes—"

"You were told nothing," Ptolemy snapped. "Because nothing was written. There is no will, no line of succession, no decree to sanctify this work. Only this body. And until it is preserved, you answer to me."

He turned to the Babylonian priest holding a bowl of oil dusted with lapis. "You've stalled for three days over the shape of the incision. If he rots, his legacy dies with him. That's your loyalty?"

The priest offered no reply.

Ptolemy stepped back, lowered his voice, and drew it taut.

"We will do this once. We will do it correctly. And we will do it without priests tearing each other apart over the scraps of a god."

He signaled to the guard. The curtain was drawn; the inner gate sealed.

Light thinned. The room darkened.

And then they began.

The Egyptian teams laid out lacquered trays: obsidian blades, flint spatulas, copper hooks, and ceramic jars of natron salted dust. They prayed to Anubis and Osiris; they told the old story of dismemberment and divine stitching. Their voices grew louder, each word folded into motion. Hands searched for the incision site just beneath the ribcage.

The first disagreement was quiet. Then it rose, like incense, until it cracked the air.

The Babylonians insisted on seven sacred washes. The Egyptians wanted to remove the brain. They argued over the liver, over whether the spleen held memory, over whether the eyes must remain open or be sewn shut.

Most of all, they fought over the heart.

One called it the seat of the *ka*. Another claimed it recorded truth. Another swore it must be weighed. The Babylonians said it must stay inside the chest. The Egyptians argued it could not.

The body darkened at the edges. Heat rose in the chamber, dampened by Babylon's river air. The nostrils had been stuffed with honeyed reeds. The skin swelled.

Then one morning, the Babylonian high priest failed to appear.

They found him in the palace well. His mouth was filled with sand. A scorpion clung to his tongue, still alive.

*****

Perdiccas arrived within the hour. His cuirass was flecked with dried blood from a riot near the Hanging Gardens. He came with Macedonian officers, walked directly into the mortuary, and said nothing to either corpse or priest.

He looked only at Ptolemy.

"If this continues," he said, "I'll exile every one of you to the Gedrosian waste and let the vultures sort your gods."

He pointed at Nes-Serqet. "You are here by grace, not by right." Then he turned to the Babylonians. "You speak when spoken to."

His eyes lingered on the bier.

"The body is the state now. You want a war? Keep arguing."

Then he left.

The room never fully recovered its voice. The authority of the regent had been declared, but it held only as long as the body did.

Ptolemy did not raise his voice again. He remained at the edge of the chamber near a cracked amphora of myrrh where flies gathered in lazy constellations. He made notes in a codex. He asked no questions, but watched carefully. He paid attention to hands, not prayers.

He shared a cup of pomegranate wine with one of the Egyptians, spoke in Greek, walked with him through the garden beneath the oleander. He asked about sacred salts, lunar transport, and embalming under moonlight. The man answered slowly, weighing each word.

Two nights later, the priest was gone.

Some said Persians took him. Others claimed they saw him on a skiff heading west. The Babylonians blamed Ptolemy. No one could prove it.

The work continued.

*****

Eventually, the body was hardened—not dry, not lifelike—merely preserved.

The stench of death had lifted, replaced with cinnabar and smoke. The scarab on the chest bore no known language. The rituals had been blended, truncated, and silenced.

What emerged was neither Egyptian nor Babylonian. It was invention; it was an empire embalmed. They placed the corpse in a sarcophagus of red ochre and black pitch. The lid was sculpted to resemble the king's face, but the eyes looked wrong—too awake, too present.

A second coffin was ordered. It remained empty.

In the corner of the embalming room, a bronze knife stood upright in a salt bowl. It remained untouched.

A scribe from the temple of Nabu was assigned to record every detail. He tracked temperatures, noted skin shifts, measured the length of each prayer. He wrote that the air grew hotter during arguments, that candles dimmed when placed near the bier, that one morning the cinnabar coating the lips began to bubble. He told no one, except a palace servant.

Two nights after the sarcophagus was sealed, a fire consumed the scriptorium.

No bodies were found—only scorched wax and ashes of forgotten prayer. The scribe's name never appeared in temple records again.

CHAPTER 5

CASSANDER'S GAME

BABYLON—PALACE UNDERCITY. The embalming slab hadn't cooled. Its obsidian surface remained streaked with oils, blood, and a chalky rim of dried natron beneath the neckrest. Strips of linen still clung to its corners, torn by haste or grief, stiff as burned skin. The chamber reeked—clove oil soured by rot, lotus resin gone bitter in the stagnant heat. The god's scent had already curdled into something alchemical.

No rites had been closed. No hymns completed. The priests who began the ritual no longer drew breath.

Now, six shadows wheeled the sarcophagus through the tunnels beneath the palace. They moved without torches at first—blind but sure, relying on memory and the glint of wall-salt to guide them. The bier had been scavenged from an old storeroom where sacrificial bulls were once quartered. Its wheels groaned at every turn, the straps binding the lid creaking as the stone shifted.

CASSANDER

One man slipped against the incline, catching himself with a grunt. Another muttered an Aramaic prayer meant for the newly dead.

None of them looked directly at what they carried.

The sarcophagus had been sealed in haste. A resin-soaked band of linen had been burned at both ends and wound in a spiral across the lip of the lid—meant to ward off evil or mark betrayal, depending on the tradition. There was no movement inside. Of course not. And yet—

"Don't speak near it," one whispered. His voice didn't shake from fear exactly, but from something inherited—ritual passed hand to hand through generations of trench-workers and gravekeepers.

No one challenged him.

Above them, Babylon slept in the thick heat of mourning. Its courtyards sagged with dust. Processions stalled into silence. But below, in the palace undercity where cisterns echoed and rats gorged on the granaries of gods, the king's body was still in play—not for burial, but for strategy, for leverage.

Torchlight flickered every few paces, casting streaks of shadow across unfinished murals along the walls. These had been painted in haste after the astrologers misread the stars. One showed a horse with no rider. Another, a throne with no legs. The king's portrait was incomplete—just a halo of red pigment and an upraised hand whose gesture could be either benediction or warning.

The sarcophagus scraped past it.

The sound echoed—high, metallic, unnervingly delicate. No one spoke.

At one turn, the cart refused to move. The slope was too steep. The youngest handler dropped to adjust the axle-pin. When his knuckles brushed the underside of the coffin, his breath caught. He jerked backward and raised his hand.

Two fingers glistened with resin—thick, amber-colored, still tacky-warm. It should not have been warm.

Drip.

A bead of resin slid from a rear seam, struck the stone, and hardened mid-run before it could spread. No one moved. One man crossed himself. Another repeated an Egyptian invocation out of order.

Still, they continued.

As the tunnel narrowed, the ceiling lowered and the air thickened. They passed beneath a crumbling arch etched with Chaldean script and flanked by twin carvings of Namtar—the demon who records fate. Each had a silver coin jammed in its mouth and a nose deliberately chiseled off.

The lead bearer paused. "We're not alone down here."

He wasn't wrong. Babylon never buried its dead cleanly. The city had long since become its own underworld. The tunnel sealed behind them with a breath of cold air. Ahead, a stone door waited—not a tomb, but a chamber for negotiation—the place between death and inheritance.

Inside the coffin, the king was beginning to harden into myth.

✲✲✲✲✲

No new rites had been scheduled. For seven days, the bronze doors remained shut. No edict explained the delay. The eunuchs refused to stand watch. The stonemasons muttered prayers as they passed. Soon, the rumor emerged: the room hadn't been desecrated. It had been unmade.

When the seal finally broke, the air inside the chamber was thick and still. No wind had entered. The oil basins had burned to wax nubs. A basin in the center of the room stood dark with old blood, its rim crusted and cracked. The scent of lotus oil had turned sour, and resin had congealed on the walls like tree sap gone to rot.

The stele tablets—carved with the names of gods and the prayers of passage—had been gouged at the edges. Not weathered. Deliberately defaced. As if someone had tried to claw the language away.

The priests remained inside.

Their bodies lay folded, posed in grotesque imitation of their duties. Each had been embalmed in parody: tongues removed, eye sockets filled with natron, linen packed down their throats until the bellies swelled. None showed signs of struggle. There were no broken bones. No defensive wounds.

The knives were missing. The scarab seals smashed. The embalming records—painstaking logs of temperature, moisture, ingredient ratios—had been burned, then soaked, then burned again. A few blackened scroll-ends curled like desiccated spiders in the ash pit.

No animals entered. No flies. No rats. Only one person had been seen near the vault since.

He was barely a boy. Perhaps twelve. Or a eunuch, too small to be remembered. No one recalled his name. He never spoke. He arrived with a pail of limewater and a cleaning rag, trailing his feet in arcs across the polished floor.

He never looked at the bodies. Only the stone.

As he cleaned the base of the altar, his fingers struck something solid. Not bone. Not stone.

Metal.

He pried it loose—a funerary pin, gold-leafed over copper, stamped with a single pierced eye.

The Eye of Horus.

It should have been placed over the heart. Instead, someone had left it in the drain.

The boy stood—silent. Something in the air shifted. It wasn't sound; it was pressure—as if the room itself drew a breath.

He didn't flinch. He finished cleaning. And when he left, he never returned. Not even to eat.

*****

By now, Roxana's silence had become its own kind of rebellion.

The midwives spoke only in euphemism. They asked about appetite, not bleeding; about signs, not sons. The word heir was never used. It carried too much weight.

She could no longer sleep. At night, she felt her heartbeat in her belly— fast and irregular. Not the child's rhythm. Her own. Her body already knew what the court pretended not to see: that she was either carrying salvation, or the justification for her erasure.

The Oracle had known it, too.

On that last night, one of Olympias's Oracles—barefoot, teeth blackened with ash—knelt and pressed her forehead to Roxana's belly. She whispered a language no one else recognized, her breath thick with myrrh and burnt laurel.

Roxana flinched, less from fear than from memory.

She didn't ask if the words were a blessing or a curse.

The girl was gone by morning. Her bed was untouched. A braid of hair, tied in ritual fashion, lay coiled on the floor.

Since then, Roxana had kept a ritual dagger beneath her pillow. The blade was dull—ceremonial—but sharp enough to make a choice irreversible.

It wasn't for protection. It was for sovereignty.

She wouldn't be used. Not again.

She began noticing the watchers—the bath scrubber with a Macedonian accent, the food-taster who recited loyalty oaths after tasting each grape. Even her old nursemaid, once quiet, had begun to pray too loudly, too publicly.

Cassander had found a way in. Or perhaps he had never left.

She wrapped a hand over her stomach and whispered to the child.

She didn't know if the child could hear her, but she spoke anyway.

They brought the ceremonial bath at dusk—wide, shallow, rimmed with painted serpents. A rite older than Babylon itself: fennel and myrtle steeped in boiled water, meant to bless the womb and coax a safe delivery. The priests had already chanted outside the door. Eunuchs had sealed the hall. Steam drifted from the basin.

Roxana stood at the threshold, one hand on her belly. She took a single step forward.

"Don't."

The word stopped her.

Eumenes burst through the side gate, tunic soaked from rain, sword already drawn. Two Persian guards followed, pushing past the servants with the authority of those who didn't need to explain themselves.

"No one touches the water," he said. "Not until I've seen it."

He knocked the ceremonial ladle from a servant's hand and pulled a pouch from beneath his cloak. Inside were leaves—nightshade, still damp.

They had been crushed and stirred into the bath, hidden beneath laurel to mask the bitterness. Not enough to kill a grown woman instantly, but more than enough for the child. Given time, enough for both.

Roxana didn't speak.

She looked at the water, still steaming, and watched a fragment of night-shade float to the surface.

Then she turned and placed a hand over her stomach.

"He's not just watching," she said. "He's already inside the walls."

*****

They still called her Queen, but Olympias of Epiros had no throne left to sit on. Sixty now—gaunt, sharp, iron-boned—she dressed in red wool and war-cloth, her hair twisted into thick cords bound with bronze charms. Her arms were marked with inked geometry, her fingernails stained with ash. Time had taken her softness; what remained was doctrine.

The poets once whispered that she bedded snakes and birthed gods, that she had lain beneath Dionysus in a thunderstorm and screamed as crows circled the roof beams. It was myth and confession in the same breath.

Now in exile, she acted like a priestess who had stopped asking permission.

Six women rode out from her sanctuary beneath the burning moon— Oracles of Smoke, draped in violet robes, veiled and silent. Their mouths were blackened with ritual dye. Their hands bore the marks of prior assignments. Each carried a blade; each had memorized the interior of a woman's body.

Their task wasn't vengeance. It was correction—holy surgery.

In the dark, Olympias knelt at the edge of a fire, her ankles cracking beneath her weight. She held a scroll inked in blood and unreadable to anyone else. She fed it to the flame and spoke aloud: "Let only the worthy drink the future."

The Oracles mounted and rode.

Cassander didn't believe in gods. He believed in order.

Son of Antipater, raised in court shadow, mocked by Alexander himself—"a librarian's son in soldier's boots"—he had been trained to wait and to remember.

He was forty-one—pale, calculating, never armored unless image demanded it. His left hand trembled slightly. No one dared ask why. He wore it well, hiding it in scrolls or behind his back.

Cassander believed cities should run on grain, not glory; roads mattered more than relics. But he understood symbols, and he knew Alexander's corpse was still speaking—perhaps louder than the man ever had.

He heard about the priestesses crossing the orchard aqueducts outside Babylon. He didn't ask questions. He gave no orders aloud. His men already knew.

They caught the first three just before dawn.

One tried to bite down on a poison pellet. A boot shattered her jaw. The second burned. The third took longer—strangled into the dust, her heels carving lines into the clay.

The fourth and fifth scattered but never made it past the reed-beds.

The sixth was different.

She was younger, smaller. Her veil half-burned, her hands raw. She dropped to her knees without command.

Cassander studied her. She didn't tremble. Her eyes were blank—not with fear, but with the absence that comes after it. There was nothing left in her to intimidate.

"This one?" a soldier asked.

"She's harmless," Cassander said. "Let her deliver a message."

He didn't say what the message was. He didn't need to.

*****

In the deep vaults of Babylon, she was known only as Asharē.

She hadn't taken a vow of silence. The ink along her tongue had simply burned her voice down to a whisper. That was the price. She had agreed to it—and she remembered why.

Asharē entered the palace through no gate. Her name never reached a ledger. No servant recalled letting her in.

She passed through steam rooms and silent halls. A square of linen was found later on a bench, still warm, scented with lavender and fig ash. It bore the sigil of her order: a spiral within a spiral, marked in ink and oil.

Some swore she knelt beside Roxana's bed, whispered to the womb, and left only a single line: *"He will not have a father, but he will not be fatherless."*

Then she vanished.

A servant found a scrap of veil tangled in a hinge near the shrine of Ea—god of underground rivers and hidden speech. Beneath that shrine, a grate led downward. It hadn't been opened in a generation.

But it wasn't locked.

Asharē passed beneath the city barefoot, her robe trailing in the floodwater. Her breath was steady. Her eyes did not search for light; they had been trained not to.

Babylon beneath Babylon was a forgotten system of aqueducts, cisterns, drainage gates. Once it managed floods. Now it collected dust and memory. Shrines leaned in darkness. Walls wept minerals. The tiled mosaics had cracked, revealing older murals underneath—scenes no temple sanctioned, stories from before the gods had names.

Asharē walked forward—not like a pilgrim, but like someone returning to a place they had never visited in daylight.

"If the child lives," Olympias had said, "the basin will appear."

The basin appeared.

It rested in a recess of stone, rimmed with broken laurel tiles. Bronze, wide as a cradle, greened with age and warm to the touch. No guards stood nearby. There was no need; the weight of the room enforced reverence.

Etched in a near-erased script along the rim: *THE FATHERLESS SHALL RULE.*

Inside the basin floated a mixture—blood-warmed milk laced with rosemary and something metallic. A single black hair curled across the surface like a sigil.

Asharē didn't pray. She didn't speak. She lowered her head to the rim, folded her hands, and waited. Above her, Babylon breathed in sleep.

Below her, the gods remembered what they had lost.

CHAPTER 6

AN UNRELIABLE TIME TRAVELER

DELPHI, GREECE, 108 CE—PLUTARCH'S VILLA. By the second century of the common era, Delphi no longer held the authority it once commanded. The oracles had dimmed, and Rome's shadow stretched over Greece, but the place still drew pilgrims, scholars, and dreamers who wanted to stand where the gods had once spoken. The city clung to the slopes of Mount Parnassus—its marble terraces, colonnades, and staircases climbing toward the Temple of Apollo. The Pythia still gave prophecies, though they were now mostly ritualized performances, half-echoes of an older fire.

Plutarch presided over this fading light as both archon and priest. His villa stood just beyond the sacred precinct: Roman in scale, Greek in spirit. Terracotta tiles warmed in the pale winter sun. A shaded colonnade looked inward onto a fountain-fed courtyard, while his writing chamber faced east to catch the first light over the cliffs. Shelves of scrolls lined the walls. The air smelled of cedar, wax, and ink.

From his desk, Plutarch could see the olive groves of the Crisaean plain rolling toward the Gulf of Corinth, silver leaves shifting like water under the morning mist. In the evening, the light turned the ruins above into amber relics. Delphi had become a place where memory lived longer than truth, and Plutarch was its curator.

He had never seen Babylon, though his name was carved into its history. That was his first deception. He was no chronicler in the modern sense, no guardian of clean dates or verified events. He was a priest, a philosopher, and above all, a storyteller who shaped men into symbols. His *Parallel Lives* paired Greek heroes with Roman counterparts not to record but to teach, to exemplify. Facts bent willingly beneath his pen until they carried the moral he required.

Born in 46 CE in Chaeronea, Plutarch lived as a Greek under Roman rule but never surrendered his cultural allegiance. He traveled widely, spoke with emperors, and still returned to Delphi, where the gods no longer thundered but continued to murmur for those who knew how to listen. He claimed continuity for Greece in an age when Rome absorbed everything into its own myths.

And so we grant him a liberty here: we place him in Babylon more as later scribe than witness—centuries before his birth—since he would learn the echoes of this epoch even if he never heard the shouts. He did not smell the resin in Alexander's death chamber or hear the priests chanting over the body, but he understood the way ambition stalked silence. He saw how empire fractured when memory hardened into myth. He could not be trusted as a witness, which is precisely why he must serve as one here.

*****

The palace at Babylon smelled of cedar and heat. The chamber of the dead king carried both sanctity and rot, while his generals circled with parchments that looked like weapons disguised as records. Plutarch was not there. Yet in the villa at Delphi, centuries later, the scene pressed itself into his imagination until it felt more real than the stones beneath his sandals.

Delphi, by his age, was a city of echoes. The gods no longer roared; they murmured. The oracles had become rituals, closer to theater than revelation. But the stones still asked questions, and Plutarch still listened. Every scroll on his desk was a voice pulling him toward that earlier chamber in Babylon: letters from Eumenes' scribes, a decree touched by Ptolemy's hand, three conflicting tales of Meleager's death. None reliable. All necessary.

He stacked them not by date but by guilt. Babylon always lay on top. Always waiting.

The records disagreed: one had Perdiccas strangling Meleager in his sleep, another described a reconciliation feast ending in blood. Plutarch favored the feast. Marble deserved the stain. History, he believed, needed bones to carry its flesh.

At his desk, sunlight slanted harsh across the parchment—too clean, too flattening, too much like fact. He hated when ink looked factual. It needed the warmth of bitterness and cyncism.

He lit an oil lamp though it was still morning, and the words softened under flame. Truth was never clean. It only needed a spine strong enough to hold memory upright before the bones dissolved.

Plutarch was sixty-two now: thick around the middle, hair thin at the crown but still curling at the neck, barefoot with heels cracked and ink-stained. His robes were too clean for his liking, his feet too honest. He had his slave Heron move the desk when the light failed him. Heron understood ink and silence better than many scholars.

He dipped the stylus, muttered a line, scratched it down, crossed it out:

"They called it a council. It was the parceling of a corpse."

Not right. Not holy. But close enough.

The generals stood in the heat of Babylon as though already grieving, though it was certainty that had died, not their king. Perdiccas held the ring, a symbol too heavy to wear without breaking under it. His caution gave him authority, and his authority made him brittle. Meleager opposed him with the raw impatience of a soldier who loved his phalanx more than any unborn heir in a Bactrian womb. He sweated through his cuirass, scarred, blunt, furious.

His voice carried the hunger of men who wanted a king they could see, not the promise of one still carried beneath a veil.

Arrhidaeus, the half-brother, stood nearby with trembling hands, a circlet that looked like an error resting above his brow. His words were few: "I am the son of Philip." Memorized, fragile, spoken like a prayer. They hung in the air without reply.

Plutarch, bent over his lamp-lit desk, filled margins with contradictions and caveats. The absence of agreement spoke louder than any single account. He knew empire was not preserved in decrees but in the stories chosen to survive them. That was the lie that kept history alive—and the lie he himself lived by every time his stylus touched parchment.

✷✷✷✷✷

The generals had met in Babylon under heat so relentless that court-yards felt like open furnaces. The palace allowed no shadows; every stone was exposed, every gesture magnified by the sun. The king's body lay in state, priests muttering over it with the practiced rhythm of incense and delay.

At the center stood Perdiccas, shoulders squared, ring of succession glinting faintly in the haze. He carried his grief like a cuirass—polished, ceremonial, and unyielding. Oral traditions revealed that Alexander had given him the ring with his dying hand, but no one had seen it: a relic without witnesses, only rumor. He refused burial, holding the corpse in suspension, as though keeping the gods themselves from departing. The funeral cart he ordered into construction was less a bier than a monument to his own undoing.

Plutarch had admired him once, from the distance of parchment. He recognized the instinct to preserve, though he later wrote in the margin of a draft: He mistook preservation for loyalty; he feared the gods would leave him behind.

Meleager, across the chamber, radiated impatience. He was built like the phalanx he championed—broad, scarred, slow-blinking, always ready to strike. A mutiny had left one knuckle split, a badge he wore like proof of his bond with the rank and file. He sweated through his armor, fury thick in his breath. He slammed the butt of his spear on stone, the sound echoing like a challenge.

"The men are tired," he said. "They need a king. Not a regency. Not a womb."

He didn't need to name her. The word hung long enough to make Roxana present without being spoken.

Arrhidaeus stood between them, Alexander's half-brother, shoulders heavy but spine bent, as if already defeated by the crown he did not wear. His face sagged unevenly; his eyes wandered; his hands shook against the table's edge. The circlet on his brow looked like a mistake placed there in haste. When he spoke, the words were memorized, stripped of conviction:

"I am the son of Philip."

No one replied.

In Delphi, Plutarch paused, stylus hovering. He struggled again with sources refusing to agree: *was* Meleager strangled in his sleep, or was a variant of the feast account more likely, this one ending in a pit of spears? He circled the second account. History needed spectacle, or it dissolved into dust.

And then there was Roxana. Veiled, confined, yet unignorable. She had already erased one rival, whether by poison or suffocation no one cared to distinguish. Her body now bore the future like a sealed verdict, the unborn child dictating the pace of empire. The generals never named her, fearing that the syllables themselves might grant her power.

Plutarch respected her from afar—not for strategies but for patience, an endurance sharper than ambition. He imagined the silence in that chamber when the arguments fell away: flies buzzing faintly above linen wrappings, men shifting their weight, no one daring to speak the queen's name.

In the margin of his scroll he wrote, in the small hand of a priest who doubted but never stopped recording:

The first woman erased from empire was still breathing.

*****

Antigonus entered the record like a siege tower rolling across a plain. One eye lost to a Persian javelin, skull bald and gleaming, his face carved into ridges of campaign-worn scorn. He moved with the certainty of geography—slow, deliberate, impossible to ignore. His voice was gravel, pitched low, as if the dust of demolished walls still clung to his throat. There was no beauty in him, only gravity.

He did not pray. He did not pretend to. If Alexander had been a god, Antigonus was the thunder that came after the storm. He had no reverence for the body swaddled in linen, no time for the incense clouding the chamber. What he wanted was weight—territory, soldiers, taxes. Things to crush beneath his heel until they formed the outline of empire.

Plutarch softened him, even when the author knew better. On the scrolls he made Antigonus logical, purposeful, a counterweight to Eumenes. In the draft margins, though, the harsher sentence survived: He believed in silence, and he made corpses of those who broke it. He crossed it out, then kept reading anyway, because even the ink resisted letting it go.

Demetrius was his father's mirror turned inside out. Where Antigonus lumbered like stone, Demetrius blazed like fire—Besieger, Dazzler, Alexander's echo in silk and bronze. He wrapped a lion skin across his shoulder, carried flute-girls on each arm, and fought as though war were theater staged for his own reflection. His hair fell gold across his brow; his smile disarmed more cities than his cavalry; and still the archives burned behind him. He promised freedom, feasts, crowns—then left only smoke.

Plutarch loved writing him, though he distrusted his own fondness. Sometimes he thought of Paris, vain and doomed; other times of Nero, strumming as Rome collapsed. He left one line intact because Athens applauded it: He was loved by women, by soldiers, by statues—though not by gods.

Back in Delphi, the priest's lamp guttered as he lingered over Demetrius. Lust, admiration, envy—he wasn't sure which bled into the ink. In the published draft he would call Demetrius "divine and disappointing," then pretend in a long paragraph the words were praise.

The partition that followed looked clean enough on parchment: Perdiccas confirmed as regent; Arrhidaeus propped up until Roxana's child was born; Ptolemy in Egypt; Antipater in Macedon; Seleucus and Peithon pushed to the edges. It read like order, but it smelled like delay and rot—Alexander himself the rot, two years preserved in oils, too sacred to bury, too dangerous to move.

Priests whispered omens. Birds refused to nest. A goat spat grain back onto the altar. Doves beat themselves to death against the temple walls. The cart under construction became less a vehicle than a shrine: gold curling under the sun, wheels tall enough to crush oxen. Perdiccas called it a procession. Plutarch called it a coronation for a man already undone.

He wrote Perdiccas as villain, then softened, then sharpened again—not from indecision, but because the man left only absences, no wounds to trace, no words worth saving. History punishes those who end their sentences too early.

Antigonus remained another problem. Plutarch once wrote, then cut, that the man governed like stone: immovable, unshakable, but increasingly cracked. Instead he let blank space carry meaning. Antigonus was the only figure who made him afraid of being remembered.

Demetrius, the beautiful ruin, was coming easier—Alexander's shadow blurred through siege towers and wine. The only one who made Plutarch feel: desire, pity, the ache of wasted design. He adored him too much, maybe. But he could not look away.

Eumenes stood apart—the scribe who believed in ghosts. Ink beneath his fingernails, scrolls strapped to his saddle, every debt and oath catalogued. A Greek among Macedonians, serving a corpse as if it still breathed. To him, Alexander was continuity, civilization, the last unrotted thing worth guarding. That made him noble—and dangerous.

Plutarch saw too much of himself there: a man who wrote what he could not control, serving a phantom he never dared question. He gave Eumenes the gentlest chapter, then buried the truth under ellipses. In the private draft he wrote: He died because he served a dead man better than the living served themselves. He copied the line three times, then struck it out. Too honest. Too modern. Too much like a mirror.

*****

There were no raised voices when Ptolemy moved. He had no taste for theater. Power, to him, was an anatomy lesson—an embalmer's art: cut where the flesh allows, stitch where it must hold, wait until the body cools before declaring it finished. In Babylon, he kept to the edges, speaking little, eyes measuring the others as though time itself would deliver his opportunity.

He never expected to inherit the empire, and he never begged for it. His plan was cleaner: take Egypt, take the corpse, and let memory do the rest. Ptolemy understood symbols. He didn't care for the mythology that gilded Alexander; he cared for the body itself—the smell of sanctity clinging to linen, the procession that would write his authority onto stone. Later, he would call himself guardian, not thief. That was the trick—the lie told often enough to feel like piety.

At Delphi, Plutarch weighed his words carefully. Ptolemy had likely commissioned his own history—perhaps even written it himself, aided by scribes and editors. He massaged the scrolls into permanence, myth burnished into fact. To challenge them was dangerous. Still, in the margin, Plutarch tried two sentences:

Ptolemy preserved the body so no one else could use it.
The distinction was everything.

*****

In Plutarch's notes, Antipater was never in Babylon. He didn't need to be. He sent letters from Macedon—short, commanding, stripped of decoration. While Perdiccas gilded his regency with silk and delay, Antipater simply ruled. He respected Alexander as one respects a storm: endured it, measured it, then waited for it to pass.

He was built for structure, not spectacle. He trusted spear more than altar. His authority rested not in incense but in pragmatism. In Macedon, he secured power through family and oath, building a dynasty while the younger men drowned in ambition. His son Cassander would finish what he began, though without the father's restraint.

Cassander came late, but the rot was early. Ice in his blood, calculation in every move, he waited until exhaustion hollowed the others. Then he struck in silence, erasing the future not with armies but with quiet murder: Roxana, the boy. Not a battlefield, not a proclamation—just a cellar, a knife, no witnesses.

Plutarch hated him, not for cruelty but for precision. Cruelty at least acknowledged passion. Precision left only inevitability. In one draft he wrote:

Cassander didn't kill the legacy of Alexander; he erased the footnotes. He left that one untouched.

He called Antipater once *"the last sensible man in a room of ghosts."* He let it stand in the published text, though in private he judged even that too generous. Antipater wanted silence more than order—a world where questions died before they could be asked.

Seleucus left hardly a trace in Babylon. He did not posture, did not stake loud claims. First a cavalry commander, then a minor functionary, he stood just close enough to the fire to feel its heat, never close enough to be consumed. When Perdiccas faltered, Seleucus stepped aside at the right moment. When the corpse was stolen, he said nothing. When the satrapies were divided, he accepted the scraps and waited.

He rose not by blood or charm but by patience. He survived long enough for survival to become strategy. City by city, eastward beyond Alexander's reach, he stitched together an empire that surprised everyone—perhaps even himself.

Plutarch struggled with him. There was no signature gesture, no lover, no betrayal to dramatize. Just endurance—steel wrapped in linen. In the end he allowed himself a single clean sentence:

Seleucus survived not because he believed in anything, but because he knew belief was a liability.

That line he did not cross out.

*****

And then there was Peithon: a name offered in the partition like a consolation prize. Media became his—reward or punishment depending on how much rebellion a man could endure. He tried to govern, tried to be more than the figure scribbled after a comma in decrees. But structure did not breed loyalty; the soldiers meant to hold his satrapy together unraveled it within a year. By the next, they turned on him.

Plutarch barely spared him space in *Parallel Lives*: a sentence, a footnote, less than the dust of memory. Only in private notes did he allow sharper clarity: Peithon didn't lose the empire; he borrowed it from men who knew how to steal better. Some men shaped history. Others faded into names you struggled to pronounce.

The map that followed was written like a will but read like an autopsy. They did not divide the empire; they carved it limb from limb—each satrapy inked across a body still warm with Alexander's myth, still fragrant with oil and resin. No one walked away with what he wanted. Borders shifted, corpses were claimed, oaths signed in smoke. Some gained nothing and still managed to lose more than the rest.

The parchment crackled with signatures that would soon sour into accusations. Promises tasted false even before the ink dried. There was no stability here—only gambits in the costume of honors: a regency without a center, a funeral without a grave, a child unborn, a body embalmed into paralysis. For a moment it resembled peace. Plutarch knew better. He had seen enough scrolls to know the difference between agreement and delay.

He wrote partition once, then crossed it out. In the margin he tried again: *The empire did not shatter at once; it remembered how to break slowly.* He paused, scratched it darker, slower, as if repetition might make it less true.

This was only the beginning. Every territory carried a motive. Every name carried a death sentence. The parchment preserved the shape of empire, but none of its breath. He did not call it a partition. He called it an exhumation.

His hand trembled. He hadn't meant to write any of this. His task had been to record logistics—the decrees, the names, the divisions etched on goathide. Instead he kept circling the men who survived Alexander only to imitate divinity in their own brittle forms.

Wounded. Radiant. False. He dipped his stylus again, wrote a line he almost believed: *They didn't divide an empire; they sliced up a corpse.* He stared at it. Then struck it out. Too close.

That sentence would wait for another time, perhaps for the *Lives*, where truth could wear the mask of moral lesson. Perhaps another writer of another age. All of Alexander's generals would fall; the scrolls whispered their ends. But he had yet to find the phrase that made those endings feel like justice.

CHAPTER 7

THE PRICE OF BURIAL

ROYAL STABLES AND THE SATRAPAL ROADS BEYOND BABYLON.
To bury a god, one must first build a god's cart. Perdiccas stood in the sweltering gloom of the royal stables, arms folded across his sweat-dark tunic, watching craftsmen labor through sweat and muttered prayers. Torches spat resin. The air was heavy with dust, iron filings, and smoke. A hinge slipped from the blacksmith's grip and skittered across the stones like an insect—an accident, or an omen.

"You call that a lion?" Perdiccas barked, striking the carved axle. "The snout looks like a goat's arse. Start again."

The artisan bowed once and returned to his bench, knuckles white. No one intervened. No one ever did—not since Perdiccas had flogged the last man for choosing the wrong timber. This was no cart. It was a shrine forged as a declaration of power.

Three treasuries fed its making: wheels of cedar and marble, hammered inlays of gold, a canopy dyed indigo and embroidered with constellations marking the night of Alexander's birth. Sixty oxen waited in bronze trappings, horns capped, hides painted with stars. They stank of barley mash and camphor oil. Even the flies hesitated.

In the far corner, Eumenes found Perdiccas bent over a whetstone, sharpening his dagger. The rasp carried through the chamber.

"You're building him like a god," Eumenes said.

Perdiccas did not look up. "Because burying a man may not be enough."

"Enough for whom?"

"The men. The world. The silence in my own mouth."

"Alexander didn't want worship," Eumenes said. "He wanted control."

Perdiccas's hand slowed. "Same thing, in the end. What he wanted, and what the world wants now—that is the gap I'm closing with this cart. The gods won't close it for us."

A boy lingered at the threshold: Menon, apprentice cartwright. His master had vanished two nights before.

"You'll speak to the foreman," Perdiccas told him without turning.

"There is no foreman," Menon replied.

"Then you are."

"I'll finish it. But I don't want coin."

Perdiccas studied him—young, pale, smudged with ash. "What then?"

"No name on the wheels. Let it be yours. Or no one's."

The general's mouth tightened. "You'll have neither coin nor legacy, only silence."

"Silence is better," the boy said, "than being cursed in three languages."

*****

For two years, the corpse waited—preserved in honey and resin; guarded by superstition; argued over in council; passed like a curse among generals too proud to yield and too fearful to strike. Threats rose. Oaths broke. Rumors spread. Still the body did not move.

And then, one night without ceremony, the cart was finished. It had consumed treasure, stalled the succession, and turned a corpse into a shrine. The cost was not just in gold, but in time and in myth.

Torchlight revealed it: a rolling temple—three tons of cedar and bronze crowned with Tyrian purple silk stitched with constellations in lapis. Each wheel bore the sigil of Zeus-Ammon flanked by roaring lions. Axles greased with ox fat and incense. It reeked of conquest—sweet, charred, holy—and wrong.

At dawn, they rolled it toward the Temple Road. The paving cracked beneath its weight, startling pigeons into flight. Sixty oxen strained against their yokes, hides painted with stars, nostrils steaming like war-horns.

Spectators gathered on balconies: soldiers in dulled cuirasses, merchants clutching baskets, priests whispering invocations too faint to bind. One priest, hollow-eyed, watched the oxen lurch.

"No god asks to be carted across desert roads like meat," he murmured.

Peithon sneered. "Then perhaps he was never a god."

Perdiccas turned, his hand on the hilt of his sword. "He is whatever the world refuses to bury."

The first wheel groaned forward, crushing a black beetle under its rim. A soldier muttered a charm. Another spat. The priest whispered once more: "Then may your god rot in silence."

They reached Susa. The fortress gates stood sealed, rebuilt atop the ruins of Darius's palace. No royal standard flew. On the wall stood Artavazd, Median-born, oxblood cloak embroidered with suns and peacocks. Archers waited behind him.

"By what right do you pass?" he called down.

Seleucus lifted the baton of command. "By order of the Regent."

Artavazd laughed. "We answer no regents. Only kings."

His father had bent the knee to Alexander. Artavazd inherited the memory, not the fear.

Perdiccas spoke calmly to Leonnatus: "Send word to Ptolemy. Tell him the body remains mine. Tell him I will see it to Macedon—or see the road buried in ash."

Leonnatus hesitated. "That will provoke him."

"He needs provoking."

For Ptolemy was already moving, whispering to the garrisons of Egypt, promising them gold, land, protection. Word spread that he meant to intercept the cart and claim Alexander for Memphis—for Osiris, not Macedon. Whoever buried Alexander would inherit him. That was the truth all men feared.

*****

That night, the officers gathered beneath a toppled obelisk. Artavazd was dragged into the firelight, beaten but proud.

"There is no king," he said. "Only a corpse and a crown without a head."

Perdiccas held up a letter, intercepted from Ptolemy:

> *The gods no longer march beneath your banners. They wait*
> *on the Nile, where bodies are not dragged across dust but*
> *sanctified. You chase Alexander's shadow. I will give him*
> *form. He will live, eternally entombed in Egypt.*

Perdiccas let the scroll fall into the dust. "He was son of ambition," he said. "That is the only father that counts."

Artavazd smiled through blood. "You don't want to bury him. You want him to walk again. When he will not, you'll dress the corpse, call it a god, and pray we forget the man."

Perdiccas's blade answered. One stroke. Blood on cracked stone. A silence no prayer could break.

Menon, standing near the cart, whispered: "You killed the road."

Later, the officers drank in silence. Eumenes murmured: "There was no trial."

"No time," Leonnatus said.

"No patience," Seleucus added.

Perdiccas stood apart, eyes hollow. "Do you think I ever wanted to bury him? I begged the gods to keep him. Still, he died. I'm not carrying him to Macedon. I'm dragging him through my sleep."

That night, Perdiccas dreamed.

The cart stood under a blank sky. The oxen were statues of salt. The wheels spun without hands. Alexander sat up—his eyes river-stone gray.

"You think you can carry me?" he asked. *"You think you know where I belong? You return yourself, not me. I am only your excuse."*

The wheels shrieked. The lions wept bronze tears. Alexander rose. *"Every man who carries me dies. That is the myth."*

Perdiccas woke choking, the cart outside softly creaking though the oxen slept.

*****

By morning, the oxen refused their feed. One collapsed. Another split its yoke. Priests muttered that the gods would not bless what was not truly dead.

Perdiccas ordered incense, gold, wine—every god's name he could summon. Nothing moved.

The cart waited at the gate, a mausoleum on wheels. Dust dulled the lions. Flies swarmed. Menon polished the wheels again, whispering: "When a god dies, the world fractures. But when a man pretends to be one—we fracture instead."

On the third day, the wind turned green with storm. The oxen stamped in unison, leaning into their yokes as if pulled by an unseen hand. The cart groaned forward—no triumph, only compulsion, as though dragged from the underworld.

Perdiccas walked at its head. Behind him, where the obelisk shadowed the plaza, a figure stood. Not man, not ghost, not king. Just watching.

Alexander. Still unconvinced.

The cart moved on.

PART II

THE WARS OF SILENCE

LOYALTY, BETRAYAL, AND PROPHECY GRIND
AGAINST EACH OTHER IN THE DUST OF
BABYLON.

CHAPTER 8

THE TEMPLE OF ASH

RUINS OF THE TEMPLE OF MARDUK, BABYLON. Cassander removed his sandals at the temple gate without any priest asking him or inscription requiring it. But this place—blackened by siege, heavy with ghosts, and sodden with the memory of gods—demanded bare feet.

He wanted them to see it: the defiance, the contempt. Yet beneath that, curiosity lingered.

He had never believed in Babylon's gods, nor fully in his own. Still, ruins like this carried a gravity that pressed even the most disciplined soul to silence.

It had been fifteen days since they left Babylon. Time no longer measured itself in stars or miles but in sweat and silence. Cassander had never been at ease with ghosts.

The soot clung to his soles. Warm, granular. Profane.

He looked up. A century ago, the ziggurat had pierced the clouds—axis mundi, the pillar where heaven touched earth. Now it sagged like a burnt tongue. The staircase had imploded inward. The altar lay in shards. The roof bowed like a ribcage of cracked bone—a god's body hollowed and eaten from within.

Still, the faithful lingered.

Figures moved behind fractured colonnades, robes the shade of dried blood or sun-bleached saffron. They watched him: lean, silent, half-starved. Survivors, but more than that—remnants of a principle: that once, the world had symmetry.

Cassander pitied them briefly, then let the feeling burn off like fog.

He walked forward, alone but never unarmed. His posture, his gaze, and the rumors stitched to his name were weapons enough. The priests had nothing left but memory—and madness.

And both could be bent to purpose.

He was thirty-four, the son of Antipater, regent of Macedon while Alexander carved his empire abroad. His father had watched Alexander absorb all glory, treating the homeland as an afterthought. That resentment—political, personal, generational—was grafted into Cassander's bones. He had grown up watching Macedon drained of its sons while Alexander wrote himself into myth.

Cassander's allegiance was not to a man or to a dream. It was to soil and strategy. He had been trained in courts where boys learned to whisper poison and smile while doing it. He had served under Alexander—briefly—and never forgiven him. He had watched his father's letters go unread. Watched Athens pawn its civic soul to fund campaigns no soldier returned from. Watched conquest turned into ritual and sacrifice into theater.

His enemies were many: Perdiccas, the regent; Ptolemy, the embalmer; Seleucus, the tactician without a throne. His allies were temporary—Antigonus One-Eye, for now. Eurydice, if she could be steered. Cassander believed not in alliances, only in timing.

Where Alexander blurred borders, Cassander intended to prune them back. He distrusted Alexander's eastern turn—the robes, the titles, the Persian marriages. He called it costume, blasphemy, betrayal. He saw not cosmopolitanism but contamination.

He came to Babylon not to barter with the gods but to annex their shadows. He understood that power lived where myth and memory converged. Whoever claimed the corpse claimed the story. But his aim was not to honor the myth. It was to cauterize it. He would not inherit Alexander's dream. He would gut it—quietly, precisely.

"History doesn't remember ruin," he told Menon. "It remembers the replacement."

His loathing of Alexander had ossified into vision. Roxana and her son were dynastic spores to be burned from the soil. Alexander's divinity was a contagion. Cassander would vaccinate the future against it.

If people feared omens, he would manufacture them.

If they whispered prophecy, he would rewrite their prayers.

If they feared silence, he would teach them to dread his voice.

And if the gods still spoke, he would outtalk them.

He stepped into the ashen nave. Memory ambushed him—another temple, Delphi, boyhood, a goat that refused to cross the threshold. His tutor had called it an omen. Cassander had laughed and kicked the animal aside. He regretted it—not from pity, but because the goat had hesitated for a reason he never learned.

This temple hesitated too. Held its breath.

Cassander let the silence gather around him. The ochre-robed men watched. A bell fractured under its own rust.

He kept walking. The empire was a carcass. Faith was inventory. If the old gods would not return, Cassander would mint new ones—ones that answered to him.

High in the rafters, a boy watched. His left eye swollen shut, fingers raw from carrying flame bowls. He made no sound. The soldiers hadn't seen him. Nor had the man walking barefoot through consecrated ash.

The boy had heard the whispers: this Macedonian was not a conqueror but a censor. Not here to loot, but to erase. And looking down, the boy believed it.

The priests called themselves the Keepers of the Ash.

Once they had been dozens—scribes, augurs, dream-interpreters. Now seven remained. Only three still spoke. The rest drifted like shadows, some lips sewn shut, some fasting into silence. Their ochre robes were stitched from veils and shrouds stolen from the dead.

Their leader was once En-Mazru, who had sat beside kings, read comets for Darius, and kept Babylon's calendar aligned with the stars. Now his stars had died. His knowledge—eclipse intervals, solstice arcs, planetary motions— had collapsed with the empire. The temple no longer marked time. Faith had burned down to ignorance.

En-Mazru's skin was cracked parchment, his cataracts milky as stone, yet vision flickered beneath. His words slipped into an Akkadian so ancient even the priests struggled to follow. His dreams, they said, always ended in fire.

*****

Cassander's arrival was not announced. But En-Mazru already knew.

The old man knelt before the shattered altar, smoke curling like a warning. His voice rasped: "The mouthless king comes. Dust in his wake. Hunger in his hands."

Cassander didn't blink. He waited. Then:

"You know who I am."

En-Mazru lifted his clouded eyes.

"You are Antipater's son. The one who does not kneel."

Cassander smiled thinly. "Kneeling is for the dead."

The priest laughed like breaking coal.

"Then you must be here to bury something."

Cassander laid out gold—thin obols stamped with Herakles, bearing Alexander's name. A lie hammered in silver. He scattered them across the scorched altar.

"For restoration," he said. "Rebuild the gate. Scrub the soot. Call back the gods."

En-Mazru murmured, toneless: "They always return hungrier the second time."

That night, the priests gathered. They brought out relics from vaults below: charred tablets, fractured charts, star calendars etched in copper. They placed them on a scorched cloth once used to dress a god. The smell of old metal and burnt linen thickened the air.

En-Mazru spoke: *"The mouthless king shall rule through silence. The serpent sleeps beneath the throne."*

Cassander touched the tablets. Dust flaked away. His eyes narrowed.

"What throne?"

"When the gods abandon the heavens, the corpse becomes the crown."

En-Mazru smiled—not kindly. He had seen kings wear the skins of gods, but this one unnerved him. Not for cruelty, but for belief in nothing.

*****

That night, Cassander's soldiers returned. Silent. Torchless. They emptied the temple's drawers—scrolls, eclipse charts, star codes. Cosmology seized like contraband.

A boy tried to stop them. He screamed in a tongue they did not know. They beat him and left him broken in the ritual bath.

Another priest drenched himself in oil, lit his body at the altar, and burned until nothing remained but silence.

Cassander did not watch. He didn't need to.

At dawn, he returned barefoot, ash caked in the cuts of his heels. He stepped onto the altar where the fire-priest had burned. Around him: nothing. Not even wind.

But silence could be shaped.

"Omens are just truths waiting for the right author," he told Menon.

Menon flinched. He always flinched. But this morning, something in him wavered. As Cassander spoke, Menon's eyes fell—not in submission, but hesitation. Cassander noticed.

Elsewhere, a boy ran. Burned fingers pressed to his chest. Beneath his robe, he clutched a half-charred prophecy tablet. He whispered the words to himself, again and again:

"The corpse is the crown."

"Faith is useful," Cassander would later say, "until silence serves the Kingdom better."

CHAPTER 9

SAND AND SPECTACLE

OUTER BABYLON, ALONG THE KING'S ROAD. The funeral procession opened as unprecedented spectacle. Flutes led the way—long, reedy Persian pipes whose cries cut through the morning haze. Behind them moved dancers from the Indus Valley, a dozen women with henna-stained palms and bronze bangles at their wrists. They swayed in spirals, their movements drifting like smoke, their bare feet barely stirring the dust.

Next came the wailers, Babylonian women draped in linen, their breasts smeared with ash. Their voices did not mourn the man so much as the order he had imposed, an order now collapsing into noise and vacancy. Over it all, the gold sun pressed down without pity.

The funerary cart followed, pulled by sixty white oxen with gilded horns and crimson plumes. Its wheels, banded with lapis and orichalcum, strained with every turn. Inside the cedar sarcophagus—sealed with pitch, bound in silver thread—Alexander's embalmed body remained intact. Decay had not yet claimed it, though the air already carried the sour trace of unspent power—unsettled and unclaimed.

Eumenes rode ahead, scrolls tucked beneath his arm. He did not weep; he observed. He calculated, adjusted, recorded—the only ritual he trusted.

He whispered to heralds who posted Perdiccas's proclamations at every crossing: *THE KING IS DEAD. THE EMPIRE REMAINS.* He doubted the truth of the phrase, but it fit a banner, and in grief people clutched slogans like driftwood.

Eumenes had never quite belonged. Born in Thrace, raised among scribes and salt traders, his Greek was too polished for Macedonian camps, his accent too revealing, his complexion too pale for the sun. He had been marked as an outsider even when holding a sword. "Quill-born," they called him—"pretty boy," "eunuch." He dressed carefully for the procession: white linen, a blue Persian sash, dagger polished, beard trimmed, hair oiled. Each detail was armor of another kind.

Alexander had trusted him, and that trust now weighed heavier than any cuirass. As the cart rolled forward, Pharnabazus of Phrygia drew close, his smile insolent.

"Still revising history while it unravels in front of us?"

"Only trying to keep it legible," Eumenes replied. "Before the illiterate carve their legends."

Pharnabazus laughed. "Too late. I've seen a coin already—Alexandria mint. His face newly struck. Altars will follow."

Eumenes looked to the horizon. "They always do. Funerals are snares. This one most of all."

The road narrowed, dust rising in clouds. Crowds gathered at shrines and roadside altars—farmers, grooms, children clutching coins like prayers. They shouted questions no proclamation could answer: Where is his heir? Who owns his shadow? One woman shrieked, "A god does not rot!" A boy thrust forward a coin marked with Isis on the reverse—an Egyptian claim wrapped in devotion.

Eumenes felt the murmurs circle him: "Clerk. Greek. Useless without a king." He pressed on, his lips tight. He needed a thread through the unraveling—something more than survival, something to prove that thought could still matter in a world drunk on spectacle.

At night, the fires dimmed. A bard went missing, leaving his lyre restrung with black horsehair, its sound more omen than music. Eumenes sat by the coals, unrolling a letter never sent:

> *To Hephaestion, in death— They treat you like a ghost. I remember you as flame. You loved him as no one else dared. I serve him still, not as you did, but because someone must keep the ink from drying before memory gives way to myth.*

Before dawn, he burned the page. The flame curled the parchment like breath withdrawing from a body.

*****

Perdiccas rode beside the funerary cart, a figure of bronze and discipline, speaking little. The empire sat on his shoulders like ill-fitted armor. Priests from every corner of the empire slaughtered sheep, bulls, and doves in rites that bled together, but no god answered. Among the ranks, muttering grew. Cavalry patrols disappeared. Newly minted coins surfaced, each bearing Alexander's face—silver prayers in circulation. Whispers spread that Ptolemy was buying loyalty with silver.

Eumenes brought word to Perdiccas.

"This is no funeral," he said. "It is a forced march wrapped in cedar and linen. If we do not name the threat, it will name us."

Perdiccas dismissed his officers, then admitted, "The coin reeks of the Nile. Only one man would dare it."

"And yet we march toward Macedon."

"If I turn back, I look weak. The priests scatter, the Macedonians riot, Roxana crowns her son. Antipater answers with steel."

"Then you will bleed your command dry before you reach Pella," Eumenes warned.

He offered a plan: a decoy cart, sent east, seeded with rumor. Perdiccas agreed. That night, Eumenes summoned Tyra—a woman who had survived satraps and betrayals, whose loyalty was sharpened by pragmatism. He gave her the coin. She took it without question, as if handling contagion. She disappeared into the camp's shadows to spread the illusion of a second bier. Soon word spread that another cart had been sighted near Nippur. Spies, drawn by scent rather than reason, began following the wrong trail.

By the seventh day, the procession stretched like a scar. No songs. No garlands. The cart's gold dulled, its wheels caked with grit. From a distant ridge, the line of priests bowed in dust like the arms of a broken crown.

Eumenes rode in silence, no longer muttering revisions. He watched for cracks—where morale faltered, where silence thickened, where memory dissolved into rumor. The decoy had worked, yet he knew it was only a pause. Perception had become the empire's last defense, truth its first casualty.

As a sandstorm brewed in the east, he thought of Hephaestion, of Alexander, of the fragile machinery beneath empire—clerks, cooks, coin-strikers. Of the bard's lyre, still humming somewhere in the dust.

He tightened his grip on the reins. Not in defiance, but in grim acknowledgment. The story was no longer his to preserve. Behind him, dragged by weary oxen, the body of a god rolled forward into history—not toward burial, but toward conflict.

CHAPTER 10

THE FIRST BLOOD FEUD

EAST OF BABYLON, TIGRIS RIVER CROSSING. The river shimmered like a blade—the brassy, beaten-metal gleam of a sword held too long in the sun. On the western bank of the Tigris the funeral procession halted for logistics: carts recoupled to flatter river barges, animals watered, men returned to labor. The corpse of the god was too heavy for any bridge, and the delay began.

Heat thickened. Animals fouled the ground. Eumenes' loyalists worked beside Thracian infantry and hired archers to unload barley and salt. The operation had been scripted, but plans bend in heat and in the presence of gold—especially gold stamped with Ptolemy's mint.

First came shouted names and a missing ration count. Then a crate turned up unsealed and half empty, eaten or stolen or both. A Thracian lieutenant swore the cart had never been fully loaded at Babylon. The ledger disagreed. When Eumenes' quartermaster raised it like a shield, the Thracian slapped it away. The breach opened.

"I saw your men swap crates in Seleucia!" a Thracian shouted, a finger hard in a Greek officer's chest.

"You're drunk, or bribed—or both," came the reply.

"You think because your commander bedded the king's secretary you own the grain?"

"Say that again," growled a dark-bearded Eumenid, lifting his spear.

A nearby horse danced sideways, sensing what the men refused to name.

The standard-bearer hesitated at the edge of the standoff, hands white on the pole. Barely twenty, fresh from Pella, he still smelled of oak sap and the straw that had padded his armor's crate.

A veteran had handed him the banner with instruction. "Hold it like your father's bones." The lapis-threaded cloth, edged in Sidonian purple, was built to be paraded.

It was snatched instead—by a rankless foot-soldier, bare-chested, eyes yellowed from opium or fever. He wrenched the pole sideways; the fabric caught on a nailhead and tore. Gold thread snapped. The cloth hit the dirt.

Nicanor saw it fall. He had fought under that standard at Issus, watched it flutter over Darius' broken chariot, felt his heart swell. Now, on the Tigris bank, it looked like a soiled robe.

"Pick it up," he said, to anyone. "By the gods—pick it up."

The air held its breath. Even the flies paused. Then a word cut through the heat—some heard "treason," others "Egypt." Debate never arrived. Violence did.

A blade flashed from a Thracian scabbard; another answered from behind. A scream. A spear. Men collapsed into each other like scaffolding giving way. Horses shrieked. A cart toppled into the river; salt sacks burst and bled.

The burning came slower. Someone lifted the fallen banner, touched a torch to it, and held the fire there with intention. The lapis hissed, the gold blackened, and the flame ate upward. Smoke rose into the afternoon, curling into the bent shape of a scorpion's tail.

Perdiccas arrived late, his horse lathered and flecked at the nostrils. He rode past fire and bodies to the vanguard guarding the bier. He dismounted without ceremony, walked to the last man breathing—an older Phoenician tattooed with Tyre's crest—and listened as the man, calm despite his wound, whispered, "The body belongs to Egypt."

Perdiccas turned to his adjutant. "Sew his mouth shut. No coin for the ferryman."

The body went under a withered tree, face down, with salt-packed dirt pressed into the ears.

That night, Eumenes reopened the ledger that had been slapped aside that morning. He wrote the names of the dead, the companies they came from, a rough count of the supplies lost, a tally of wounds. For the Phoenician he left only a mark, a smudge—enough to remember that something had happened, not enough to name who. Some stories are not denied; they are merely delayed.

OUTSIDE BABYLON, THE NEXT NIGHT

They still called it a villa, though the word no longer fit. Dust and silence had stripped it. Vines were skeletal; pergolas had collapsed. Paths were cracked and weeping weeds. The central pool held only stagnant water and the broken spine of a clay amphora, half submerged like a forgotten offering to a god who no longer collected tribute. Somewhere under the stonework, the blood of the former owner likely lingered—a stain swallowed into limestone, a signature erased.

Just after sunset the previous night, a cry had carried on the river wind—sharp, unnatural. Not pain so much as protest, the sound men make when they violate a covenant they did not know they'd sworn. Cassander listened for it again, but the night was quiet, the kind that settles only after the irreversible.

He had chosen the place for its vantage. From the upper portico he could read the eastern horizon—the Tigris in moonlight, smoke from the camps rising like incense—and imagine each gust as a report. Quiet slowed the news, and he preferred to savor it.

It arrived on foot. The messenger knelt on the marble, mud on his legs, salt burning in the welts on his face, breath ragged. He waited until Cassander answered with a small tilt of the chin.

"They clashed at the crossing," the boy said. "Two units—Eumenes' men and Thracian hires. A supply dispute. Salt rations, barley—"

"Not interested in inventory," Cassander said.

"The standard. The king's. Someone pulled it down. Someone else lit it."

Cassander studied the boy's face, not for truth but for the hesitation that betrays invention. He saw only exhaustion and the fear reserved for messengers who bring omen instead of order.

"And the reaction?"

"Six dead. A Phoenician taken alive. He said something before they opened him." The boy faltered, then finished: "That the body of their god belongs to Egypt."

Cassander turned back to the rail. "Then the funeral has finally begun."

He dismissed the boy. The footsteps faded into the hush. The breeze shifted, carrying the acrid sting of burned cloth, a note of something older than fire. He didn't need confirmation. He had felt the flame before the messenger spoke.

"You've been watching the same fire I have," a voice said behind him.

Roxana stepped into the moonlight, veiled, unmistakable. He did not turn; he didn't need to.

"I was told your quarters were sealed," he said.

"I told the guard to seal them. Not myself inside them."

She came to the rail beside him—not close, but close enough that a trace of myrrh cut through the scorch.

"I heard what happened at the river," she said. "They say the smoke curled into a scorpion's tail."

"Of course it did," he said. "The gods send their warnings after the knives are drawn."

"There were witnesses," she said. "They'll remember who lit the torch."

"Let them. Memory is soft. History softer."

"You move pieces for advantage. Ptolemy moves his. Eumenes records with a shaking hand. Yet none of you has touched the body. You burn symbols and argue over carts, but you haven't opened the coffin."

"Because it isn't time."

"And when it is?"

"Then we stop pretending we're in mourning."

Her eyes burned behind the veil. "I won't let my son be ruled by men who worship only strategy."

"You think you'll have a son?"

"I know I carry an heir."

"The gods name sons. Empires make heirs."

She turned to go. "Be careful what you burn, Cassander. Some standards catch faster than others."

The wind shifted toward Babylon. Cassander stayed on the portico long after she vanished. In the courtyard below, a campfire sent up a spiral of smoke that bent into the shape of a noose.

"Flammable," he said to the darkness. "We'll see."

*****

Later that night, under a brittle moon, Enlil Mannu—last ritual archivist and priest of Marduk's House of Esagila—slipped from the tent. Once he had presided over sacred washings for satraps. Once he had anointed Alexander with cedar oil under the ziggurat's shadow. No one watched priests anymore. He carried no lamp, only a linen-wrapped bundle held against his ribs with the care one gives a saint's bones.

The remnants of the standard were still warm.

He knelt in the sand. "Hear me, Bel," he whispered. "You who spoke through kings and omens. Forgive what we allowed. Forgive what we burned." The old syllables scraped his throat. Ritual Babylonian felt like summoning the voice of a dead relative one no longer fully remembers.

Charred gold clung in patches to the lapis weft threads; geometry blistered and split. A corner of purple remained, marked by a burn like a finger bone— or a lightning stroke—drawn by an invisible hand. Resin and smoke rode the fabric with something older. Something holy.

He walked down the embankment. The silt took his feet like the skin of an unanointed child. No guards watched. No orders had been given. This was not duty; it was devotion. Generals and accountants had sidelined his kind, but the gods remembered, and he remembered the gods.

He dug a shallow grave just above the floodline—too shallow to endure, deep enough to be found—and laid the cloth down as a parent lays down a child not yet ready to leave the world. With ash still on his fingers he drew a spiral over the mound and murmured in a tongue older than Gaugamela, older than Siwa, older than the needle Alexander had used to thread divinity through empire.

A jackal called once in the reeds. In the auguries, a lone jackal near water meant a misplaced soul.

Then the wind rose without warning, hard and insistent. It pressed his robe, teased the sand over the mound, hissed through the reeds. The gust curled him in a circle and lifted smoke from abandoned ash pits and oil-stained torches, turning it back across the river. The day's smoke had drifted east toward Susa. Now it went west—toward Babylon, toward the temple, toward the throne with no king.

Enlil Mannu did not speak again. He lowered his head. The gods had seen the fire, and they were waiting.

"The gods do not always speak in thunder, but more often in silence after defilement."

—Fragment from the Lost Tablets of Harran (c. 322 BCE)

CHAPTER 11

PILGRIMAGE OF THE DAMNED

PTOLEMY'S GARDEN, MEMPHIS. He fed the fish by hand. It was an old habit, carried from boyhood—Nile canals, palace pools in Aegae. His mother had called it weakness. "Only cowards need pets." But in Memphis, the ritual hardened. The limestone basin gleamed with lapis and obsidian. The water moved slow, as if wary of him.

Beyond the wall, the stench was growing. Not garden rot—corpse rot. The god's body seeping brine. Servants whispered of flies that would not die.

The fish circled in silence. Bred for aggression. Watchful. So was he.

Memphis hummed beyond the walls. Older than dynasties. Older than Greek ledgers. A city of double meanings, where even silence carried theology. Priests walked the causeways. White bulls groaned. Children ran alleys thick with incense. The city had taught him patience. He had learned.

He dropped a pellet. The largest fish struck fast. He smiled faintly.

The trap had taken months. Not warbands. Not charges. That was

Perdiccas—loud, costly. Ptolemy moved differently: quiet, patient, a violence that behaved like drought—slow, unnoticed, then absolute.

He had planted guides. Paid for forged papyri. Placed them in the right hands. A route almost true. Almost. A forgotten Phoenician road, warped by rivers and time. Then the priests—one Babylonian, one Macedonian defector—each whispering of omens. Never shouting. Whispering.

A servant approached. Silent. Kneeling, scroll in hand.

"They've passed Emesa," he said. "The false pass is four days ahead."

Ptolemy did not read. He watched the pool. One fish swam lame, fin torn. Weakness showed early.

"And the guides?"

"Still in place. Maps accepted. No deviation."

"And our men?"

"Two inside. Ledgers and night watch. Secure."

"And the priests?"

"Speaking of blood-liver. Of dreams."

He nodded. The Nile wind stirred his robes. Memory tugged—Siwa, the desert march, the oracle that named Alexander a god. Strange boy. Certain the world would follow him beyond its edge. For a time, it had.

But gods rot. And myths, once embalmed, ferment.

He wiped his hands on a linen cloth embroidered with Alexander's sigil—the faded sun-disc. He folded it and handed it back. "Tell the serpent to shed its skin."

The servant bowed and left.

A smaller fish strayed too close. The strike came sudden. Water clouded red. Ptolemy leaned forward, watching his reflection fracture.

"Such appetite," he murmured.

Would Perdiccas see the trap before it closed? Or die convinced the map had failed him?

He did not smile again.

NORTHERN SYRIA, NEAR THE SHADOW PASS

By the seventh week, even the oxen balked. Tongues cracked. Hooves slipped on dust where no true road lay. What had begun as a western arc had bent north, then west, then north again. The Euphrates now shimmered far to the south. The old road abandoned.

Eumenes rode with a map. The parchment buckled in the heat. Ink smeared. A geometry of arrogance. A plan written by men who thought the land obeyed.

He drew alongside Perdiccas.

"This is not the route to the Cilician Gates."

"All roads bend when they climb," Perdiccas said.

"We are not climbing. We are circling. This is no road. It is a snare."

Silence.

Eumenes pressed. "You broke the path. Or let it be broken."

Perdiccas turned, eyes narrowed against the sun. "Do you accuse me of treason?"

"I accuse you of pride. Of trusting maps over instinct. Of dragging us into another man's design."

Perdiccas dismounted. "Every report was clear. Antioch to the fords. The southern passes were flooded. This was the only open cut."

"And you trusted that? You think maps cannot be forged? That rot does not bloom in a courier's pouch? You've been played. Not in battle—in thought."

The general's fingers shook faintly on his cuirass. Eumenes saw.

Behind them, the column sagged. Men walked like revenants. A Thracian scout screamed at dawn that a boulder had moved. A mule died mid-step, eyes wide. The king's cart groaned under twenty oxen. Axles bent. Perfume braziers gone cold. The stench of decay lingered. Bells rattled like omens.

Roxana did not sleep.

She watched. Counted guards. Heard the silence. Not queen. Not wife. Not mother. A vessel in flesh. Dream-haunted: Alexander on a throne of obsidian, cradling a serpent-child. Or his face splitting to stone beneath a mask. She woke to silence thicker than breath.

That night, she stepped from her palanquin barefoot. Pale. Robes loose. Firelight made her spectral.

She found Perdiccas by a bloodstone, goat steam rising.

"You are feeding us to the dark," she said.

"Roxana—"

"No more ceremony. We are lost."

His jaw locked. "Alexander would not have allowed this. Not the silence. Not this decay."

"Alexander is dead."

"Yes. And I wonder if your ambition died with him, or wears his corpse."

"You would question me here—?"

"I remind you," she said, low and steady, "that I carry the child of a god. And your hold thins by the hour. Even the oxen smell betrayal."

She stepped closer. "I should be in Ekbatana. With my son. Not here, beside a corpse."

"You swore he was safe."

"He is," Perdiccas said, too fast.

"Then why do I dream of fire?"

She turned. "When the trap closes, don't expect the dead to defend you."

She vanished into dark.

That night, the wind carried two crooked notes—flute or memory. Guards swore at pale figures on the ridges. Fires twisted blue, then green.

Perdiccas doubled the watch.

Eumenes stood at the torch ring, reading the same letter again. The false path works. They follow ghosts. Let the box close. He knew the hand. The calm smile. He burned the letter, but the smile lingered. Had he misread the war itself? Or was war the misreading?

At dawn, scouts returned shaken.

"The path ends."

"No exit. Box canyon. Walls high. Floor flat. No way forward. No way back."

Perdiccas said nothing. He walked toward the cart like a man to his sentence.

Roxana emerged barefoot. Hair loose. Eyes hollow. She lifted a goblet from the altar. Looked into wine. Saw Alexander's grin staring back. She dropped it. Shattered glass bled across the dirt.

On the ridges, signals flared—one torch, then three, then none.

They had not reached the Cilician Gates. They had been led into a throat.

The king's body had never weighed more.

PERDICCAS

CHAPTER 12

THE THEFT OF THE KING

THE FALSE PASS, NIGHT. They called it a road, but it wasn't one. It was a scar through the hills—narrow, broken, twisted. A place caravans hurried through by daylight, a place priests refused entirely. A fissure where things went in whole and came out wrong—if they came out at all.

For nearly three weeks the procession had dragged west. Sleep came in jolts, food in fractions. Time measured itself in bruises. Perdiccas had heard the scouts' warnings: unstable rock, the unnatural tilt of the cliffs, the way sound died against the walls. But he pressed forward. He had left caution east of Babylon.

The cart carried more than a body. It carried the verdict of empire. If he could deliver it to Aegae, into the tombs of the Argeads, then perhaps the line would still hold. Perhaps the empire might still recognize itself.

But doubt crept in. The coffin grew heavier with each mile. Villagers bowed to it; soldiers lowered their voices around it. The dead king had become an object more than a man. Objects draw gravity. Gravity draws thieves.

Rumors spread: that Ptolemy had left Alexandria, that a temple was rising in Memphis dedicated to one man. Then the letter arrived, sealed in violet wax:

> *The King spoke to me in his final hours.*
> *He did not wish to lie in Macedon.*
> *His desire was for Siwa.*
> *That is where I will take him.*

Perdiccas read it three times—not for clarity, but for the audacity. Siwa—the desert shrine where Alexander had once gone alone, returning with silence and the name "son of Zeus-Ammon." No record existed of any such wish in his final days. Ptolemy was forging belief out of myth. And belief, once stolen, rarely returns unbroken.

They entered the False Pass at dusk. The cliffs closed in. Torches were lit early. Then came the fires above—dozens of them, evenly spaced along the rim. Horns followed, low and unbroken. Horses reared. A cart splintered against stone.

They descended. Ptolemy's men disguised as phantoms—linen over chain, kohl-rimmed eyes, obsidian blades. They struck the rear guard first. The supply wagons burned. Eumenes shouted orders into a wind already lost.

The coffin cart came unmoored. The oxen bolted. In the smoke, six figures emerged—robed, marked with symbols not Macedonian, not Babylonian. They draped the coffin in embroidered cloth, lifted it like a shrine, and disappeared into the canyon dark.

By dawn the pass was still. Thirty men dead. Twenty missing. The cart stood gutted, a single wheel turning slowly in the ash. The tracks led west. To Egypt. To Siwa.

Perdiccas stood amid the wreckage, his command scattered like bones. Eumenes limped into view, silent. They watched the wheel turn.

Later, in Memphis, Ptolemy would stand before the priests and declare: We are not burying a king. We are building a god.

The survivors whispered another story. That one of the veiled men had turned back before vanishing into the smoke—just long enough to meet a soldier's eyes.

Some swore it was Iollas—the wine-pourer. The one who had stood behind Alexander on his last night. The one already recorded as dead.

But then again, so was the man in the coffin.

And that had not stopped anything either.

CHAPTER 13

THE GOD WHO
WOULD NOT SLEEP

AT THE SYRIAN GATES. The wind shifted before the smoke. Heat came off the stone, carrying burnt myrrh and something fouler—charred cloth, old oil. Perdiccas raised a fist for halt; no one needed telling. The air had gone thin and metallic. Fire hissed somewhere in the ruin. A vulture cried once and was quiet.

The Syrian Gates had been a checkpoint shrine cut into the saddle of the pass, a place of bread, omens, and warnings. Now it was a blackened throat. Columns were scorched and flaking. An Apollo frieze lay shattered in the forecourt. Smoke curled from the rafters without prayer or forgiveness behind it.

Eumenes dismounted first. The others held back, hands on reins and hilts. Even the horses balked.

Perdiccas swung down last, knees stiff from days in the saddle. His temper felt like the rock—brittle, ready to shear. The gold thread of his cloak was dull with dust. Ink stained the crescents of his nails.

"This was to be our turning point," he said. "Halfway home."

They ducked under a lintel whose inscription had been scraped away—by fire, or by will. Heat doubled inside. The place smelled like a forge. Or a tomb.

At the center sat a coffin. Not Alexander's. A rough wooden box, unadorned. No bronze. No royal sign. Inside, thousands of Macedonian drachmas poured over a burial cloth. They caught the torchlight like pooled blood. Curled among them lay a serpent—green-gold in the glow, black eyes reflecting everything and nothing.

"It's a message," Eumenes said.

"A god's," Perdiccas answered, "or a thief's."

The coins were arranged—rings and spirals—Egyptian solar work Perdiccas had seen carved at Karnak and sketched in stolen margins. The serpent did not strike. It watched.

Perdiccas turned. "Form the circle. Bring the scribe."

They gathered in the atrium under wavering light, armor and faces wet with heat. No one met his eyes. Even the younger officers—raised on Chaeronea and Issus—looked unsure what war story this was.

Perdiccas dictated an edict: the royal body sacred, any tampering a desecration punishable by death; the regency renewed in his name and Alexander's; Ptolemy named a heretic, a violator of divine order.

His voice held. His hand did not. When they brought the wet clay tablet, the torch dipped. He lifted his seal, then stopped. The seal felt small. The words already felt brittle, as though law could still outpace legend.

No one stepped forward to press a seal beside his. Eumenes looked away. Boots shifted on ash.

Perdiccas lowered the tablet and set it aside. He dismissed the council with a nod and walked into the courtyard alone.

The moon was up. The sky above the Gates was spare and close. A jackal called somewhere beyond the cliffs.

By morning the serpent was gone. No tracks. No carcass. No trail. The guards swore they had held their posts. One claimed it slid under a bedroll; another that it coiled around a column and vanished.

The whispers moved faster than orders. *Alexander has chosen another.* Some said the serpent had taken a man's breath for its body. Others said Alexander himself had slipped the coffin—roaming again, sleepless, hunting a temple not yet built.

At morning watch a guard spoke Ptolemy's name. He was lashed—not for blasphemy, but for saying what others thought.

The column moved out the next day. They left the box where it lay. No one offered to carry it. No one asked why.

Perdiccas kept his silence on the march. That night he unrolled the edict. The seal was smudged. The clay was cracked. He pressed a thumb to the edge, not to mark it—just to feel something give.

The gods were silent. The king was gone. The column went west to the sea. Perdiccas, once steward of ritual and rule, walked under a sky that did not answer.

The god would not sleep.

Neither would he.

PART III

THE KNIFE AND THE CRADLE

THE BIRTH OF EMPIRE'S GHOSTS.

.

PTOLEMY

CHAPTER 14

PROPHECY IN MEMPHIS

THE NECROPOLIS-TEMPLE, LOWER EGYPT. Nothing here was finished: not the walls, not the gods, not the story being staged.

Memphis lay at a threshold between worlds—a city of crossings that had learned to outlast dynasties. Ptolemy entered the half-built temple barefoot, walking ahead of the stolen coffin as if leading a guest to an epitaph still being written.

The sarcophagus followed. The oxen were washed in beer and cedar ash; cloth wrapped their hooves to keep the approach silent. Linen soaked in oil bound the cart wheels to mute their grind. Even the dust seemed trained to fall without sound. Pain, if present, would not be heard.

Banners hung in three scripts: Greek for the generals, Demotic for the priests, and an older sign for the wind alone. The texts did not agree. One named Alexander Basileus. One named him Nesu. The third offered only a solar spiral cut so deep the pigment bled through the fabric.

Crowds lined the way without cheering. They knelt, bowed, or watched through cloth held over their mouths. Most had never seen the king alive. What they saw now was not a man, but a perfected absence.

The temple compound was a patchwork of gates and stones, with a central sanctuary cleared and sealed in haste. Workers had whitewashed old inscriptions, but the heat cracked the gesso and the older images pushed back through. A jackal's tail showed behind a sun disk; a lioness's outline surfaced beneath a winged thunderbolt. In Memphis, memory behaved like limestone—forever exhaling its ghosts.

Inside, torchlight wavered. One flame burned green. Priests called it a sign. Greek engineers said copper had spoiled the oil. No one resolved the point, and the omen stood.

Memphis had once ruled the Two Lands—long before Greeks, Persians, or Libyans. It had been crown and cradle: seat of kings, forge of laws, a city where gods were named and laid to rest. Tradition said Menes founded it and united Upper and Lower Egypt. Thebes later challenged it; Alexandria would eclipse it; yet Memphis remained the axis by which Egypt read itself.

Just south of the Delta, where the river split like a scribe's pen, the land learned to bloom. The cult of Ptah took root here, and with it the craft of making: speaking, shaping, giving form to intent. To build in Memphis was to turn idea into stone. Its walls had held palaces, embassies, docks, gardens, and a temple district so vast that even gods could be imagined lost within it. To die here was to be prepared for eternity. Saqqara rose to the west with stepped horizons, pyramids older than memory, catacombs of mummified bulls, and tombs carved with prayers no one had spoken aloud for a thousand years.

Alexander understood the city's importance when he arrived in 332 BCE. The priests greeted him with pharaonic rites: echoes of the sed-festival, the double crown, the union of reed and papyrus. They knew how to survive new gods. Alexander performed as required—made offerings, listened to counsel, walked the processional ways. Then he moved on. Memphis was too rooted, too heavy with ritual. He wanted the geometry of beginnings.

He marked a harbor between Lake Mareotis and open water and ordered a city of straight roads and clear views. Alexandria would serve the living, not the dead.

In death, or something close to it, he had returned. It was not his choice. He came not to be crowned, but to be claimed.

Ptolemy chose Memphis by calculation. This was Egypt's sacred core. Its walls had outlasted kings. To place Alexander here—even for a time—was to borrow that endurance, to recast him not only as conqueror of Egypt but as a god native to it. In the same act, Ptolemy—watcher, embalmer, former bodyguard—worked to become more than Macedonian: heir, vessel, priest to a god who never fit any single coffin.

At the center of the sanctuary a raised dais waited, dressed with lotus and ivory. The cart halted. The oxen were led away, bells loose around their necks so their thin ringing skittered along the stone.

Ptolemy stepped forward alone. His robes fell in ordered folds. Torchlight gleamed on his scalp. A pale scar marked his right temple, a relic of a battle no one discussed. He stood before the sarcophagus neither as satrap nor general but as something still inventing its own divinity.

He took a flint blade from a copper bowl and opened both forearms—shallow and precise. Blood darkened the basin where crushed lotus steeped. No one moved to stop him.

Behind him, priests—native and foreign—braided their voices. Greek carried the grammar of victory. Demotic answered from the throat, a water-deep cadence. A third voice joined, hoarse and irregular, a tongue no longer written but still kept by temple lives.

Ptolemy dipped his hands, marked brow and chest, then traced the sealed linen where Alexander's heart would have rested.

"He has chosen Egypt," he said. The walls carried it. "He lives again through me."

Somewhere in the darkness a priest clenched his jaw. Egypt had words for men who borrowed eternity too soon.

Outside, the mints had already begun. New dies cut that morning set a portrait not in mourning but in declaration: lips parted, hair bound with rays, eyes wide and alert. On the reverse, a serpent coiled the white crown of Upper

Egypt, its tongue a flame. Boys in falcon dress threw the first coins into the crowd. People received them as offerings—or as proof.

Within the sanctuary, the body lay under the torches, limbs stiff with resin, face flattened by tight bandage. The green flame kept burning despite new oil and fresh wicks.

At the veil's edge, a general named Menes watched. "He is embalming himself in myth," he said. The man beside him said nothing and tightened his grip on his sword.

That night, in the market along the necropolis wall—between perfumers, scribes, spice sellers, and courtesans—a blind oracle spoke without pause. Three scribes wrote. None agreed on syntax; the layers of language were too many. Still, the fragments converged: a storm of knives in the north; a crown too heavy for its bearer; he walks again, but not in one body; the tide will claim what the desert cannot keep. One scribe swore the cadence matched a prophecy spoken during the Persian eclipse. The archivist filed the scroll under divinations and marked it with a crescent and a question.

In the tomb chamber, beneath linen and gold, the king did not stir. The green flame burned on.

CHAPTER 15

RIVER OF KNIVES

NILE DELTA, LOWER EGYPT. The river did not want them. It had said so from the first reeds. Earth dissolved under their feet. Causeways broke. Oxen collapsed. Every mile past Pelusium swallowed more of them. The cart leaked a trail of ichor that stained the marshes. Even the priests refused to name it aloud.

They were no longer procession or army—only a column of ghosts, chasing the weight of a corpse.

Perdiccas kept riding. Not for victory—he could no longer imagine what living looked like if he stopped. The Sinai crossing had burned them out. Heat. Hunger. Silence. Satraps in the rear withheld supplies. Messengers arrived with nothing. Soldiers stripped silver from armor, buried it as charms against a curse. No one touched the cart. They called it the ghost's box, the cursed wagon, the vessel. One recruit spoke Alexander's name. The veterans beat him insensible and left him to the vultures.

Still, Perdiccas pushed forward. Each dawn he rode alone, ahead of his officers. He no longer asked for reports. No longer gave orders. At night he drank little, chewed meat too dry to swallow, and read over the last edict he had failed to seal.

By the time they reached the Delta, the army was a chain of funerals across the silt. The Nile broke into fingers, channels winding through reed-thick islands. Paths doubled back. Maps failed.

Two elephants went down in a side channel—riders and beasts dragged under. The men on the banks did not move. A mahout tore his headdress. Another cut his thigh and walked into the water.

On the tenth day they reached Canopus. A rope bridge crossed the channel. Narrow. Two men wide. Engineers swore it would hold. The reeds bent in dissent.

At dusk the first companies crossed—archers, then supply men. The ropes sagged. A rivet snapped. Someone ran. Someone turned back. The bridge went out like a joint giving way—slow, then all at once. Men screamed. Shields floated. A standard sank.

Perdiccas waded in himself, dragging a soldier from the current. He reached the bank with a gash over his eye and a leg torn open. His horse drowned.

That night no fires were lit. Officers did not come. Eumenes tended the wounded in silence. They outnumbered the living.

When the moon rose, three men entered the command tent without summons—Peithon first, then Antigenes, then Seleucus. They said nothing. The argument had ended days before. Only execution remained.

Perdiccas, half-asleep, reached for his sword. His hand closed on linen. He looked at Seleucus as if trying to recall whether friendship had ever truly existed. They cut his throat with a hunting blade. Not quick. Not cruel. A kindness—for themselves.

His body was wrapped in a cloak and buried beneath a tamarisk leaning over the swamp. No marker. No rites. By morning the army spoke of fever, collapse, judgment. Silence had earned its due.

News reached Memphis as whispers first, then dispatch. Stories bent with every retelling—drowned in armor, cursed by the king's ghost. By the time the scroll reached Ptolemy, the truth no longer mattered. The regent was dead. The line was broken.

Ptolemy read the words aloud in the sanctuary. The body lay near, still shrouded in silk and resin. His voice carried across the stone. No theater was required; the moment already believed itself sacred.

That evening he entered the inner sanctum alone—guards at the gate, priests dismissed. He poured oil on a bare altar, lit it with the green torch, and watched the flame rise. He said no prayers. He believed the ritual was complete. That the war was memory. That the king was his.

But memory does not obey. War does not end when claimed.

In Macedon, Cassander wrote to loyalists. In Phrygia, Antigonus gathered troops under pretense of border duty, his eye east to Babylon. Seleucus drafted letters to rivals. Eumenes rode into the eastern satrapies with no banner, only scrolls and a small portrait of the dead. He withdrew, not fled. He wrote to remember.

He had seen myth break loose from its stewards—power shifting from ritual to theater, inheritance to performance. He knew what remained would not restore empire. It would splinter heaven. The age of generals had begun to speak in the language of gods.

The Nile swelled with silt that summer. The tamarisk tree stood over his grave. The war did not end. It changed languages.

And in the quiet, the god slept.

But not for long.

CHAPTER 16

A BROKEN OATH

LOWER EGYPT, THE WESTERN DESERT, AND BABYLON. They buried Perdiccas in the sand as hawks and rumors circled.

No tomb. No priest. No rites. Only silence and the wind.

The priests had refused to follow. The omens had turned the moment they crossed the Nile's western arm. No pyres were lit. No chants rose. Even the body's position—half in shade, half in glare—looked undecided, as if the desert itself would not claim him.

At first the word spread he drowned near the Fayoum. Then poison. Then betrayal. Then the knives of his own men.

In the end, the only truth was the corpse. Everything else dissolved in the heat.

Roxana stood over the shrouded form. The desert pulled at her cloak. None of the men met her eye—not the Thracians, not the Macedonians, not even the Persians in her guard. Loyalty had gone with the last of the water. Columns fractured. Officers bickered. Scouts disappeared. Horses wandered back riderless.

It was no longer a procession. It was a siege turned inward.

She thought of her father's court in Bactria—where power had a grammar, performed in gestures, silks, and scents. Here there was no language. Only knives.

That night she bent over maps with Eumenes. One lamp threw their shadows across the tent. Outside, the wind hissed at the seams.

The map was a ruin of its own: sweat-stained, creased, its ink bled at the rivers. Half the cities no longer belonged to the empire whose name was scrawled across them.

"They slit his throat," she said, her voice low and steady. "With his own dagger. That's not just murder. That's display."

"Or convenience," Eumenes said. "A weapon close to hand. They wanted us to know it wasn't chance. They wanted doubt."

His fingers hovered above the Euphrates, tracing something invisible.

"Not guilt?" she asked.

"Doubt fractures faster," he said.

"And Perdiccas?"

"He believed too much in his own cleverness. That makes a man easy to kill."

Her gaze stayed on him. "You served my husband from the start. Before Babylon. Before India."

"I was with him before Issus," Eumenes said. "I saw the boy they crowned become something no one had words for. He trusted me to live in that silence."

"And you never betrayed him?"

"I couldn't afford to."

It was not flattery. It was calculation. Cold, but clear.

"You're Greek," she said. "And still they never accepted you."

"My father made wagons," he said. "I had wit, not birth. They called me secretary, foreigner, opportunist. I learned not to need them."

"Then you and I have that in common," she said.

"We also share a problem."

His finger pressed the bend of the Euphrates. Babylon.

"Cassander writes now in his own hand. Not his father's. He smells blood. Half the generals still call your son king, but none know who speaks for him."

"And Arrhidaeus?"

"A puppet. Strings pulled by Antipater, Cassander, Seleucus. To them he is no man, only a throne."

She drank her sour wine. "And what do you see, Eumenes, when you look at my son?"

"The last chance for meaning," he said.

That silenced her. It was not sentiment. It was stakes.

"Then we move," she said. "Back to Babylon."

"And if Cassander holds the gates?"

"Then we burn the gates."

For the first time in days, he smiled. But it was not victory's smile. It was cost's.

"Who profits most?" she pressed. "Ptolemy?"

"Ptolemy profits. That is not the same as ordering it."

"Seleucus?"

"Always silent until he speaks."

"Cassander then?"

"He plays at games. But yes—he benefits most. Council in Babylon, claims of collapse, invoking Antipater's name. It smells of theater."

"Then who gave the order?"

"Perhaps no one we can prove. Which leaves everyone suspect."

"Everyone but the corpse," she said.

The land dried before the water ran out. Villages emptied ahead. Wells sealed. No birds, no merchants, only wind. It was as if the empire exhaled them.

Arguments filled the gaps left by thirst. The days bled together.

One evening, Eumenes asked, "Do you ever wonder what the Argead name means anymore?"

"It means my son lives," she said.

"It also makes him target," he replied. "The name once split a continent. Now it barely holds a column together."

He listed the kings of the line, from shepherd ancestry through Philip.

"Philip made Macedon cruel," she said.

"And Alexander made it myth," he answered.

"Now we have Arrhidaeus."

The name hung like smoke.

"He is not a man. He is a shield," she said. "And shields break."

They broke camp before dawn.

Roxana no longer rode beneath banners. Her guard—all eastern-born—stayed close. She no longer trusted Greek accents.

Rumor moved faster than fact. One afternoon a falcon brought a sealed note.

"Cassander declares a council in Babylon," Eumenes read. "He says the regency has collapsed. That the child is unguarded. That his father will restore order."

"Is my boy alive?" Roxana asked.

"No harm mentioned. Only that he is under protection."

"Whose?"

"That's the question."

By dusk her decision was set. Camped on a ridge, she stood watching the sun die into sand. Behind her, fires were lit in small circles. The silence heavier than the wind. In her hands, Perdiccas's signet ring. He had pressed it to her palm before Egypt, when ambition still called itself destiny. Now it felt like debt.

She held it to the flame until it burned her fingers. Then let it fall into the coals. The seal hissed, warped, disappeared.

Eumenes came to her side. "You've chosen," he said.

"I didn't need to. The world chose for me."

Alexander was already stone and story. She had waited for some omen, some sign from him. None came. He was gone.

Her son was the pulse left in a collapsing empire. She turned from the fire. Stars were cold above. Babylon lay ahead, across rumor and sand. She would walk into it not as widow but as mother—and as power.

By morning the men noticed the change. Not grief. Not pride. Not fear. Only momentum.

When one of the captains asked where they were headed, Roxana gave no answer.

She didn't need to.

OLYMPIAS

CHAPTER 17

THE EMPTY THRONE

BABYLON, MACEDON, AND BABYLON AGAIN. Cassander had always hated Babylon. It wasn't the heat, though the air felt spoiled—too ripe, too wet, like fruit left too long in the sun. It wasn't the dust, which clung even under layers of incense.

It wasn't even the gods, whose images crowded every wall—winged bulls carved into gates, half-stars and man-beast hybrid figures recessed into lintels in scripts that made his mouth ache to pronounce. He hated Babylon because it was not his—not in memory, not in blood, not in spirit.

It belonged to dead men and their myths. He had been sent there once as a boy, a Macedonian among sharper minds, to study under Aristotle. He had walked beside the son of Philip—Alexander, the boy who would turn into a god. The boy who asked questions that were not questions, and whose answers Aristotle treated as revelation.

Cassander had asked once about justice.

Aristotle had barely looked at him and said, Justice depends on who holds the scale.

When Alexander asked, the old man stopped pacing, smiled, lifted his hands. If Achilles had lived, would he have built an empire or destroyed one? How many cities must exist before they feel less real than a myth?

Cassander had watched. He had listened. He had bitten the inside of his cheek.

The game had been rigged from the start. The questions were only ever for Alexander. The rest were audience.

Now Alexander was gone. Perdiccas drowned in Nile silt. Eumenes had vanished with the queen and the boy-king. The empire was breaking apart.

Cassander pressed a hand to the limestone wall. Justice depends on who holds the scale.

He held it now.

The throne stood empty.

So he returned—not as conqueror, not yet, as steward, as placeholder, as a man willing to wait.

Babylon would serve, not as capital but as crucible, a furnace to burn through illusion until only what could be ruled remained.

He chose Nebuchadnezzar's older palace. The walls were thick, the corridors wide, the silence deep.

He had no title here, no decree, but no one stopped him. The satraps were divided, the regents distracted. He entered not as heir but as custodian of uncertainty.

He scraped the lions from the north wall, whitewashed Ishtar and Ea, brought in Macedonian carpenters, replaced cedar screens with lattice from Aegae.

His advisors joked he was measuring drapes. Cassander did not laugh.

He sealed the gates, replaced the water clocks with Greek ones, gathered the Babylonian scribes beneath a throne draped in violet. He said nothing.

At his side moved three shadows: Antigonos of Pellene, his childhood companion, blunt and loyal, useful with a knife. Meno, the Athenian eunuch, sharp with words, keeping satraps in line by scroll and seal. And finally Ophis, a Babylonian seer, robes stained with myrrh and mildew, predictions vague enough to serve.

Cassander trusted none of them, but tolerated them as a fever tolerates sweat.

They made him less alone.

By day he debated epigrams and ordered roses for the halls.

By night the questions came: Do they still dream of him? How old is the boy? Can Olympias be stopped at Larissa?

No one answered quickly. They knew the questions were not for knowledge but for proof of fear.

He was not mad, but he had begun to lose the symmetry of things. He punished gardeners for trees that leaned east. He studied the map room but kept his eyes on the floor, not the constellations above. He wore armor with care, robes with grace, but his eyes twitched when he disliked an answer. His jaw tightened before rage.

Because he was not king. Not yet.

He was dismantling memory, piece by piece, until the absence of power itself became unbearable. Then he would sit—not as Aristotle's forgotten pupil but as the one who had learned the lesson best.

MACEDON, A YEAR EARLIER

Antipater could no longer piss standing. He sat by the brazier in Pella, rubbing swollen knees, snapping at the air—regent once, now old and failing.

"You think he's ready?" he spat.

Polyperchon stood across from him, soldier's sash on his shoulder. They had fought at Chaeronea. They had buried Philip.

"He listens enough," Polyperchon said.

"But not to me." Antipater's cough rattled phlegm and blood. "Cassander hears only what flatters him. He mistakes the rooms of power for the throne. He sees conspiracy in mirrors, offense in silence, ambition in loyalty. He wants a crown, not a kingdom."

"Then warn him off."

"I tried—in Egypt, in Syria, in every message since the Nile. He sends back orders. Orders! From a man who's never held a city, never kept peace between tribes, never bent a satrap to his will. He thinks Babylon makes him Macedonian."

"And so?"

Antipater stared at the fire. His hand hovered over parchment, then withdrew. "Will I name you? Or him?"

Polyperchon said nothing.

"My own blood," Antipater muttered, "but hungry in the wrong ways. He thinks ruling is removing obstacles. But you—" He stopped. Looked across the hall. "You endure."

The fire hissed. The shutters rattled.

"I must decide soon," he said. "Before they smell weakness."

Polyperchon bowed his head. But Antipater saw the flicker in his breath—fear, not of ambition but of cost.

The pen stayed dry. The name unwritten. But both men knew what now lay on the table—and who would come for it.

*****

In Babylon the scribes waited, styluses poised over wet clay beneath the purple throne. Cassander walked the chamber, the walls still carved with Alexander's triumphs. They would not be erased—yet. Only reframed.

"Two kings," he told them. "Philip Arrhidaeus. Alexander IV. One broken. One too young. Both sacred. Both useless."

"What name first?" a scribe asked.

Cassander touched the violet cloth. He said nothing. Let them argue over sequence. He had already won.

Eumenes still roamed with Roxana and the boy, hiding in ravines beyond satrapal reach. The child still lived—Cassander knew he must—for now.

But not as king. As blur. As co-signature. As balance that meant nothing.

Meanwhile Cassander held the army, the grain, and the ink. His agents countersigned decrees. His seals released shipments. The coin bore Alexander's face but passed through his hand.

And bodies vanished—handmaidens, envoys, a priest who dared anoint the boy. The priest was found crucified near the ziggurat, a placard above him: He dreamed of kings.

Cassander ordered the wood burned, the sand salted. That same day a rider came from the west, dust-choked, carrying a scroll sealed with a lion's paw—Olympias.

He read it three times, then burned it. The lion cub does not share its cave.

Cassander watched the parchment curl to ash. "No," he said. "Then let the cave burn."

EUMENES

CHAPTER 18

THE KNIFE AND THE CRADLE

THE WIND OFF THE EUPHRATES CARRIED THE SCENT OF ASH AND MYRRH—ritual perfumes stretched too far from their purpose. History did not stir.

They sat on opposite sides of the fire, silence narrowing after weeks of flight. Eumenes had set aside his breastplate but not his sword. Roxana had abandoned her mantle but kept the knife in her boot. Neither trusted the dark, or each other. Both trusted only the mission.

"The city's already shifting," Eumenes said, drawing slow lines in the dirt with a stick. "Cassander's men control the accounting offices. The priests wait. The veterans watch. They'll act once Antipater declares."

Roxana leaned closer to the fire, her hood low. "And the boy?"

Eumenes delayed his answer. "Moved from the nursery—into the ceremonial wing. Discipline. Ritual instruction. They're turning him into a symbol."

She watched the flames. "Then I go in. Alone."

"That gains nothing."

"Delay gains less. Every day he forgets. Every day someone else takes my place."

Her eyes fixed on him. "You think I should walk in as queen?"

"No. As ash. As mourning. As shadow." For a moment they let the wind speak for them.

"Will you go after him?" she nodded. "Cassander?"

He let the silence hang. "Not yet. Ptolemy holds the body. Antigonus builds power in the west. Seleucus plays both sides. Cassander thinks short-term. I play longer."

Roxana's smile was sharp and bitter. "Alexander played all of them at once."

Eumenes returned a sad smile. "We are not him."

She drew her cloak around her.

"If I don't come back, find someone to tell the boy who he was. Who I was. Don't let him believe power is inheritance."

"He won't need to," Eumenes said, rising. "He'll see it in your absence."

They parted before dawn. She left no tracks.

*****

She entered Babylon beneath a mourning veil, carrying nothing that could betray her and everything she could not bury.

At the outer checkpoint, guards barely looked at her. The papers were sound, the ash convincing, her trembling hands deliberate. Grief was common in Babylon; few looked twice.

Two older women walked beside her—companions too worn to draw notice. A bent eunuch followed, half-lame, dressed like a forgotten servant. He passed without question.

Two days earlier she had shed her name. Eumenes had ridden north with noise and fire to draw Cassander's attention. She moved south in silence.

No one followed. No one stopped her. That, too, unsettled her. She told herself her son was here—not only by instinct. The city itself gave hints. Babylon's silence carried weight, as if something sacred had been locked away and ordered to remain still.

The city's form had not changed—rings of temples, groves, canals, all turning inward toward the palace. But the rhythm had shifted—not toward gods, but toward opportunists. Authority was paper, seal, and office—not prayer.

At the palace gate, a young eunuch studied her documents with nervous care. Antipater's seal was intact. He stepped aside.

She entered the palace without notice. History remained still.

They lodged her in the western wing once used for satraps' lesser wives. Perfume clung to the air, mixed with mildew. She accepted the rooms with lowered eyes. Within an hour she had tested windows, listened to hinges, mapped sightlines. She slept on stone, ate only what she carried, sang lullabies deliberately broken, listening for silences that did not belong.

The boy was close. She felt it not as vision but as pressure. Her chest tightened near certain corridors. Her jaw set passing guarded doors. The body forgets, but mothers remember.

Eight months since he had been taken. Her attendants gone. Letters unanswered. Mina vanished without word. Now she was inside the palace, yet shut out of all that had once been hers.

The boy had been remade.

Confirmation came from a temple girl. Roxana sat by a dry fountain, sifting dust. The girl beside her hummed a tune—off-key but familiar.

The hawk and the sea. "Where did you learn that?" Roxana asked.

"The golden boy sings it in his sleep," the girl said.

That night Roxana vomited quietly into a bowl—not poison, but certainty. The next morning, she found him.

The sacred education wing was cold, orderly. Scrolls lined the walls. A shrine to Alexander gleamed in the corner.

The boy looked up as she entered. No shock. Only a blink, as if testing memory. "Your hair is different," he said.

She dropped to her knees. Hummed the lullaby wrong. He whispered the reply. Stepped forward, half a pace.

She opened her arms. He did not enter. But he did not retreat.

It was enough—for now.

The next morning she began reclaiming space: her chamber, the corridor, the rhythm of footsteps. She replaced the basin eunuch, lined vents with bitter herbs, sharpened a hairpin to bone. Slept beside the boy.

He turned toward her in the night.

BABYLON — OUTER COURTYARD OF THE SATRAP'S HALL

The air hung heavy with sweat and incense. Cassander stood at the colonnade's edge, armor polished, eyes hollow from lack of sleep. "Egypt," he said. "What do they say?"

"Ptolemy will host the body," Eumenes replied. "Memphis will be the new seat of the divine."

"Ptolemy hosts nothing. He steals."

"The crowds cheer him," Eumenes said.

"That can be managed. Perdiccas is dead. Egypt's claim is theft. Which leaves me—"

"The boy," Eumenes said.

Cassander's eyes snapped toward him. "The boy is safe. He learns discipline. He is a symbol."

"No. A blessing for another's throne."

Cassander stepped closer. "Alexander left no heir. Only fragments—body, name, rhetoric scattered like ash."

"Then why guard the fire?" Eumenes asked.

"Because someone must. Better me than jackals at every border."

Antipater was returning. There would be regency—formal and binding. Order, not riddles.

"Order," Eumenes repeated.

"You'd rather war?"

"I'd rather memory."

Cassander turned away. "Tell Ptolemy Babylon will speak for the empire. If Roxana appears, remind her what happened to Perdiccas."

Eumenes bowed only with his mouth. "She needs no reminder."

*****

Dusk. A eunuch brought a parcel to Roxana's quarters—gold-threaded linen, Cassander's seal.

Inside: a bronze disc, polished bare. A mirror.

Her reflection stared back—thinner, hollowed. She passed it to the boy.

"It isn't for looking," he said.

She hurled it against the wall. Bronze shattered, a shard slicing Alexander's shrine.

She gathered the pieces. Chose one. Drew it across her palm—shallow, enough to feel. Not pain. Promise.

That night the shard lay across her lap. The boy curled against her. She hummed the lullaby in the right order.

He finished the last line before sleep.

She closed her eyes.

Outside, Babylon slept beneath its own reflection. The river mirrored firelight and rumor, each ripple carrying the whisper of a name not yet spoken. In the courtyards, priests counted hours by dripping oil; in the upper chambers, Cassander dreamed of scales.

Roxana did not sleep. The shard lay cooling in her hand, its edge thin as prophecy. The boy's breath rose against her shoulder—steady, untroubled. She watched it, counting each exhale as proof of a world that still remembered her.

Beyond the walls, torches guttered. A sentry paused, hearing nothing, and told himself the silence was peace. It wasn't. It was waiting.

Somewhere in the archive halls, clay tablets dried unfinished, the words for king and blood beginning to blur. By dawn, one would replace the other.

She pressed the shard flat against her palm. The knife was no longer a weapon. It was inheritance sharpened thin.

ANTIGONUS

CHAPTER 19

THE FIRST BATTLE
OF THE DIADOCHI

BABYLON, 320 BCE. The shard pressed into her palm still gleamed faintly in memory—inheritance sharpened to a blade.

Antipater entered Babylon like a corpse refusing burial. His body had betrayed him weeks earlier—some said at the Cilician Gates, others at Thapsacus. His breath rasped; his legs were bound in linen so he could stay in the saddle. But he dragged himself from Europe to the heart of the empire with one purpose clenched in his teeth.

He would not die in Macedon. He would not die beside Cassander. He would die in Babylon, where gods were made and kings unmade. He would name the regent himself.

Cassander waited in the eastern palace courtyard, shaded by incense smoke. Dust still clung to his face, but his cloak had been freshly oiled. He had learned to polish his fury. "You should have sent word," he growled.

Antipater dismounted like a man falling. Persian orderlies caught him. He did not look at his son.

"I did."

Cassander blinked. "Then why—"

"Because you'd have burned it. I wanted witnesses."

His voice was low, unshakable—the last groan of an ancient door. He walked past Alexander's training ground, past the pool where Parmenion's betrayal was whispered, into the hall of scrolls, where the empire's truths still dried in the kiln.

There Polyperchon waited.

The old general had come the night before, summoned by Antipater's hand. He traveled cloaked, mistaken for a courier until the final gate. His beard was white, his left eye clouded, his hands trembling but not uncertain. The right eye still burned.

"You're late," Antipater said.

"I'm old," Polyperchon answered.

They clasped forearms—not as friends, not as allies, but as relics. They carried the memory of Philip—the one-eyed wolf who had carved Macedonia from tribes and rot. They remembered the drills in cold mountains, the oaths sworn before Alexander's name was spoken with reverence.

Antipater had never loved Alexander, but he had obeyed him—for Philip's blood, for the momentum of conquest. What disturbed him most was not the victories but the certainty in the boy's eyes.

"I sent you east because you remember," Antipater said.

"Remember what?"

"That we were men before we were myths. Before Babylon opened its gates like a whore."

Polyperchon was silent, then said, "But the boy was more than us."

Antipater's eyes narrowed. "He flew too close."

"Yes. But the world caught fire in his wake."

Antipater withdrew a linen-wrapped clay tablet. His hands shook with age and finality.

"I have the seal. I have the right. And no time left." He forced his voice clear. "Tomorrow I will name you regent. Not because I trust you. Because you still fear the gods."

Polyperchon gave a small, tired smile. "I never stopped fearing them."

The torches hissed. The scribes froze. The archive held its breath. "And Cassander?"

Antipater's eyes clouded. "He was raised on stories, not sweat. He thinks kingship is inherited. But you and I know—it must be dragged into being."

Polyperchon pressed the scroll to his forehead—not in reverence to Antipater, but to the weight now his.

"So be it," he said. "The road waits. And the gods are watching."

The next morning, the eastern archive bristled. It was a chamber for records, not ceremony. But Antipater's cedar chair became a throne. His breath wheezed through every sentence, yet his hand was steady as he sealed the clay.

Cassander stood in shadow, arms crossed.

Polyperchon entered at first light. No armor—just a Macedonian cloak with a lion brooch.

The decree was read aloud:

> *"I, Antipater son of Iolaus, conclude my office. By the seal of the king, I name Polyperchon regent of the empire. He shall protect the blood of Alexander. Cassander, my son, shall serve beneath him. As is proper."*

No cheers. Only reed pens scratching. Copies for Susa, Persepolis, Sardis, Aegae.

Cassander stepped forward. His voice was quiet, sharpened by silence.

"You hand the empire to a ghost—a man who lost more sons than battles. Over me?"

Polyperchon stayed silent.

Antipater met his son's eyes. "You wanted power. You never asked what it was for."

Cassander's jaw locked. "You'll regret touching that seal," he told Polyperchon. Then he turned and left. The thread snapped. The first war of the Diadochi had begun.

*****

Polyperchon left the Hall alone. They would say Antipater trusted him. He knew better. The seal was a chalice, already poisoned. Antipater had made him both steward and scapegoat.

By nightfall, Cassander's scribes were already at work. Not soldiers—scribes. Not blades—bribes. New tablets pressed, seals forged, decrees rewritten. One elevated Arrhidaeus. Another gave Cassander stewardship. A third offered vague reassurances of Roxana and her child. Each was plausible. Each dispatched east.

Eumenes received the first quietly, hidden among pomegranates and dried apricots. He studied the clay, the seal, the grooves. Then he dictated his own:

"The boy is not merely king. He is constellation—born under lion, flame, and falcon, foretold by Zoroaster, by Apollo, by the stars of Marduk. Let no man call himself guardian of heaven's child lest he answer to heaven itself."

No seal. No name. Just myth, fired and copied, carried east.

Commanders laid tablets side by side. The question was no longer which was authentic. It was which felt true.

That evening, Cassander skimmed pebbles into the Euphrates. Seleucus came and sat beside him.

"You're losing the east," Seleucus said.

Cassander kept his eyes on the ripples. "Truth isn't what happened," he said. "It's what survives."

Seleucus nodded once. "Truth is a local custom now."

In the archive quarter, two kilns burned through the night. One fired Cassander's counter-decree. The other, Eumenes' prophecy. By morning, both were dry. Both were en route. Neither bore a name—only words, and the weight of war they carried.

CHAPTER 20

THE MOTHERS OF EMPIRE

BABYLON, 320 BCE. Antipater asked for no procession. He had already played his part in the theater of empire. At the end, he wanted only a mule cart, a shaded road, and enough silence to die properly.

The physicians urged against travel. He waved them off with the same withered hand that once commanded legions. Macedon was calling—not the court, not the war camps, but the soil.

He wanted to be buried near Philip at Aegae, where the mountains held tombs and the wind spoke an older tongue.

His body betrayed him again. Fingers curled inward. Lungs thickened. He had not eaten since the regency proclamation. He no longer needed to; his seal was passed, his power spent.

At dawn, the cart was readied—linen, waterskins, the clay copies of his decree. Servants packed quietly in the courtyard. Antipater stood once more in

Alexander's garden, where phalanx drills had once been traced in river stones, where he had named a regent in front of gods, men, and his son.

He did not expect Cassander. The boy had vanished after the proclamation—some said to Seleucia, others whispered he had taken the archives. Let him sulk, Antipater thought. Ambition sharpened in the dark, but it never escaped time.

Yet Cassander came—not through the front gate but by the side path through olive trees. No sword. Only a dagger wrapped in waxed cloth.

Antipater turned slowly, recognizing the shape before the face.

"You waited too long," he said.

Cassander did not answer.

The strike was clean, just beneath the ribs. Not immediate, but certain. Antipater's knees gave. His hand gripped his son's wrist—not to defend, but to recognize.

"I named you too late," he said. "Or too early."

Cassander held him upright. "You named the wrong man."

The old regent sagged, then fell.

By mid-morning, the cart still stood empty. Cassander had the body burned in secret, the ashes scattered without rites. The seal remained untouched, carved into clay. But the brake was gone. The balance cut.

Cassander returned to the chambers. The physicians were executed. The cart dismantled. The scribes shuffled. In the kitchens, onions boiled in goat milk. The palace went on breathing, unaware that the last man who remembered Macedon before the boy-god was erased.

And far away—in Epirus—a woman walked barefoot into a grove of iron oaks, preparing to speak with gods no man dared name.

*****

The smoke from Antipater's cremation never reached the women's quarter. The silence did.

Roxana sat in late-morning light, brushing her son's hair as he slept across her lap. His breath rose and fell in the rhythm of deep dreams. Lately he had begun speaking in his sleep—Greek blurred with Persian vowels, Babylonian words she had not taught him. He was becoming something the palace could not name.

Polyperchon entered. He moved stiffly, joints worn by too many campaigns. His cloak carried cedar oil and sweat. He paused under the archway. He did not bow, but he offered her silence.

"I hear the boy dreams in more than one tongue," he said. "That's how it begins—with voices."

Roxana did not look up. "He dreams of burning rivers. Horses without mouths."

Polyperchon smiled faintly, half amusement, half fear. "I once heard your husband speak in his sleep. Mid-battle. He gave orders to gods."

"And you followed them," she said.

"I did."

He stepped closer. His gaze lingered on the boy's small hands. "He looks like him."

"No," Roxana said. "He is him. That is what terrifies them."

Polyperchon circled the room. He touched the brazier where herbs smoldered. He stopped at the alcove where a clay lion sat under an oil lamp.

"You should know," he said, "Antipater is dead. Burned, quietly."

"I felt it," she said.

"He was going home. Cassander chose otherwise."

Her eyes lifted, sharp. "Did you try to stop him?"

"Would you have?" Silence spread.

"You are regent now," she said. "My son's guardian."

"And you are his mother," he replied. "Which is stronger?"

She did not answer.

He crouched beside the child, joints cracking. His calloused hand rested on the boy's shoulder. "I don't want the throne. I want the line to survive."

"And Cassander?" she asked.

"He wants to be remembered."

Polyperchon rose. He seemed older, bent beneath the seal pressing into his back. "You'll be watched. But not alone. He should not be hidden too long. The world forgets children faster than it remembers gods."

Roxana's hand covered her son's. "Let the world forget. For now, I need him to live."

Polyperchon lingered in the doorway, torn between warning and blessing. In the end, he offered neither. He simply left.

EPIRUS — THE TEMPLE OF DODONA

The oaks groaned. Their roots split earth like prophecy clawing upward. Leaves clattered like coins. The priests said the gods still spoke here—in tremors, in birds, in blood.

Olympias returned barefoot. She entered with her circle of oracles—five women older than memory, eyes ringed with coal and ash. No guards. No generals. Only women, and gods.

She had not been born Macedonian, but no woman carried its gods more fiercely. Daughter of Neoptolemus of Epirus, descendant of Achilles by blood or story, she had come to Philip's court as alliance and had stayed as queen. She bore him Alexander. She told him from the cradle he was divine. She fed him snakes. She raised him on Zeus and Achilles until blood and myth were one.

She endured Philip's infidelities. She survived his insult when he married again. When he was struck down at Aegae, some said her silence was too cold. Afterward, she lived through her son, writing him letters of omens and prayers, believing in his divinity not as symbol but as fact.

She was not in Babylon when he died. They never let her come.

Now only a grandson remained—a puppet king, a watched child. Olympias did not care for empire as the world measured it. She cared for blood. Macedon was a family, not a territory. Men had failed to protect it. Now it would be the mothers.

The altar at Dodona was oak, cut by bronze axes a century before Philip's empire. Burnt barley, animal bones, a blackened arrowhead lay at its base.

She raised her arms. The grove hushed.

"I have called your names—Philip, Alexander. Now the boy. My blood's blood. Your grandson."

The oracles chanted a broken tongue, older than tribes, older than kings. Their voices cracked like firewood.

Olympias stood with sleeves soaked in wine and myrrh. She lifted the obsidian dagger from her father's tomb.

"I name Alexander the Fourth, son of the god-king, Basileus of Macedon."

Lightning split the sky without rain. The oaks shuddered. The oracles threw oil into fire. Flames leapt. Behind the gates, Epirus cried out. They could not see her, but they heard the naming.

The dynasty had spoken—not by seal, but by her.

BABYLON, LATER THAT NIGHT

Roxana lit a candle in her archway as the wind shifted. A lacquered box lay waiting—black wood, crimson thread. She opened it. Inside was a dagger of obsidian. No note. None needed. She knew it. Olympias had once held it to her own wrist in Susa. Now it was here—not a threat, but a signal.

She turned it in torchlight, veins of stone catching fire. Then she extinguished the flame.

Their networks spread in silence. Olympias rebuilt hers with priestesses and seers, planted in temples across Greece. Roxana built hers with midwives and scribes, cooks and widows, kindness traded in small gifts. Together they wove a web not of soldiers or decrees, but of women. At its center, a boy who dreamed of fire and voiceless horses.

Far apart, in different cities, two candles burned at the same hour—one in a grove of gods, one in a palace of spies. Both flames were prayers. Both were warnings.

ANTIPATER

CHAPTER 21

THE SIEGE WITHOUT WALLS

CAPPADOCIA. Two candles died at dawn—one in a grove of gods, one in a palace of spies. Their smoke traveled farther than any rider.

Eumenes of Cardia read the first scroll beneath a pale sky, the mountains rising like unsheathed blades. The wind snapped at the parchment's corners. His horses shifted, steaming in the cold. He rolled the scroll shut and held it longer than needed—not to weigh the message, but the hand that had written it.

It bore Cassander's seal, or something close. The wording was careful—too careful. It named Arrhidaeus sole king. It spoke of Roxana and her son in the past tense.

The second scroll came three days later. No seal. No lie. Only thunder.

It was carried by a man with a branded arm and no tongue. The ink was blood-colored, the script fractured—half omen, half decree. Olympias had named the boy Basileus beneath the oaks of Dodona, with fire and storm as witnesses.

Eumenes read it twice, then handed both to his Persian captain, once a guard of Sogdiana's roads.

"Make copies. Distribute both."

"Even the forgery?"

"Especially the forgery. Let every satrap ask which truth he believes."

His force was growing: loyalists from Lydia, mercenaries from Media, Macedonians too proud to bend. But it was not an army yet. It was a signal—a mirror held up to a crown.

He let the scrolls ride ahead of him. The question was no longer truth. The truth no longer mattered. but which lie the empire would choose.

BABYLON

The heat pressed down like ritual. Even at dawn the air smelled of cedar smoke and coin.

Cassander stood behind a gauze-curtained balcony as the procession wound through the plaza. At its center rode Philip III Arrhidaeus, lashed to a white horse, crown slipping left, an attendant straightening it every few steps. Drums thudded, horns groaned, flowers were flung in rehearsed arcs.

Boys chanted in Greek and Aramaic: "The king is present. The king is eternal."

Cassander turned away before they finished. The wording did not name Alexander IV. It merely omitted him.

Inside the eastern archives, scribes bent over clay: new levies, new rosters, a new chronology. Today's ceremony had been inscribed as the "Reaffirmation of Sovereignty." Antipater's regency decree was already removed from the shelves.

"What news from Sardis?" he asked.

A young officer cleared his throat. "The satraps are divided. Some quote your decree. Some Olympias. One swears to Eumenes."

"And the boy?"

The officer hesitated. "They call him 'the claimant' or 'the echo.'"

Cassander traced the ridges of the tablets where his father's hand had once pressed wax. "Let them echo. Echoes fade."

He tapped the wax map east of Babylon. "Polyperchon?"

"In name."

"And Roxana?"

"No public appearance. But—rumor. The boy was seen on the palace roof, wearing a lion-skinned helmet."

Cassander's gaze fixed, quiet. "Never let him be seen again." The officer bowed.

Cassander returned to the balcony. The crowd was dispersing too quickly. There had been no cheering. Only silence—not the kind that fades, the kind that waits.

OUTSKIRTS OF BABYLON

Polyperchon squinted into dust. The riders on the horizon might have been his, Cassander's, or ghosts. The villa, once a satrap's retreat, now housed a fractured council, dwindling stores, and a child who asked too many questions. Reports were grim: mutiny in Macedon, Pella overrun, advisors dead by poison. The scroll ended simply: "Cassander has taken the palace."

He let it fall—not burn, not break—just fall.

Roxana entered without ceremony. Torchlight showed cracks in the ceiling, dust like powdered bone on her shawl. "You've read it," she said.

"I have."

"I warned you."

"I know. And I deserved worse."

She waited. "And now?"

"I have no decision left. The satraps have chosen. The gods are silent. All that remains is a boy—and a promise to a dying man."

"You mean Antipater."

"No. Your husband."

They stood in silence.

"He listens now," she said. "He mimics Alexander's stance. Hands on hips. Eyes like a hawk."

"The boy becomes the myth," Polyperchon murmured.

"Or the myth becomes the boy."

They did not speak of Arrhidaeus. The truth hung between them: two kings cannot last.

"If we stay, Cassander comes. If we run, we vanish," he said.

She unrolled a parchment sealed in black wax, Dodona's sigil burned into the edge. "Olympias has called us."

Polyperchon did not ask what it said. He only looked to the horizon. "Then we ride at dusk. Not for battle. For belief."

EPIRUS — DODONA

The oaks groaned before the storm—iron-barked, older than temples. The grove spoke in creaks and silences. Olympias stood barefoot in the mud, yew leaves knotted in her hair, robe black. Around her, seven Oracles knelt, hair bound with thorns, wool dyed ash. A drumbeat. Scattered barley. Fire sparked from flint and breath.

She raised her arms. "The gods do not name kings. Mothers do." Thunder rolled.

She held a scroll of rawhide, stitched from a sacrificial bull—inked in blood, sealed with her thumb. Before her stood a clay effigy of her grandson, crowned with myrtle, clutching a spear and a lion's tooth.

Her voice rose: "In the name of Philip. In the name of Alexander. In the name of Macedon and Epirus—I, Olympias, mother of Alexander, name this child Basileus. Let the oaks bear it. Let thunder carry it. Let no man crown another."

Lightning split the oak behind the altar, cracking it in two. Birds scattered in a black wave. The Oracles cried out. Olympias did not move.

BABYLON, THAT NIGHT

Roxana lit a candle as the wind shifted. Polyperchon sat beside the boy. Alexander looked up from carving a lion. "Do emperors run away?"

Roxana met his gaze. "Not if they ride first."

In her palm she held the obsidian dagger from Epirus. She touched its edge, then closed her hand. The boy had grown. He no longer asked where his father was. He asked where his sword was. They would leave Babylon—not with blades, but with names.

CAPPADOCIA, BEFORE DAWN

Eumenes wrote while the camp slept, frost clinging to saddles. He did not write in Greek or Persian, but in the old Macedonian tongue—the language of hills and oaths, nearly extinct. He was no Macedonian; they never let him forget. But he had bled for their king. That gave him the right.

He wrote not to a court, but to a mother.

> *I have read your decrees and your prophecies, true and false.*
> *I have seen words twisted until even truth forgot its shape.*
> *But I remember when a word meant more than wax. I*
> *remember the man who made us kneel. I bore his coffin.*
> *I hoped you might keep his son safe. That hope is gone.*
> *So let this be my only word: the boy lives. I will fight for*
> *that. Not for omens. Not for ghosts. But because once, a king*
> *put his hand on my shoulder and said, Guard what is not*
> *yet born.*
> *That vow holds. I will not write again. This letter may not*
> *reach you. It may reach Cassander instead. Let that be my*
> *gamble.*

He signed with no name—only four dots, the mark of Alexander's inner circle. When the letter reached Babylon, a priest of Mithra carried it disguised as spice trade. Roxana unwrapped the clay herself. She read it aloud.

The scent of cedar lingered, like the pyre where Alexander had ceased to be a man and become myth. She read it again, slower. The boy carved a lion from driftwood. He looked up once.

"Will the man come here?" he asked.

Roxana shook her head. "No. But we will go to him."

PART IV

ASHES OF EMPIRE

THE LAST EMBERS, STILL BURNING IN THE DARK.

CHAPTER 22

FLIGHT INTO SILENCE

OUTER GATE OF BABYLON – HOURS BEFORE DAWN. The gates of Babylon did not open for them. They sighed—just enough to let a memory slip past.

Roxana rode ahead, posture rigid beneath the darkness of the night. A woolen cloak veiled her face, but tension rippled along her jaw, her eyes tracking every shift in the dark. Behind her, the boy walked barefoot, dragging a wooden sword through gravel. Too large. Too real. He held it like a relic. It bounced against his ankles in a rhythm the living could not name.

Polyperchon brought up the rear, reins slack in one hand, a scarred olive branch clutched in the other like a question left unanswered. He hadn't spoken since they passed through the eastern breach—just a hole in the wall, plastered with mud and forgetfulness. The guards hadn't even looked up. Not paid. Just hollow.

No banners. No bridles. No songs. Just twelve riders and a future they weren't sure belonged to them, slipping beneath stars already turning away.

Thais of Ecbatana walked beside the boy. Older. Wiry. Dust-tough. Her robes stitched with survival. Her mouth never stopped—half-chant, half-prayer to a god Babylon had scraped from its stones but not from her bones. Her voice wove a veil over them. Sound as shield.

Roxana trusted her more than any man.

In her saddlebag, sealed in waxed lambskin, lay a small object left in the talons of a dead falcon. The courier had collapsed beside a meat stall near the Ishtar Gate, mouth full of dirt, fingers sliced to the bone. But the token remained: an ivory seal braided with wolf-hair.

Olympias. No inscription. Just a stamped mouth in profile—teeth bared. Tongue missing.

"Come to the place where the gods still listen," Roxana whispered. Epirus.

But not directly. That path was sewn with knives. Macedonian cities throbbed with Cassander's spies—men who read prayers backward and poisoned the bleed.

They turned north. Through fields that forgot names. Paths worn by smugglers, servants, and runaway priests. Wheat gone to salt. Vineyards crumbling into dust. They never spoke Eumenes' name aloud. Roxana had seen the glint in Polyperchon's eye when she said "north." Not trust. Recognition.

At a checkpoint past an Assyrian cistern shattered by time, the boy stopped. Tilted his head. Sword upright.

"He's here."

Roxana turned. "Who?"

"The man with no nose."

Polyperchon froze. Thais spat three times into the dust.

The air went metallic. Dry palms rustled like breath. No figures. Just the feeling. They moved faster.

A rider snapped his horse's leg cutting across salt-ridge. Left behind. No debate.

That night, camp without fire. Roxana found Polyperchon at a dead fig tree, sharpening a dagger—not a sword, but something meant for necks.

"You still think we'll reach Eumenes?"

He tested the edge. Wiped the blade clean.

"He won't trust you."

"But he'll trust you."

He shrugged. "He respects desperation. And dynasties. You qualify." A beat passed.

"And what do you respect?"

"Children who live long enough to matter."

Roxana nodded once, breath steaming.

"Then let's get him there."

Behind her, Thais whispered:

"Don't speak his name. Even gods can be hunted if they shout too loud." The boy no longer hummed. But he held the sword as if it remembered itself.

*****

The sun rose behind a fractured watchtower west of the Tigris, dragging gray light through a dust veil that never lifted.

Four days on the road. No birds. No insects. Just a child speaking to ghosts—half-memories, half-warnings, all in fragments. They stopped at a ruined Parthian tower, half-collapsed, jagged like a molar. Polyperchon signaled a halt.

No fire. No salted meat. Only wooden spoons, dried fruit, water passed slowly.

Thais crouched, sniffed the air. "Two fires. One for heat. One for watching."

Polyperchon climbed the wall with a fingerbone spyglass. His shoulders sagged. "Pairs. Maybe three. Not soldiers. Eyes."

Roxana moved instantly. She pulled a decoy from the saddlebags—robes, headdress, a wooden mask painted in her likeness.

The woman stepped forward. Lysandra. A dancer who moved like someone else's memory.

"You'll have an hour," Roxana said.

"I only need thirty minutes," Lysandra replied.

She rode south. Toward surveillance.

Roxana turned north. They approached a collapsed Roman bridge. Only a tree trunk and stone ribs remained.

She tied a rope to the boy's wrist. "Hold this."

"Was that you?"

"No. But she's helping."

"Will she die?"

"I don't know."

Polyperchon cursed—lame horse, stone in the hoof. Offered to shoot it. Roxana refused. "We walk."

Single file. Cloth-wrapped hooves. Light fading. Dust rising. At the far side, the boy coughed—not from illness, but from fear exhaled too late.

Thais placed honeycloth to his lips. "Too many dreams in that chest," she said. "They'll wake if we don't bleed them out."

They did not sleep. Polyperchon sat, dagger across his lap like a relic. Roxana traced stars she didn't trust. Somewhere, a woman wore her face and walked into blades. Somewhere, the second signal fire burned.

Above, the sky withheld judgment. It often did.

*****

By nightfall, they reached the shrine at the edge of a gorge—a discovery shaped more by hunger and terrain than intent.

It sat half-swallowed by the hillside, a lean stone frame marked by seven carved stars and a mother's hand protecting a flame. There were no offerings left, no clear indication of the god once worshipped here. The maps gave it no name. Locals hadn't spoken of it. But something had stayed.

Roxana dismounted first. She circled the ruin slowly, letting her fingers trace the worn grooves in the stone. The scent inside was thick—cedar burned long ago, spoiled milk left to curdle in heat. Not rot. Something suspended.

Thais stopped just short of the lintel.

Her voice dropped. "She stayed," she said. "Not the god. The mother."

Polyperchon didn't challenge her. His shoulders were too low for arguing.

Roxana sat in the dust, cross-legged. The boy leaned against her side, too tired to eat, too restless to sleep. She fed him mashed fig from her fingers. He took each bite without complaint, his eyes never leaving her face.

The air shifted overhead—drier now, sharp with salt and stone. On the far wall, barely visible, someone had once painted a lioness standing over an altar. Beneath her paws: two cubs circled in bone. Time had blurred the lines, but Thais recognized the shape and laid her thumb to it.

"This story isn't about salvation," she said. "It's about who remembers."

Roxana studied the cubs. She imagined the brush that had drawn them. The hand that trembled, or didn't.

Let memory carry this, she thought. Not just the lion, but what she shielded.

Later, when the boy finally slept with his head in Thais's lap, Roxana unwrapped the seal again. The ivory caught no firelight—there was none—but held its warmth anyway. The braid of wolf-hair had frayed. She turned it between her fingers, waiting. Hoping it would change. It hadn't.

"Come to the place where the gods still listen." The words had hardened. Once a call, now a test.

"We move west tomorrow," she said. "Northwest into the highlands. He needs mountain air. He needs time."

Polyperchon looked up from his seat, sharpening a bent spearhead. "You think Eumenes is still willing?"

"He might not be," she answered. "But he believes in Alexander."

Polyperchon frowned. "And if that's no longer true?"

Roxana didn't pause. "Then he'll believe in what's left of me."

They sat in stillness until the hawk passed overhead—just a single shape, circling without hurry. Its wings cast no omen. Its hunger was its own.

The night closed in, heavy and without promise.

*****

The Cappadocian foothills rose slow and sharp, ribbed with scrub brush and exposed stone. The road had long since lost its name. What remained was a track worn by goats and traders who no longer came.

Roxana led. No one challenged her. The boy slept behind her in a muleman's arms, the wooden sword still clutched in his hand. His knuckles stayed white even in dreams.

They reached a broken Roman relay station by noon. Weeds burst through the mosaics; columns listed like drunk men. Roxana knelt beside one pillar and began clearing the dirt.

She drew with her finger—paths remembered more than mapped. Spring runoff. A collapsed mine road. A cavalry post that might still hold a trace of Eumenes' camp. She didn't speak to the others. Her voice narrated only for herself.

"Here. South ridge. He quartered cavalry here. Flooded by end of month. There's a cut-path through the pass—dug by miners. Old. Forgotten. That's the way."

Polyperchon joined her. He watched the lines she made, the way her hand trembled only once. "You believe he's still up there?"

"If he is, he's watching the plains. Looking for smoke."

Polyperchon tapped a boot against stone. "And if he's not?"

She rubbed the drawing clean with the flat of her palm.

"Then we make him real again. Even if all that's left is ash."

He studied her face—not for strategy, but to understand what had hardened there. She was no longer asking his opinion.

"You weren't like this before," he said.

"Before what?"

"Before Egypt. Before Babylon. Before the boy."

She rose, eyes on the horizon. A distant glint caught the light—a mineral seam or a blade unsheathed.

"I was someone's wife," she said. "Now I'm the warning."

*****

That night she did not sleep. By moonlight, she wrote three letters. One for Eumenes—coded and brittle with effort. One for a mercenary captain whose loyalty might bend but hadn't yet broken. One for Olympias.

Each was burned after sealing. Not out of fear. Because the words had already done their work. They lived now in breath and memory.

Later, she walked the edge of the camp. The moon hung low, bruised and silent. She found the boy sitting upright. Eyes open.

"Why are you awake?" she asked.

"Because you are," he said.

She sat beside him. He leaned into her without speaking. "Do you remember your father?"

He blinked once, then looked away.

"Still in my belly, he called you thunderborn," she whispered. "Said you'd be louder than anything that came hunting."

"Am I a god?" the boy asked.

Roxana reached into her cloak and gave him a piece of salted bread. "You're my son," she said. "That's louder."

*****

They waited until the last star before crossing Shinarak Gorge, where the Cappadocian border splits like torn fabric. The gorge ran deep—carved by centuries of glacial retreat. Its pass was narrow, no more than two hands wide, with no rail and no room for mistakes.

They crossed without speaking. Scouts first. Then the mules. Then the riders, each leading their horses on foot.

Roxana carried the boy on her back, his arms looped around her neck. He didn't stir. His body was limp with exhaustion, but his grip on the sword never faltered.

Midway through, Polyperchon slipped. He caught the edge. The man behind him didn't. One breath of sound. A fall too steep to hear landfall.

They kept moving. The road didn't wait for grief.

By the far side, Roxana's palms bled. Her breath came sharp and hot through her teeth.

A Thracian rider collapsed to his knees, sobbing—not from fear, but from memory. He'd crossed this gorge in another life, behind Alexander. Now he crossed it for a boy no one dared name.

Polyperchon left him. No judgment. Only distance.

*****

That night, in a clearing where the trees let the stars look down without interruption, the boy began to hum. The sound was soft at first—a rhythm older than melody.

Thais joined in, instinctive. Her voice wove into his like she'd known it before.

Roxana stepped closer. "Where did you learn that?"

The boy didn't answer. His eyes were open, but looking somewhere else.

Polyperchon grimaced. "It's a death song. Hittite or older. It should not come from him."

"It comes now," Thais said.

The tune swelled. It trembled the dust around their feet. They didn't light a fire. They didn't look away.

"He's listening to something," Thais whispered. "And it's listening back."

Roxana didn't speak. She listened, too. To the earth, to the sky, to the space between breaths. She saw the road stretched behind them—burned, empty, and lined with names the world no longer wanted.

Ahead: stone, shadow, a narrowing thread of belief. She looked at the boy. She made herself a promise.

If something came for him, it would go through her first.

CHAPTER 23

MY BLOOD SHALL RETURN

They reached Mount Argaeus at dusk, its cleft swallowing the last of the light like a secret sealed shut. The boy squinted as the trail curled between twin basalt ridges, blackened and fractured like old wounds left to weather. His cloak snapped in the cold air, and the pony beneath him shifted—bored of the climb, but not tamed by it.

Roxana rode beside him, her veil drawn back. Dust veiled her hair, but her eyes still caught the fading sun like obsidian. She pointed with her chin.

"There," she said. "The Argaeum."

The name hovered in the air, as if it had waited years to be spoken aloud.

Up the slope, a cluster of dark stone structures clung to the mountain. Temples, yes—but not for the living.

The site carried an old gravity. Seleucid and Roman troops had long avoided the passes, and even the local cults approached the peak as if petitioning a god that answered only in silence.

The boy frowned. "It looks… broken."

"It was," Polyperchon muttered, reining up beside them. His beard had bleached to chalk, and his voice scraped like stone on leather.

"Before you were born. Before your father carved his name into the world's spine."

The mules climbed the final switchbacks in silence. Juniper rustled in the dry wind, and the cliffs bore the marks of rituals older than their memories—votive niches worn faceless, half-legible prayers cut into the dark tuff.

The boy looked up, watching a hawk circle with deliberate slowness.

"It smells like rust," he said.

"Juniper," Roxana corrected, but she understood.

"The mountain leaks iron when it rains." He didn't ask how mountains could bleed. He nodded, as if it already made sense.

They rounded the last bend. The stronghold emerged from the cliff—not built, but exhumed. Arches. Terraces. Mouths carved from the mountain's own jaw. Moss coated the stone steps like dried scabs. Overhead, an eagle relief glared from above the gate, its right eye chiseled out by time or blasphemy—only the left remained, watching.

"Your father spared this place," Roxana said, her voice hushed as they approached. "His advisors said burn it. Remote, unaligned. A fire temple buried in basalt. But he stayed. Three nights."

Polyperchon's hands flexed around the reins.

"He said nothing. Not to his men. Not to me."

"What did he do?" the boy asked.

"He listened."

"To what?"

"To the stone. To the fire beneath it. To the voice that remains when conquest ends."

The boy turned his gaze to the temple. He didn't speak.

Ahead, Polyperchon's men moved like ghosts among the terraces—clearing aqueducts, restoring the sleeping quarters. Thin tendrils of smoke rose from hidden chimneys, funneled through natural vents that kept the fires invisible. A handful of smiths, engineers, and worn-eyed scouts bowed—not deeply, but in a way that suggested memory, not rank.

They passed under the gate. No banners hung. No horns sounded. Only the dull rhythm of their footsteps.

Roxana dismounted with care. Her muscles ached from the climb.

The boy moved to follow, but she caught his wrist.

"This is where we wait," she said.

Polyperchon stood beside her, every year now visible in the slump of his shoulders. His voice came slower. Firmer.

"Not for long. Cassander's at Pella."

"Then why bring us here?"

"Because you're no longer a queen," he said. "And he—" he glanced at the boy, "—is no longer a child. He's the hinge on which the war will turn."

She looked beyond them to the eastern caves, now half-converted into living quarters. Smoke-smudged walls. Hearths lit again.

If myth had bones, this place was its ribcage. "This was his," the boy said, brushing the wall with his palm.

Polyperchon nodded. "One of the only places he didn't conquer. He remembered it instead."

They stepped into the inner hall—a courtyard carved between cave and sky.

Water ticked from the stone cisterns in slow, deliberate rhythm. Light slanted through shaft-holes cut centuries ago to catch the sun at noon. Incense burned somewhere unseen. The air carried it like memory refusing to scatter.

"His name is here," Polyperchon said. He led them to a cistern wall.

Roxana lifted the boy to see.

There it was. A single line scratched deep into the basalt in ancient script. My blood shall return.

Alexander read it silently. His fingers curled slightly.

Roxana felt the tension in him—as if he were straining toward something only he could feel. "Do you believe it?" he asked.

She bent, kissing the crown of his head.

"I do."

Terrace | Map | Messages | Omens

Later, on the upper terrace, Polyperchon stood hunched over a map drawn on the back of a Hellenic battle banner. Roxana leaned on the parapet beside him, watching her son chase a goatling between the ruined columns.

The boy laughed—once—and the sound pierced something in her chest.

"We'll hold here," she said.

"For a time," Polyperchon replied. He traced a finger along a mountain pass. "But I'll need to return to Pella."

"Cassander's not waiting," she said.

"No." He folded the edge of the map. "He's already crowned Arrhidaeus. The farce is official. Macedon has a king who doesn't know he's king, and a regent who plays god from behind a curtain."

"You sound tired."

"I am." He looked past the parapet, toward the flickering torches below. "Antipater thought naming no heir would buy time. He assumed the contenders would kill each other before the dust settled. But now the throne's a carcass, and the vultures have grown patient."

Roxana studied him. "And what are you?"

Polyperchon didn't answer right away. His gaze drifted to the boy, now crouched over a beetle, whispering to the wind.

"I'm the one who gets him to the other side."

She nodded. "Then leave tonight. Take only your best. You'll need the hours."

"And you?"

"I have the mountain," she said. "I have women who remember more than men record. And I have the son of the king."

Polyperchon grunted. "And the mountain still listens."

That night, villagers from the lower settlements left offerings at the base of the trail—goat skulls, twisted juniper branches, folded charms made from reed and soot. No candles. No procession.

The mountain needed no invitation. Its heir had returned.

*****

By dawn, Polyperchon's chamber—once a fire altar—had become a war room. The stone walls still radiated a subtle warmth, not from flames, but from memory. On a low table sat five scrolls sealed in wax, delivered by messengers who hadn't dismounted.

He opened the first.

Ptolemy had declared himself guardian of the divine corpse. Memphis was his now—recast as holy ground. Priests had begun carving his image beside that of the pharaohs. One scroll called him "Protector of the God-Body." Not a title—a claim.

The second spoke of Seleucus. He had returned to Babylon, nominally as satrap. But the orders from Macedon were returned unopened. He'd seized the treasury, restructured the garrisons, replaced Greek scribes with Babylonian astrologers and Persian swords. The note read: He rules from the shadows now, not the regent's light.

Cassander had made no move to contest it. He no longer feigned interest in Babylon. No dispatches. No denunciations. His ambition had narrowed to the throne halls of Macedon.

And in the west—Antigonus. His banners now flew over Celaenae and Sardis. The old Argead star returned, stitched in gold thread. His messengers claimed loyalty. The scroll repeated one phrase three times: In defense of unity.

Polyperchon rubbed his temple. The words sounded less like coordination than the tuning of war drums.

The empire had splintered into instinct.

Every satrap an heir. Every letter a blade.

But no one called themselves king. Not yet.

Only Roxana's son had the blood to pull it back together. A boy with Alexander's eyes. A child still whispering to hawks and stone.

He pressed his ring into the wax of his reply. Not an order. Not yet. Just a signal. The war had already begun. They just hadn't admitted it.

*****

They dressed Arrhidaeus in silver—not gold—by Cassander's decree. "Less garish," he said. "More civilized."

But everyone knew the real reason. Alexander had worn gold.

The coronation took place in the old palace courtyard. Once a training ground. Once a garden. Now swept clean of history, bleached with lime, drained of ghosts. The olive tree where boys once practiced swordplay had been removed. Nothing shaded the dais but sky.

Cassander stood behind the throne. Not beside it. One pace right. Shadow stretched long.

He carried no scepter. Wore no crown. Just the weight of precision—hands folded, eyes steady, mouth set in permanent judgment.

The trumpet blew too soon. A pigeon startled from the eaves.

No one laughed.

A priest in yellowed linen read a blessing older than most gods still remembered. The syllables hung brittle in the air, understood only by the dust that had clung to the columns since Philip's time.

Arrhidaeus sat slack-mouthed, drooling once, then blinking slowly. His tunic bunched at the waist. His lips moved without sound. He stared at the banners as if they might whisper his role back to him.

Cassander's fingers curled tighter around the edge of the throne.

No one interrupted the rite. No one believed it mattered.

When the nobles knelt, they did so with the slow, performative precision of men playing at conviction.

Lord Alketas knelt last.

Too late. The delay was brief, but fatal. His knee cracked audibly. Cassander didn't flinch, but he saw. Alketas would be dead by the full moon.

Lady Myrto of Amphipolis had already vanished. Illness, they said. Fever, perhaps. But her retinue had left before sunrise, and her seal had been broken from the council scroll. She had help. No one said who.

In the colonnade, Polyperchon stood without insignia.

He had returned, but not declared. A quiet threat. Beside him—taller than memory, robed in black wool and fury—stood Olympias. She hadn't asked permission to enter. She hadn't needed to.

Some whispered she brought snakes. Others said she had spoken to the statue of Philip the night before and that the stone had wept. She remained standing when the others bent.

Her spine didn't know how to bow.

"Look at this," she muttered, low enough only Polyperchon could hear. "Philip's bastard shell."

"Arrhidaeus was legitimate," he replied, voice even.

Her scoff held fire. "Philinna danced in taverns before she danced in beds. That boy is a shadow made flesh."

Polyperchon said nothing. His eyes were on Cassander. "That," he said, "is the real danger."

Olympias's gaze didn't follow. "Then pull the throne from under him."

Polyperchon exhaled. "That would crown you again."

Her smile didn't reach her eyes. "I never abdicated."

*****

At the final moment, Cassander stepped forward and raised the olive-band crown. The room silenced—not in awe, but obedience.

"By the will of Macedon," he declared, "and the gods of the House of Argead, our line continues, unbroken."

Arrhidaeus said nothing. He blinked three times, his fingers trembling at the hem of his robe.

The crown was placed. The farce was sealed. Outside, Pella carried on.

Markets remained open. Bakers kept kneading. Children threw dice against temple steps. There were no garlands, songs, or anthems. Just a single proclamation nailed to the agora wall. It curled in the breeze like something already forgotten.

A cobbler read it, spat, and walked on. "Silver for a puppet," he said. "Bronze for the rest of us."

No one repeated it. But no one corrected him.

*****

Some time later, Roxana read the new proclamation aloud. Her voice held no ceremony—just breath, steadied against the wind that pushed through the Argaeum's upper terraces.

"The son of Philip, Arrhidaeus, was today affirmed in the palace court at Pella. By will of the late regent Antipater, and with the blessing of the temple priests, he assumes ceremonial duties in the line of Argead kings."

Her son sat cross-legged on a basalt slab, heels knocking rhythm against the stone like a war drum forgotten by time. He squinted at her, then out across the valley below.

"Is he king now?" the boy asked.

She folded the parchment. "They say he is."

"But he's not."

"No."

He tapped his foot again. A slower rhythm now. Thinking. "Father was king. And then me."

"You are."

"Then why do they pretend?"

She let the silence do its work before answering. "Because pretending keeps them safe. And truth does not."

The boy looked away. The clouds had begun to fracture, leaking orange across the high ridges. Down in the valley, the goat paths gleamed like old bone. He said nothing, but picked up a fragment of broken pottery and began scratching it against the wall behind him—tuff stone, soft enough to mark.

She stepped closer. At first she thought it was a sun. Then she saw the horse beneath it.

"Bucephalus," he whispered.

She knelt beside him. The image was crude but deliberate: flared nostrils, storm legs, a starburst on the brow.

"He comes back sometimes. In dreams."

She brushed the dust from his wrist, her touch feather-light. "I know," she said. "So does your father."

CHAPTER 24

THE SHAPE OF
WHAT REMAINS

The girl had been caught at the gatehouse wearing the blue sash of a temple acolyte and carrying no weapon but a sealed scroll. She walked into Pella like a ghost into a chapel—unhurried, unswerving, unreadable. When the guards searched her robes, they found a satchel of powdered myrrh and a twist of dried hemlock tucked behind her ear.

Cassander had her brought to the old council chamber—the same hall where Antipater once lectured generals with maps inked on sheepskin. It was bare now, save for a brazier and a dead wasp drifting in the wine jug.

He waited until the door shut behind her. "You're too young to be this reckless."

The girl—sixteen, perhaps seventeen—lowered her hood. Her hair was braided with black thread. Mourning braids. Her wrists were ringed in charcoal.

"I'm older than you think," she said. "In Epirus, we count time by blood-lines, not birthdays."

Cassander smiled, but the shape of it had no conviction. "And how many bloodlines have you outlived?"

She did not answer.

He rose and circled her, as if appraising an unfinished sculpture. Her san-dals were worn to leather string. Her fingernails were bitten raw. But she did not bow. She did not blink. "Who sent you?"

"You already know."

"And what did she offer?"

"She didn't offer," the girl said. "She called. I answered. I serve."

Cassander turned back to the brazier, stirring the coals with a bronze rod. "Of course. That's her favorite weapon—requests dressed as inevitability."

He poured himself wine and gestured toward her with the cup. "Do you drink?"

"I fast." "Of course you do." He drank.

"She could've sent a letter. Or a corpse. Why a girl?"

"She said you wouldn't listen to anyone else."

He laughed once—briefly, the kind of laugh a younger man might mis-take for power. "She's right," he said. "I don't."

He drained the cup. "What does she want?"

"She wants the line restored. The rightful line. She wants the boy crowned, the gods invoked. She wants a funeral pyre for your lies and a chorus to carry your name into silence."

The girl stepped forward, her voice low and deliberate. "She says: You sever roots and call it pruning. You burn scrolls and call it law."

Cassander's face stayed neutral. "She says: You speak for kings who no longer breathe. I speak for one who still does."

He stepped closer—two paces, close enough to catch the myrrh and ash threaded in her hair. "You think that boy will rule anything?"

"He already does."

"From shadow. From rumor."

"From memory. And soon—from decree."

He reached into his cloak and pulled a coin from his pouch. Held it between them. His face on one side. The reverse, blank. He tossed it.

She caught it.

"Do you see your king on that coin?"

She looked down, then met his gaze. "No," she said. "But I hear him in the forge."

Cassander's mouth twitched. He turned away. "Tell her this: if she surrenders now, she'll be buried with honors. If not—she'll be left for the birds."

The girl tucked the coin into her sash. "She says you were always afraid of birds."

He froze.

She added, quiet: "She says they remember the shape of things. Even when men forget."

Cassander looked past her. Past the stone walls. Past memory. He thought of a black-winged jay that had once stolen his brother's ring. The bird returned for days, circling the courtyard as if mocking them.

He crushed the thought. "Escort her out."

Later, alone in the chamber, he stood by the brazier, staring at the coals. He summoned no scribes. Drafted no reply. At dawn, he ordered the roads to Pydna sealed. The siege resumed by noon.

Above Pella, the birds kept flying. But their shadows stretched farther.

*****

The Nile shifted color by the hour—jade in morning, ochre by dusk, then gray as the stars returned. It moved like a living record, reflecting not just the sky, but the man who now watched over its edge.

Ptolemy hadn't truly slept since Perdiccas died—since the moment he laid claim to the corpse. At dawn, he walked barefoot across the temple's mosaic tiles, still warm from the previous day, the scent of embalming oils and cedar ash trailing in his wake.

Behind him, priests followed at a distance, their heads bowed—not in grief, but in anticipation, as though awaiting new commandments not yet written.

Alexander's body lay under a canopy of sycamore and lapis. Columns framed the tomb like an altar, ringed with bronze masks and incense bowls. Before the guards and scribes arrived to deliver new offerings, Ptolemy always came first. He stood in silence beside the sarcophagus. Listening.

He claimed there were breaths still caught in the space between the ribs. No one dared argue anymore.

Outside the tomb, a column of veterans curved around the necropolis—old Macedonian infantry with weathered faces and fractured memories. They brought their tributes not with pride, but with gravity: a bronze ring dulled by sweat, a snapped javelin point, a lock of a grandchild's hair. Each item laid at the threshold like a prayer with no answer.

There was still no funeral. No royal decree. No official mourning. Only the shrine—expanding each day, reshaped by the gravity of devotion.

Ptolemy had begun dressing in white at dawn. Not out of mourning, but mimicry. Linen robes, bleached with goat milk and salt, hung loose over one shoulder. He had seen Alexander wear the same in Siwa, during an eclipse. Now he wore them as a second skin, a daily invocation.

He called it custodianship. But the word didn't cover it. He had begun to wonder—quietly, without telling even the priests—whether the mantle of godhood could be transferred. Not denied. Not destroyed. Redirected. Made useful.

The priests had already begun asking him to interpret dreams—visions of a second sunrise, of rivers reversing their course. Visitors arrived with poems naming him Ptolemaios Soter, Deliverer of the West. A flock of herons had circled the tomb at dawn three days in a row, then vanished toward the sun.

He recorded each omen in a scroll bound with lionhide, hidden in a chamber behind the tomb. It was not grief he documented. It was pattern.

Alexander had become too large to bury. And if something could not be buried, it could be wielded.

Kingship no longer interested him. Pharaoh was a title, a mask to speak through. But divinity—divinity had no term limit. He studied it now: its symbols, its hungers, the infrastructure required to make belief endure.

Alexander had claimed godhood through ancestry and conquest. But the empire had died with him. Ptolemy would try another method.

He would become divine by proximity—by tending the corpse, by managing its access, by staging its silence as prophecy.

The shrine would not be a tomb. It would be a generator. And if the body was never buried—never allowed to decay, never confirmed in death—it could never contradict the stories told about it. That was the brilliance. The dead do not argue.

Already, the tomb had begun to whisper. Not in sound, but in certainty. It pulled pilgrims from every quarter: generals, mystics, war orphans, and soldiers who insisted they had been born the day Alexander died. They left offerings, took nothing, and walked away altered.

The priests said the oils never congealed. That the air above the sarcophagus stayed warm even at night. That doves had begun to roost atop the columns and did not scatter when approached.

Ptolemy began to dream of lungs large enough to house storms. The breath inside them carried voices—some familiar, some ancient, none complete. He never spoke of these dreams. He rose, washed in lotus water, and resumed his vigil.

He told others it was devotion. But what he measured each morning was the length of eternity—and whether it had room for more than one god.

But Alexander had never made room in life. And Ptolemy understood: to rise beside a god, first learn to bury a man.

*****

Pella had stopped burning. It simmered now—heat trapped in the marrow of its stones, radiating from tiled rooftops and the flesh of men too exhausted to sweat.

In the Hall of the Kings, the air congealed like overcooked incense. Smoke curled from censers along the colonnades, not in tribute but as distraction.

Philip III Arrhidaeus sat on the canopy throne, a body dressed as a monarch, his presence preserved by protocol more than will. His robe—once a symbol of divine inheritance—now hung loose, too large, as if sewn for another man, long gone. The circlet slid down his brow. His gaze drifted without meaning.

A court eunuch leaned close, whispering the familiar phrase. "Raise your hand, O king."

Nothing.

A servant stepped forward, gently lifted the royal hand, held it aloft. Applause followed—crisp but empty, the kind that vanishes before it finds conviction.

A herald took center court—not Cassander, of course, but one of his shadows. The man's Macedonian bore the clean edge of formal schooling. Behind him, Babylonian scribes echoed his words, translating for an empire that no longer asked for truth—only continuity.

"The will of the House of Macedon endures," he announced. "Let it be known: the throne is occupied. The line unbroken."

No mention of Roxana. No mention of the boy. The omissions had been practiced into fluency.

Macedon no longer held court. It issued statements.

Cassander's reach had grown without coronation. His orders traveled farther than the king's voice, carried on coin and decree. Let the eastern satraps whisper of ghosts, he'd said once. I will give them salt, roads, and rule.

A week before, the statue of Alexander—commissioned years prior but never unveiled—was dismantled. Itimaru of Uruk, the sculptor favored by the king himself, was not informed. At dawn, soldiers entered the courtyard, removed the drapery, and struck the bronze head from its base with a hammer. It landed in a dry pond and rolled beneath a bed of weeds.

By nightfall, the metal had been melted down.

New coins emerged from the forge—Cassander on one side, youthful and forward-facing. The reverse bore no image. Blank. Unclaimed. By morning, the coins had reached the southern markets.

A boy digging between cobblestones found one, still warm from the sun. His mother haggled over lentils a few paces away, her voice lost in the rhythm of barter.

The boy held the coin to the light. "Who's this?" he asked a vendor.

The man squinted. "No one."

"But there's a face."

"Not on both sides."

"Was someone there?"

The vendor shrugged. "Once."

From the upper colonnade, Polyperchon watched the exchange unfold without moving. He leaned against a cracked marble pillar, the same place he had stood since first light.

No guards flanked him. No scrolls waited in his hands. The guards referred to him as the observer. It wasn't a title, but it kept them from asking more.

He had once been sent by Antipater. No one had officially recalled him. So he remained—unseen, but never absent.

Seleucus, still fortifying Babylon's gates beyond the Tigris, had sent no word. Neutral, for now. But Polyperchon had learned to read absence. Silence before storms was not stillness. It was calibration.

In the square below, a new statue rose from the same plinth where Alexander's likeness had stood. The sculptors debated its form—some called it a flame curling into a hand, others said it was a hand made of smoke. Either way, it was metaphor, not monarch. A monument to transition.

The design had come from Pella. No seal accompanied the delivery. None was needed. Every artisan knew who paid the wages now.

Polyperchon was once called slow. But slowness was a weapon, too. He watched not because he lacked conviction, but because conviction without precision turned into waste.

He was waiting for a silence to end. Then he would answer in iron. But the target had not yet earned the blow.

That morning, inside the Hall of the Kings, he had stood behind the same fractured pillar and watched the ritual unfold—the eunuch's whisper, the lifted arm, the applause rehearsed into submission. He had said nothing. No one expected him to.

Later, as the columns emptied and the sun carved new shadows across the floor, a guard leaned toward another.

"Even silence is a kind of report."

Polyperchon heard it. He made no sound in reply. His gaze didn't shift. His hands stayed still.

He simply watched, as one who had served a living kingdom and now kept its unfinished ghost.

That night, high on the slopes of Mount Argaeus, Roxana sat alone beneath the cracked dome of the sanctuary. The oil lamps stuttered in their terracotta bowls, each flame casting long, uncertain limbs along the chamber walls.

The shadows in this place moved slowly. Too slowly to be accidents of light. On certain nights, they reminded her of court dancers in Susa—on others, of vultures that circled too close and stayed too long.

The world below had narrowed to rumor. The empire's noise reached her only in gusts—blunted by altitude, weathered by time. Letters no longer came. That had ended during the second winter. Even before then, the couriers from Epirus had brought only what Olympias allowed her to see.

So she had learned to listen in other registers.

There were silences, and then there were silences. The mountain's own silence broke at dusk like brittle bone. The guards, whose loyalty had settled into habit rather than duty, no longer spoke unless pressed. Polyperchon, when he visited, said little and looked long. She had seen him study the stars—not for omens, but for the shape of someone who had once returned as myth.

And the temple itself had gone quiet—not with neglect, but with intention. Its stones had been taught silence. Now they spoke it back.

She understood them.

The sanctuary had once belonged to a cult of astronomers—celestial mathematicians who marked history by comet rather than crown. Their calendars were carved into the beams overhead. Roxana slept beneath constellations cut from stone centuries before her son's birth, and each night she reached toward them, fingers tracing paths she imagined he might one day follow.

Outside, the wind dragged its weight across the cistern wall like a voice too tired to finish speaking. Somewhere near that wall, her son was awake. She heard it—the soft, patterned tap of carved wood against stone.

His lion. He called it "Father."

The questions had stopped after his seventh birthday, but she knew they hadn't vanished. Children learn where the silence begins—and what not to disturb.

She had stopped praying for Alexander's return the day she realized how eagerly the world consumed his absence. There had been no burial. No cenotaph. No coin with her child's face. Instead, erasure—his name redacted from scrolls, his bloodline excluded from the mosaic of power.

Only here, in this forgotten height above Pydna's reach, did the child still exist as heir—not to a throne, but to memory.

She no longer measured time by solstice or grain weight. Now she counted instinct.

There had been a tremor in her chest that week. Small, but precise—the kind that moved through the ribs like a signal from beneath the skin.

Olympias still lived. She was certain of it. And if Olympias lived, so did the war.

Not the war of horses and phalanxes, but of lineages—of locked-door oaths and ink scraped from vellum.

In her second year on the mountain, she had found the old spindle again— the one Olympias had sent, wrapped in lambswool. The carved message inside remained unread. She kept it beneath her pillow, unopened, its silence a more potent spell than anything inscribed.

Roxana crossed to the window. The night outside was thick—colorless, unlit. She had ordered the torches extinguished. Light drew attention. And attention was a currency she no longer spent.

The legend would be shaped here, or not at all.

She laid a hand against the stone sill, its chill climbing into her wrist.

And she whispered: "You are still his. They may hold his empire. But I have his blood. And they will choke on it."

CHAPTER 25

THE TOMB OF SMOKE
AND MIRRORS

MEMPHIS – NECROPOLIS ENCLOSURE AND INNER SANCTUM.
The first stones were hauled at dawn, sweat still clinging to the backs of the masons as if the air itself had turned to syrup. No hymns marked the labor. No architect had signed the plans—because there were none. Only sketches in sand, redrawn each morning with a jackal's rib. The limestone came from the east, quarried in silence and left unblessed. The mortar was thickened with Nile silt and powdered lapis from forgotten tombs.

What rose from the dust was not a temple. Not a tomb. Not yet.

And it would not be the only one.

Ptolemy had already sent stonecutters to Siwa, where the Oracle once named Alexander son of Amun and Zeus. Another shrine would rise near the old temple, carved from white sandstone and crowned with copper lions.

In Karnak, he commissioned a second—smaller, more symbolic—a cenotaph meant to align the king's memory with the solar cults of Upper Egypt. Others whispered of plans for Alexandria, for Naucratis, even one for the Nile delta itself, where no body would rest but where his name alone would sanctify the air.

He spoke of these shrines not as tombs, but as mirrors—reflections of a living divinity dispersed across the land.

"Wherever the Nile flows, he shall reign," he told his inner circle, voice low, fingers stained with dust. "Not as a corpse. As current."

To the public, it was tribute. To the priests, heresy in fragments. But to Ptolemy, it was control.

If he could not hold Alexander in life, he would hold the shape of his afterlife—scattered across Egypt like constellations drawn from stone, each shrine a nerve in the new god's nervous system. And at the center, always, this one: Memphis. The anchor. The breath.

Ptolemy watched from the upper colonnade, draped in Macedonian wool ill-suited to Egyptian light. He had taken to sitting on a dark throne looted from a failed Apis cult near Sakkara—its legs carved to resemble lion paws, its backrest shaped like the horizon glyph that marked divine rebirth. A week ago, it had belonged to no one. Now, it belonged to a man learning to command silence.

He refused to call it a tomb. "It is a shrine," he told the stonecutters, waving off their chisels. "A sanctum. A vessel for his living breath."

No inscriptions were permitted. No dedications. No funerary steles. The priests asked if they should summon scribes, begin the rites. Ptolemy only shook his head.

This was only the beginning.

Even as limestone rose from the earth in Memphis, he was already dreaming of something larger—something eternal. A final shrine, not carved into old rock but drawn onto the future. Alexandria—the city of the god's name. Still new, still half-drowned in salt and sea-wind, but destined—he believed—for greatness. He walked its foundations in his mind by night: a golden tomb encased in glass and bronze, surrounded by columns etched not in words, but in silence. The body would rest at its center, visible to all, yet unreachable. A beacon for pilgrims. A throne of absence.

"It will not be a tomb," he told his inner circle. "It will be a lighthouse."

He never explained what that meant. Not fully. But he sketched it on papyrus when he thought no one was looking—curves, chambers, corridors. A god's travelogue.

His men thought him obsessed. They were right. If he could shape the place where Alexander was remembered, he could shape the way he would be remembered. The founder of the city. The guardian of the god. The man who refused to bury a corpse—and instead built a kingdom around it.

"This will be remembered, not merely written."

He told himself this was reverence. He told no one that he was afraid.

Afraid that naming it a tomb would mean admitting that Alexander—his brother-in-arms, his rival, his god—was truly dead. That his own power was scaffolding draped around a hollowed-out myth. That every title he now held—satrap, commander, steward of the divine body—was less real than the warmth he sometimes still felt when he placed his hand against the stone sarcophagus.

That warmth. That pulse.

It began with the soldiers. They came in secret at first—off duty, eyes lowered. Veterans of the long campaigns. Men who had bled under the banner of the sun-lion. They left tokens beside the sealed sarcophagus: a ring. A sharpened stone. A cracked flute. One Macedonian hoplite unwrapped a boiled egg, placed it on the ground, and muttered something about rebirth before saluting the stone and limping away.

A rumor took root like a seed in old bone: the chamber was warm. That it breathed. That the marble lid was not marble at all, but a gold-veined sheath—conductive, alive, waiting.

Temple novices said that if you stood very still, you could hear a second heart beating beneath the stone.

"When will he be buried?" the priests asked.

No one would say it aloud, but the question carried a shadow: Why hasn't he decayed?

Ptolemy began sleeping beside the tomb.

Not every night. Just the ones when the dreams returned. He had a mat woven of lotus stalks and dyed camelhair, stiff with salt from his own sweat. A small brazier glowed at his feet, perfumed with lemongrass and myrrh, though he refused to call it incense. No prayers were spoken. No offerings poured.

He did not pray to Alexander.

He listened, however.

*****

At first, the dreams came like broken whispers—fragments of old battles, laughter from a boyhood he barely remembered, the voice of his mother murmuring about fate and figs. But then, the voices shifted. Focused. Sharpened. One voice began calling him by name—not as a man, but as a title.

He awoke once with blood on his hands and sand in his teeth, certain he had spoken aloud in his sleep. The guards said they heard nothing.

"He is not dead," Ptolemy said the next morning, eyes rimmed in red. "He is reigning. In silence."

By then, the site had grown strange. Pilgrims began arriving—not only Greeks and veterans, but Egyptians, Phoenicians, even a family from Judea who claimed their daughter had seen the tomb from across the river in a vision. They brought trinkets, hair, food, weeping into their palms as if mourning a lover they had never touched.

But Ptolemy saw something else: a power taking shape. Not by conquest. By belief.

Still, the priests grew restless. They needed rites. Doctrine. Instruction. But the theology was being dismantled as quickly as it was formed.

And so the tomb remained: unsealed, unwritten, untouched. A shrine with no scripture. A sanctum that pulsed without prayer. A theocracy without theology.

They began to call him Akhu—the Luminous One—in whispers.

Not to his face—never aloud. But in the palace corridors and kitchen courts, among temple scribes and market fishwives, the rumors took shape like clay left too long in the sun. Some said Ptolemy no longer ate mortal food, only drank wine steeped in crushed pearls and honeyed resin. Others swore they had seen him walking barefoot at dawn through the Necropolis gardens, his skin flashing gold beneath a veil of flies, unbothered by heat or rot.

No one touched him anymore. Not servants. Not generals. Not priests. When decrees were handed to him, they were placed on black cloth. When he passed through the sanctum, incense was lit not to honor him, but to absorb the scent of his passage—to preserve it. The god was buried, yes. But the man guarding him was ascending.

Far away, in the mountain passes near Cappadocia, the rumors drifted like ash into Roxana's camp. A merchant spoke of a tomb that breathed. A shrine ringed in fire. Of Ptolemy himself—gilded, embalmed in life, refusing burial rites for the child's father because he believed the man inside still dreamed.

Roxana did not answer. But that night, she marked the stars again. Not for navigation. For reckoning. She did not believe in gods anymore.

Not since Babylon. Not since the fever had taken him—and left the empire with no pulse but smoke and rumor. She knew what power looked like when it began to rot from within. She had seen it in the palace scribes, in the way men started inventing omens to match their ambitions. In the soft collapse of generals who still signed letters in Alexander's name, as if that would bring him back.

Now they said Ptolemy was gold. Not just robed or painted—but clad, sealed, transformed. The tomb glowed, they said, and he with it. That he had taken to speaking in riddles, refusing food for days. That he called no councils yet issued decrees. That even his own men no longer met his eyes.

She imagined him not as a man but as a figure in bas-relief—half flake, half flame. A priest of his own invention.

She pitied him. She feared him. But she also understood him.

If Alexander could not be ruled, then someone would rule his shadow.

*****

In Memphis, the envoy from Cyrene arrived in midwinter—barely announced, pale from weeks at sea. He had come bearing scrolls, gifts, and news from the western ports, but none of it seemed to matter. Not here. Not in the city of ash-veiled silence.

He was led blindfolded into the outer sanctum, where no fires burned and no names were spoken. Women in blue linen sprinkled dried coriander over the flagstones. A single horn sounded from within, low and long, like breath passing through a crypt.

At first, the envoy assumed it was a funerary rite. Then he saw the shrine. Not a monument. Not a tomb. Something else entirely. A square chamber without symbols. A sarcophagus sealed in uncarved stone. And behind it, him—Ptolemy, draped in gold leaf and linen, lips unmoving, hands raised not in greeting but benediction. He did not blink.

The envoy bowed.

He did not understand what he had seen.

He left that night without completing his mission. Later, in his journal, he wrote only one phrase: "The king does not rule Egypt. The tomb does."

And Ptolemy—once a general, now something else—stood at its center, uncertain whether he was guarding a god or becoming one.

Not thunderous. Not divine. But familiar. Soft. Like a whisper pressed against the skin of the world. They did not say his name. They summoned it in their dreams and nightmares.

He awoke once, shivering, hand clenched to the floor. The sarcophagus glowed with a pale sheen, its outline sharper than the firelight could explain.

"He is not dead," Ptolemy murmured, eyes wide. "He is reigning in silence."

By dawn, the courtyard was filled with pilgrims. Not all were soldiers. Some had traveled from Heliopolis. Others from the Delta. A group from Byblos arrived barefoot, their robes stitched with lapis, claiming they had seen a falcon of green fire descend over the city on the night Alexander's body entered the gate.

The theology—what little there was—spread by breath alone.

Rituals were memorized. Incantations whispered. No scrolls were kept. No records carved. Even the libations were performed without chant, without drums. The gods, it was said, could no longer be summoned by formula. Only presence. Only proximity.

One young scribe from Thebes—Apirion—attempted to capture the rites on papyrus. He worked in secret, hiding his ink under a basket of barley and salt. He had almost completed the first scroll when the guards found him. Ptolemy spared him. No punishment. No explanation. Only exile.

He had him exiled.

"Words are coffins," Ptolemy said. "Let none be built for the living god."

By midwinter, the priests no longer entered the inner sanctum. They made their offerings from behind a veil of cedar slats, muttering through cloth. One of the older men—High Reader Menekhkare—resigned without speaking, simply placing his staff on the temple steps and walking into the sand without a single sandal.

Still, Ptolemy remained, and the tomb of Alexander grew. And then he began to dress in gold.

Not jewelry—skin. Thin leaf pressed onto arms and shoulders before ceremonies, a practice lifted from old priest-king rituals of the Delta. At first it was symbolic—sun-born authority, a glint of Ra's favor. But then the gilding became habitual. Daily. Intimate. He insisted on being anointed before entering the inner sanctum, his chest lacquered in oil before the metal was laid. No one was permitted to watch but two mute servants from Thebes, their tongues removed, their eyes kohl-lined against the weight of what they witnessed.

He said it was for protection. But those closest to him began to murmur: that he feared infection from the corpse. That he believed the tomb radiated not warmth, but a divine fever—one that could burn or convert. That the gold was not armor, but insulation.

He saw fewer people. Spoke less. Ate alone.

And still, every night now, he slept beside the sealed sarcophagus, glowing faintly in the firelight—half-man, half-icon, gilded and silent as the god he claimed to serve.

Columns now bordered the outer wall—fluted but unmarked. Incense fires were kept burning in stone bowls that had once flanked the altar of Amun-Ra. And in the center, always, the sarcophagus: sealed, unapproachable, wreathed in blue smoke and guarded by silence.

To peer beneath the lid was heresy. To speak of burial was treason.

Egypt was becoming something it had never been—a theocracy without doctrine, a state held together not by dogma but by dream.

And its first dreamer—the dreamer who would become a god himself, if only by proximity—stood thinner each day, lit from within by something only he could hear.

Outside the shrine, the city held its breath.

And inside, the tomb no longer waited. It began to listen.

CHAPTER 26

THE NIGHT OF CLAY SCREAMS

PELLA, AUTUMN, 316 BCE – TEMPLE QUARTER AND ROYAL ARCHIVES. They said Olympias returned to Pella from Epirus like a goddess rising from the underworld—veiled, righteous, and draped in the fury of a mother wronged. The truth walked slower than myth. She did not arrive with armies. She arrived with scrolls.

Letters, seals, and witness oaths from Epirus. Edicts claiming regency on behalf of her grandson Alexander IV. A bloodline still sacred to many, especially in the north, where the name of her husband, Philip II, could still quiet a market square.

By summer's end, she held the city. By autumn, she held the throne. And by first frost, she would hold the rope.

It began with the gates thrown open at midnight. Olympias had returned to Macedon not as a regent, not as a grieving queen mother, but as reckoning. She entered cloaked in mourning black, her shoulders squared by silence, and Alexander's name etched into every scroll of legitimacy she carried.

The Argead bloodline, she claimed, had been desecrated. Now the city would be cleansed.

Polyperchon rode into Pella quiet and weathered, with dust on his boots and the scent of old laurels still clinging to his cloak.

His limbs had stiffened with age, and the fire in his lungs no longer burned clean—but there was no mistaking who he was. Macedon remembered. Even the silence in the streets tilted slightly when he passed.

He had come not for glory, nor to chase ghosts, but because the ledger of loyalty had grown too thin to ignore. He had stood beside Philip at Chaeronea, crossed rivers with Craterus, buried Hephaestion, watched Alexander ascend into myth. If any man had a claim to the bones of the empire, it was him.

So when Olympias called, he answered. They called him the last lion of Macedon, and for a moment, the streets remembered how to bow.

She arrived cloaked in mourning black, her hair threaded with silver, her eyes lit by something older than vengeance. She carried no crown. Only the sealed edicts of Epirus, the name of her grandson—Alexander the Fourth— and the full weight of a legacy Macedon no longer knew how to carry.

It was Polyperchon who cleared the roads. Who walked the hill-forts into silence. Who reminded the northern commanders that blood was thicker than strategy, and that dynasties don't end with whispers—they end with choices.

He did not ride at the head like a conquering warlord. He walked beside her carriage with his hand on a blade he hoped not to use. And the people stepped aside. Not out of fear. Out of memory.

He told them this was not a coup. It was a homecoming. And for a time, it was.

When the reigning puppet king, Philip III Arrhidaeus, was seized without protest, Polyperchon offered no defense. The king was a shadow—half-broken in mind, easily bent, tethered to Cassander's camp.

The guards surrendered him without a fight—her stepson, half-witted and twitching from years of manipulation, torn from his bed and shackled to the temple pillars where kings once stood to receive prophecy.

Three days without food; on the fourth, a chalice of honeyed wine was brought to his lips. No one knows what was in it. He died with his mouth open, trying to form a word no one understood.

When he died, the old general said nothing. Eurydice, his wife, was dragged through the square in a gown soaked with funeral oils. Olympias did not speak to her. Instead, she had the executioner lay a noose across the girl's lap and whisper, "Choose."

Eurydice hung herself beneath the statue of Artemis. The wind twisted her body like a banner. Polyperchon stood in the courtyard, fists clenched behind his back, feeling history shift under his boots.

The killings did not stop there. They had only begun.

The names were read by torchlight. Each one echoed across the colonnades. Officers escorted from their homes to the temple courtyards. Wives pulled from weddings, sons taken from study, old rivals executed not by decree but by ritual. Generals. Treasurers. Tutors. Priests. Anyone who had pledged to Cassander's house was stripped of title, property, and breath.

"They must see what justice looks like," Olympias said as fire and sword consumed flesh and bone. "Let them remember what happens when the divine is mocked. They burned Alexander's name from their ledgers. So now I burn theirs."

One by one, each was dragged into the Royal Stoa, tied to the old marble lion, opened at the throat with knives that had not been oiled in decades. Blood pooled between the columns like wine from a cracked amphora. The floor had to be sanded down each morning to keep the stone from turning slick.

One boy, barely twenty, marched out for delivering a letter bearing Cassander's seal. They cut out his tongue, pressed it between two wax tablets, and nailed them shut—proof of betrayal, archived in flesh.

In the temple of Dionysus, four priests were buried alive for failing to anoint Alexander as divine son of Ammon. Their screams were muffled by wine vats stacked atop the trench.

A mother who pleaded for her son's life was given the option to die in his place. She agreed.

Olympias had them executed together—hand to hand, bound at the wrist.

At first, Polyperchon tried to rationalize it: oaths betrayed, bloodline denied. He told himself Olympias was burning rot from wood. But each morning, the executions grew more elaborate.

The victims younger. The reasons thinner than ash.

One afternoon he stepped into the war chamber and found blood drying across the cartographic table, the lines of the empire streaked with red. It had soaked into India, smeared Egypt, turned the Aegean black.

He left before the next name was read. After that, the fire in him dimmed. He stopped attending the tribunals. He gave no commands, no counsel. He sat in the garden alone, speaking to no one, carving the names of old campaigns into scraps of olive bark and burning them by hand.

When the fever came for Polyperchon, there were no physicians. Olympias was purifying the state. His aides lit a single oil lamp and left water by the door. He died without fanfare—a man who had once led legions, now wrapped in a travel cloak, bones rattling under furs.

They found a silver ring on his finger—the crest of Alexander's first campaign—and a note scrawled in his trembling hand: "The lion followed the flame. He did not expect it to consume the forest."

No pyre. No eulogy. No honor guard. Only the slow whisper of smoke over the rooftops, as Pella turned once more toward silence.

*****

At first, Macedon and Greece watched—rooftops, porticoes, cupped hands. Some prayed. A few, emboldened by grief or memory, cheered her name.

"She is avenging Alexander," they said. "She is unmaking the blasphemy of regicide." For a time, the myth held.

Then came the children.

Three royal pages, still in training under the old code, loyal to a murdered tutor, were led into the square at dawn. Twelve. Thirteen. Fourteen. Armor oversized, almost comic. Stripped of tunics, they were bound and lashed until their backs resembled scrolls seared and rolled in coals. The guards, at Olympias's command, turned to the crowd and held out the whips.

No one moved. So she took the lash herself.

And something shifted—not just in the onlookers, but in the air. The wind dropped. The silence was no longer reverence. It was retreat.

The funerary priests ceased their chants. Carpenters left pyres half-built. Gutters ran thick and slow with blood. Crows fed openly in temple gardens. Bodies lingered. No brooms.

Pella began to smell of rust, sour milk, and unanswered gods. This—saturation, not violence—was Olympias's fatal misjudgment.

She believed terror could hold the people together; that divine inheritance could be reinforced through fire; that if she poured enough of herself into Alexander's absence, it would seal. But the kingdom had buried Philip. It had wept for the boy who became a god.

What they feared now was not Cassander. It was her.

So Cassander waited. No grand declarations. No banners. He watched from Thessaly as Olympias reduced Pella to ritualized despair. He let her name curdle on aristocratic tongues. He waited for her oil to run dry. He let the winds of Pydna do what armies could not—strip her banners and scatter them like leaves.

When he marched, it was not with vengeance, but provisions—grain, blankets, olive oil. Scribes carrying amnesty, clemency, stability. He brought no gods. Only order.

And the people let him in.

No barricades. No last stands. By the time his standard climbed the western tower, Pella had already hollowed out. Market stalls sagged under spoiled fruit. No proclamations were read. None needed.

Her loyalists dissolved—borders, cellars, silence. Even the palace guard stood like forgotten statuary. They had not been defeated. They had been corroded.

Olympias had not been overthrown. She had been left behind. Not by enemies—but by a city that no longer recognized its own mythology. She stood alone, not surrounded by traitors, but by people who no longer believed in anything.

When the summons came, she did not flinch. War cloak hem stained, she stared at the messenger as if he were late to a funeral. She said nothing—not a word, not even in her native tongue.

It was not humility. It was refusal.

Cassander denied her a trial. He feared the scaffold's echo. Even ashes carry embers, he'd said. Even silence can be too loud.

She would not be tried. She would be erased. The records are deliberately vague.

"All that survives is a single phrase: She was handed over to the families of the dead." A fiction meant to sound civilized. No one agrees which family. Or if any did.

Cassander's brilliance lay not in what he destroyed—but in what he refused to touch. He gave vengeance permission and turned his back.

Olympias was placed under guard in the south watchtower, in a stone cell that once held Thracian hostages. Torches unlit. Meals untouched. When they came, they did not come in force.

Three noblewomen walked the corridor—wives and sisters of the newly dead. No blades. Braided cords. Sealed orders. Soldiers looked away.

The sky had no color. No torches. No lamentations. Even the guards turned their faces to the wall.

No one followed.

What happened in the chamber is unknowable.

One account claims a ceremonial sash once worn by Eurydice. Another insists Cassander's captain did it himself. Some say she stood unbound, eyes forward, refusing the floor.

Some say she laughed. Others say she sang—a lullaby from Epirus, meant for a son who would never hear it.

Her body was never displayed.

A dry well behind the barracks. A slab beneath the parade ground. Ashes mixed with ox blood in the marshes. Choose your rumor. History chose none.

No rites. No names. No libation. Morning: silence. The queen was gone. The mother of Alexander. The last true flame of the Argead line. Not slain, not martyred, not entombed.

Just… gone.

*****

Then came the fire.

Cassander summoned priests and scribes to the Royal Archive—not as a king seeking wisdom, but as a man ready to shut the doors on an age. He did not raise his voice. He didn't need to. Authority lived in the silence after.

"No more oracles. No more gods in governance," he said. "Let there be no gods in politics. Let history begin again."

At his gesture, the clerks carried tablets forward. Armfuls. Some chipped, some still oiled. Records from Babylon, Siwa, Memphis. Lineage, legacy, sacred names: Son of Ammon. He Who Walks Between Worlds. The Living God of Two Lands.

One by one, into the brazier. Flames accepted them without hesitation. Characters blistered. Clay blackened. Words meant for eternity cracked like bark in wind.

Centuries collapsed in minutes—vapor, soot, silence. At the edge, an old priest trembled under linen. He stepped forward, removed his amulet, and hurled it to the floor. It bounced once, caught firelight.

"You are not Philip's heir," he said. "You are the son of silence."

No reply. No visible anger. A nod from the attendant. The old man was led away—neither honored nor killed in sight.

His name was never entered. The amulet vanished before the ashes cooled.

In a far corner, beneath a fractured lintel scented of scorched cedar and resin, a boy—sixteen, perhaps—watched the flames as if trying to remember how they moved. When backs were turned, he knelt, reached with the edge of his tunic, and lifted a tablet not yet broken. Cracked corner, but the name at its center remained.

He wrapped it in linen. Pressed it to his chest. Slipped into the hall's shadow. No one called after him.

His name is lost. The tablet's fate unknown. But the scream of scorched clay lingered in the rafters until dawn.

Olympias was buried in secret. Her name, once spoken beside gods, now moved only in whispers—half-formed, hesitant, as if breath itself might root a new myth.

Rumors surfaced—tavern, market, amphitheater. The Queen Mother executed without rite. Macedon did not rise. Doorways filled. Alleys murmured. Shutters watched.

No riots. No cheers. Only silence.

It settled like dust. Coated temple lintels, lecture corners, market tents. Bakers flipped scales upside down. Scholars left genealogies blank. Storytellers changed subjects mid-line.

Even the temple bells refused to ring.

Some called it a curse—beginning when Olympias's blood touched earth. Others said there was no curse, only a kingdom too tired to remember itself.

Cassander read the silence rightly. Not reverence. Not allegiance. Not submission.

It was fatigue.

Macedon had buried too many kings, erected too many statues, given itself too many gods and seen them bleed. Nothing left to worship. Nothing left to avenge.

So Cassander gave them what remained. Festivals—earthbound, secular, stripped of ancestor veneration.

Coins with no gods—only tools and harvest. Prayers sanctioned, if spoken behind closed doors, too soft to echo.

He ruled in the boy's name: Alexander IV—barely nine, hidden in Cappadocia—had not set foot in Macedon since before he could speak. Yet in Pella, he was now installed in absentia, as if the myth still required a body. His name on decrees. His profile—a child's sketch of a dead man's jaw—on coins. A scaled throne placed beside the dais, draped in silk and shadow.

No one sat on it.

Still, attendants bowed. A courtier later wrote, without irony: it was like watching an empire kneel to a ghost it was learning to forget.

In the Temple Quarter, the fires burned three nights. Clay tablets cracked and hissed like dying serpents. In that smoke, Macedon began to forget the names that once made kings divine.

Cassander remained after the others left.

The archive smelled of ash and boiled ink, the air heavy with what had been history. He stood beneath burned rafters, staring into embers. The amulet—gone. The priest—gone. The tablets—gone.

Only silence remained.

He placed a hand on the stone table where ledgers had been catalogued and looked up at the ceiling where Alexander on Bucephalus once galloped. Paint peeled. Outline fractured.

He did not speak. He only stood in the ruin he had made clean and breathed the stillness.

It was done. Cassander was already planning winter games.

*****

The letter arrived without a seal. Folded with care, weighted with a pressed sprig of fennel, bearing one word in Cassander's hand—"Now."

Roxana read it three times beneath the olive canopy. Wax softened in the heat; ink bled at the corners, as if the word itself resisted being whole.

She did not weep. She did not speak. She lowered the parchment and stared at the horizon where mountains blurred into wind.

Alexander IV played in the courtyard shade, sandals off, drawing a map in dust—a lopsided triangle of lines and circles he called an empire. He didn't look up.

He had not seen his mother cry in years. He did not notice the tremor in her hand as she reached for her cup.

She had protected him in absentia. Held back summons as long as possible. But smoke had reached even here. Peddlers and wine merchants brought rumors: the Queen Mother dead; the Argead flame snuffed in a whisper. No edicts bearing Olympias's seal. Only Cassander's men, watching the road.

They brought bread. Salt. A new crest.

And now, this letter. For weeks she knew the question was coming. Now it stood before her, dressed in courtesy, written with terrifying brevity.

Bring the boy to Pella—to the throne that devoured his father and now his grandmother? Or keep him spectral a little longer: a name, a coin, a child not yet devoured by men who burned clay and called it justice?

She had no illusions about Cassander's mercy. But she knew the danger of delay. To resist marked them as dissidents. To obey made them hostages.

Between those poles sat her son, drawing lines with no borders, no armies, only loops.

That night, she sat alone on the rooftop, shawl the color of dried blood, watching the northern sky. Cold clung to stone. She did not pray. She thought of Alexander, who had held this child and promised a world remade. She thought of Olympias, proud and furious, who died without a grave. She thought of herself—not queen, not widow, not prisoner, but hinge—the single pivot on which a dying house still turned.

If she sent the boy, he would be absorbed. If she held him, they would disappear more quietly. Either way, the myth ended with her.

He approved a new anthem for the opening ceremony—written by a court poet no one remembered. No Argeads. No gods. Harvest. Victory. Laurel. Stone.

In the archive, marble floors polished, ash swept.

He would wait a little longer before requesting the boy's formal appearance. Better as reconciliation than coercion. Macedon was tired of blood. It wanted civility, appearances. A child-king might help—for a season.

Far from Pella, Roxana lit a small oil lamp and placed it near her son's sleeping mat.

She sat beside it until morning, the letter in her lap—unread now, but not forgotten. She knew what it meant. Not the word. The pause after.

Now.

CHAPTER 27

ATLAS OF SHADOWS

Cassander believed Roxana and the boy were somewhere between Babylon and the Anatolian highlands—hidden among old loyalties, protected by Polyperchon, or sheltered in one of the mountain sanctuaries still beyond his reach.

It had been nearly two months since her last message. No courier. No envoy.

The empire might have fractured, but the old Persian Royal Road still carried orders and rumors alike. Riders changed horses every twenty stadia, and the routes wound like veins through satrapal strongholds—Thessaloniki, Perinthos, Ephesus, Smyrna, Mazaka. Alexander had used them to conquer the world. Now Cassander would use them to reclaim what was left of it.

The wax was still warm when he sealed the scroll. Not with Alexander's sigil, but his own—newly cut, its lion mane etched into spears. Succession by conquest, not consent.

He stood over the brazier, silent as the scribes bowed. The hall was full, but no one spoke. Even the courtiers—plump, powdered, political—sensed something final in the air.

"She's not returning," Cassander said at last. Not a suspicion. A declaration.

Seven weeks since Babylon fell quiet. Seven weeks of vague replies from temple guards and satrapal aides. Seven weeks of nothing.

"She ran. With the boy."

He moved across the floor mosaic of Philip II—the father, the unblinking ghost who'd once marched against Athens and left kings bleeding in the snow.

"She was never one of us," he said. "A Bactrian wife, a child born in the East—she knew the Macedonian heart would never bend to that. So she disappeared into story, and took the heir with her."

He turned then, meeting the eyes of every man in the chamber. "We do not rule myth. We bury it." He raised the decree, written in four tongues, sealed in five.

"Send these to Smyrna. To Ephesus. To Mazaka and Comana and the temples in the hills. Let no path remain untouched."

He did not raise his voice for the next part. He didn't need to. "Ten talents for the general. Fifteen for the woman. Fifty for the boy—alive, untouched, and unspeaking."

He dropped the scroll onto the coals. The ink hissed. Copies would be dispatched before the wax cooled. "Let the mountains know," he said. "We are not looking for a child. We are hunting a threat."

There was no applause. Only the crackle of fire and the smell of iron. By nightfall, the first bounty rider galloped from Pella.

By dawn, the myth had begun to spread.

It was not the kind of night that warned you. No wind screamed down from Argaeus. No animals stirred in the paddocks. Even the oil lamps seemed reluctant to burn. The silence clung to the stones like breath withheld.

Roxana waited until the third watch. She had been watching the sentries shift their weight for hours, listening to patrol rhythms, memorizing the sounds that did not belong.

The boy was awake. He sat quietly, the carved lion pressed to his chest, watching the torchlight outside their chamber door rise and fall as the flame guttered.

He didn't ask if they were leaving. He simply whispered to the figurine: "Are we going home?"

Behind them walked Thais of Ecbatana, barefoot and murmuring. Each step was marked by verse—protection chants from her mother's temple in Susa, strung with fire-syllables and bone-rhymes. She touched the boy's shoulder at the doorframe, not to guide, but to shield him from anything listening.

Polyperchon joined them past the aqueduct—the same spot where, years ago, he had knelt before Alexander. Now he rode again, no emblem on his cloak, no horn to announce his passing. Only memory, and the weight of what must be kept alive.

The road west was not lit. It wound through ash trees and old goat paths, worn thin by centuries of feet. They rode without fire, without speech.

They were not just fleeing. They were disappearing.

> *To Roxana, widow of Alexander, and mother to the*
> *bloodline that remains, You were not exiled. You were not*
> *pursued. You were given time to mourn and return. That*
> *time has passed. Your silence is now sedition.*

—Cassander, Regent of Macedon and Guardian of Order

RELAY STATION AT MAZAKA, CAPPADOCIA — TWO DAYS AFTER THE DECREE LEAVES PELLA

The relay post at Mazaka was little more than a stone house built into the slope, tiled roof warped by frost and sun. A shrine to Hermes had once stood outside—now reduced to a cracked plinth and a rusted offering bowl full of goat teeth and wilted fig skins.

Mazaka was a hinge—older than satraps, older than the name Cappadocia. The Hittites had once crowned kings there; Medes and Persians had paved its high passes; Alexander's scouts had ridden its air in spring and found it thin for horses but excellent for watching armies gather. To the Greeks, Mazaka was a provincial fortress with pretensions. To the locals it was the spine—where oracles muttered to wind and rebel priests still lit fires to the old codes.

The rider arrived at dusk, second horse blown, satchel marked with the lion seal. The postmaster met him at the steps. The rider did not dismount.

"From Pella," he said. "Immediate transcription. Signed Cassander himself."

The postmaster broke the wax, scanned the lines; his lips parted, then closed. "We'll copy it by moonrise," he said.

Inside, he unrolled the decree and did not begin writing. Not yet. He opened a locked cabinet and pulled a different sheet—half-filled with names, notes, rumors: a quiet ledger kept by mountain priests and loyalists. He added a line: Child and Queen rumored near Argaeus. Cassander declares open bounty. Fifty talents. Fire signal to Comana. Delay reply one day.

He folded the note, sealed it with a pebble marked with the triple-branch of the Temple of the Mother. Then he copied the original decree—careful, reverent, as if recording a prayer he didn't believe in. Outside, the rider watched the road. He would leave at dawn, never knowing the message had already split in two.

COMANA, EASTERN CAPPADOCIA — TEMPLE RIDGE

The fire was seen before the message arrived.

High on the ridge above the sacred precinct, an acolyte spotted the signal flare after moonrise—amber, three short bursts and a long. Not a local code. This one was older. A war-signal.

Comana was not a city. It was a breath between empires—temples and granaries carved into slope, a sacred bridge between men and gods. The temple of Ma—goddess of war and wilderness—kept servants bound since birth, hiding dynasties beneath ritual. Alexander had left it untouched. Comana kept no maps—only ridgelines. When its fires were lit, they were never for show.

She did not call the high priest. She went straight to Arsames, the archivist who had served four dynasties. He read the pattern, then the wall-map etched in soot and bone ash.

"Mazaka," he murmured. "They've found something."

A tablet was pulled from a sealed niche—one of Cyrus's, in the Old Tongue. The ritual to unlock it took seven minutes. The reading less than two.

"When the lion hunts the son, light the ridge. When the boy rides east, follow the birds."

Arsames rubbed his temple. It was happening again. He lit a second fire—blue. The signal passed along the eastern ridge toward Argaeus.

The moon was a sharpened crescent when they left Mount Argaeus for Mazaka. The outer gate sealed for night, but the camel path beyond the aqueduct wall was passable—if you didn't mind sand in your teeth or ghosts at your heels. Roxana walked first, sandals wrapped in linen. Her son held close beneath a soot-hemmed cloak. She did not speak. No farewells. Only gestures. Only faith.

Thais of Ecbatana followed, chanting in three languages—temple verse from Susa, fire hymns of mountain kin, a bastard Greek lullaby that replaced "sleep" with "survive." She carried salt and wormwood, slapping it once against wayposts to mark the path as sacred.

Then Polyperchon. Shoulders creaked but eyes still held command. No standard—only a carved walking stick shaped like a trident, banded in brass. He arrived at dusk unannounced. Roxana said nothing when he fell in behind them. She didn't need to.

The path narrowed to goat-trail. Two posts, lichen and old soot. Once painted red. Now gray with time. Polyperchon dismounted first. Roxana carried the boy the last paces. He was half-asleep; the air shifted—cooler, sharper, and he opened his eyes. Before them, tucked into stone, stood the sanctuary: a long stone hall, half-sunken, roof held by olivewood struts and mountain silence. It smelled of oil and something older—ash, or dried blood scrubbed away. A place where names were remembered, not spoken.

Thais crossed herself in three traditions, whispered a final charm. A single priestess—no longer young—offered a shallow nod and a basin of water. Roxana washed the boy's hands, then feet, then her own.

Polyperchon remained outside, watching ridgeline and stars fade.

"I thought you'd take us to a fortress," Roxana said.

"I did," he replied. "But the kind that lasts."

The boy wandered to painted tiles—lions, suns, winged figures not quite Babylonian. He touched the lion, once with gold in its eyes. They still caught light. Outside, a hawk circled twice then vanished. Polyperchon watched it go. He had marched behind Alexander across the world. Now he would march for his son—through silence, through shadow, through a war that refused to end.

They stopped for water in a hilltop village. The well at the square beside a toppled statue—Persian or Greek, no one could tell—was small solace. Roxana drew the bucket. Two boys sat under a fig tree. One whispered and ran. The other—ten years old—stared at the heir and at the lion. The young Alexander returned the stare. The second boy dropped his fig and knelt. Roxana turned to Polyperchon. "That's how it begins."

"One village. Then ten. Then the road opens," Polyperchon said. They left; the elder placed a hand over his heart: "May the mountain carry him." The story would reach Smyrna before them.

*****

Back in Pella, Cassander received seven papyrus scrolls in five days. None agreed.

One: near Mazaka. Another: south to the sea. A third: Roxana had died giving birth to a second child (a cruel rumor). Cassander sat in silence while a court musician plucked a syrupy lyre. He dismissed him with a gesture that made his hand ache. The mosaic of Tyre beneath his feet seemed to mock him.

"If they wished to surrender, they would have sent a herald," he said.

"They're not hiding. They're performing." He stood abruptly. "Send new riders. Offer temples gold to speak against her. Tell Ephesus this is rebellion, not sanctity." He stared across the olive groves. "They think they can make him a god. I will make him a corpse."

At Ephesus, the high priestess inside the eastern portico of Artemis did not open her eyes as the acolyte read Mazaka's report. She breathed cedar smoke, turned her head to the north wind, listened.

"The mountain flames have been seen," the acolyte whispered. "And now children bow at wells."

The priestess stirred. "They carry something older than legitimacy. They carry symmetry. The shape of return."

"Should we intervene?"

"No," she said. "We receive them."

"But Cassander—"

"Cassander is loud," she said. "The gods are patient." She laid an olive wreath at Artemis's feet.

By torchlight at a defunct waystation altar near the Lykos, Polyperchon wrote letters himself. No seal—only a cut of wolf fur tied to each scroll, an older symbol than any dynasty. Messengers were local: the village fig-boy, an old woman who once lit candles in Persepolis, a mute with a dagger etched with her name. The text called to those who remembered the march east: the Queen walks with the boy. They seek the coast, not for flight but reckoning. If you would stand between them and betrayal, come now.

He watched them ride into the dark one by one. "We will not enter Ephesus alone," he said quietly. Roxana did not respond. She didn't have to.

Near the Lykos River, in disputed lands—satrapies in old maps but a bruise in lived maps—the air hardened. Cappadocia and central Anatolia were contested memory: Persian fire temples, Greek inscriptions, Assyrian gods in caves. The land belonged to no single story, which made it dangerous. Cassander had sent messengers and coin—but coin meant little where roads forked by allegiance to the dead.

The sun began to harden as the path turned to gravel; the road narrowed too cleanly—as if cleared not for passage but purpose. Polyperchon raised his hand without turning. The guards—six now, old captains, shepherds with scars, a Thracian exile—halted. Roxana drew the boy closer beneath her cloak; he hummed to the lion. Then a voice: "Polyperchon." Not shouted—spoken. From the rocks ahead, five men emerged: not local, armor too polished, feet too quiet. One stepped forward, a gilded torque at his throat. Cappadocian accent layered with Macedonian schooling. "You were meant to ride south, not stir the old dust. This isn't your road."

Polyperchon studied him. "Is this Cassander's decree? Or your ambition?"

The man smiled. "Cassander gives orders. We give outcomes." Two more men emerged—trap as diplomacy. No banners. Thin javelins. Not negotiation.

Polyperchon didn't shout. He shifted his weight. Leather and river stone cracked through the stillness. The Thracian moved first—javelin upward; blood on gravel. Shepherds drove hooked blades. The speaker tried to flee—Polyperchon was there. His staff—iron-core, brass-tipped, trident-shaped—struck once: neck to spine. The sound was final. Not cinematic. Just the end of breath. The fight lasted less than half a minute; dust took longer to settle.

Roxana hadn't moved. The boy looked up in certainty. "They wanted to stop us."

"Yes," she said, pulling him tighter. Polyperchon stood over the dead with the quiet of a man who no longer kept count. One guard began to speak; he raised his hand. "Burn them. Leave no bones for rumor." Then to the guards: "No more waiting. We move at dusk. We do not ask again. The next man who bars this path will not speak long enough to regret it." The Thracian grunted. The procession re-formed. The road narrowed again—but now the silence around them had changed. It was not waiting. It was watching.

*****

They entered Ephesus three days later at midmorning, without trumpet or standard. The Gate of Artemis cast long shadows—columns fluted scars, capitals chipped by time and fire, still upright and watching. The temple's roof flashed gold. Ephesus had swallowed Lydian queens, Persian satraps, Ionian priests and Macedonian warlords. It had been razed and rebuilt; it had never been forgotten. Now it prepared for something stranger: a new revelation.

Word had outpaced the horses. What began as coastal whispers bloomed into declarations. By the north gate the crowd swelled into thousands—on roof tiles and amphorae, weeping or singing songs older than Babylon. Fishermen said the sea had gone calm the day the Lykos was crossed. Tokens, coins with

Alexander's face, clay offerings—people brought them all. They didn't call her name; they chanted one word, over and over: "Heir."

The boy walked, hand in Roxana's; the lion tucked into his satchel. His eyes half-hidden, he kept glancing at the people—watching, not frightened. Thais walked ahead scattering cedar and salt. Polyperchon followed, staff in hand, silence as his armor. He had led armies into Asia; now he led a procession through myth.

At the Temple's base the high priestess emerged—not with heralds, but a simple bow, acknowledging presence. The gesture neither lowered status nor rose to submission. In that moment something shifted. The people felt it before understanding it. They had not gathered for spectacle—they had gathered for confirmation. The Queen had returned. The heir lived. The silence after Alexander's death was breaking, not with trumpet, but with footsteps.

In Pella that night a wine jug shattered against the Tyre mosaic; red streaked blue tile like blood in surf. The sound echoed and choked. Two servants left without waiting; one left a sandal. Seven scrolls arrived in under an hour: no contradictions. They had entered Ephesus on foot; priests received them; people called the boy divine; some whispered Alexander himself walked behind them. Cassander stood at the marble table, fingers white. Veins pulsed. "She means to crown him," he said, barely audible. "She means to turn mourning into theater. Into something holy."

He sent word to Lysimachus: the coast is slipping. "If she reaches Smyrna," he told a general, "she won't need armies. She'll have belief." He looked into the brazier; flames coiled like questions. "Make them disappear," he said.

No names. No titles.

Just an order—cold, unblinking—from a man who understood, too late, that he was no longer writing the story. He was chasing it.

If he couldn't stop it, it would crown a kingdom in the space he failed to fill.

CHAPTER 28

FUGITIVES IN THE WEST

The road from Ephesus had turned slick with rain and hoof-pocked clay. By the time they reached the walls of Smyrna, the boy's cloak was damp at the edges, and Roxana's fingers had gone cold beneath her gloves. But her eyes stayed sharp. She did not look tired anymore. She looked like she had spent her last reserves of sleep somewhere back in Caria and had decided that was the end of it.

The gates opened without challenge. War had trained the guards to let dust-covered travelers pass without questions, so long as they bore no banners.

Smyrna was not yet a city of refugees, but it was listening for the sound. The crack of empire—that particular silence that followed dead kings and lost wages—was beginning to hum beneath the marble colonnades. Merchants still shouted their prices, but they didn't look you in the eye.

Polyperchon walked a step behind Roxana, not out of deference, but cal‑culation. He wanted eyes on her first. If she was recognized, he'd know it by the sudden hush in the market or the hand that didn't go back to the scales. The boy walked between them, half‑muddied, chewing on a strip of dried fig, his eyes scanning everything: the perfume sellers, the chained monkeys, the creaking mastheads at the port.

They moved through the Market Quarter like ghosts in daylight. A child's voice called out in Persian, singing a lullaby. Thais, barefoot as always, finished the end of the verse under her breath.

*****

At the harbor, they found a sailor from Phocaea willing to sell space on a grain freighter bound for Byzantium. He didn't ask names. But he looked too long at the boy and said, without smiling:

"If you're going north, take the winter with you. It's already dead here."

They secured berths under false names. Polyperchon paid in old coin, stamped with a lion and a trident. The sailor ran his thumb over the worn face and muttered something in a dialect no one had spoken since Alexander crossed the Halys.

That night, in a salt‑stained storeroom above a fishmonger's stall, Roxana wrote a letter to Eumenes. She did not ask how many soldiers he had. She did not ask where he would strike.

She wrote: "If your sword still holds, let it hold for him. We move north under the cloak of Orion. The child breathes. He dreams of his father at night. We dream of you in the morning."

She folded the parchment carefully and passed it to Polyperchon. He didn't speak. He pressed a coin into the fold—a cavalry drachma, silver‑black with age, Alexander's profile almost gone smooth—and sealed it in wax with the hilt of his knife.

"He'll understand," Polyperchon said.

They gave the letter to a trusted rider—Thracian, silent, with a scar across his neck and eyes that had seen three kings die. He rode out before dawn with the stars still visible over the water.

The wind rose behind him.

By nightfall, their freighter slipped out of the harbor under low cloud and sea mist. No flags. No names. Just a boy asleep in the hull with his lion figurine clutched in one hand, and a mother who no longer prayed—only watched the horizon.

*****

In the east, near ancient Media—what we now call western Iran—harsh wind brought sand into the tent seams and made the ink freeze in the inkwells. Horses shivered in their hobbles. The plain of Gabiene was flat as a coin, blanketed in frost, and bitter underfoot. Eumenes stood at the edge of camp beneath a tattered awning, watching the sunrise like a man reading a ledger he already knew would not balance.

Behind him, the fires of the Silver Shields sputtered in their braziers. Veterans, all of them. Men who had marched behind Alexander when the world was still being named. Now they sat hunched and murmuring, drinking broth too thin to carry heat, sharpening blades they no longer planned to use for ideals.

They still respected Eumenes. But they respected their families, their pensions, and their memories more.

A scout rode in from the southwest, dust-caked and blinking from the cold. He slid off his horse before it stopped moving and offered no formal salute—just a pouch, knotted twice.

Eumenes opened it alone. He knew the script before he saw it. Roxana's hand—unmistakable, narrow, precise. Measured like poetry spoken from behind a curtain.

> *"If your sword still holds, let it hold for him.*
> *We move north under the cloak of Orion.*
> *The child breathes. He dreams of his father at night.*
> *We dream of you in the morning."*

He folded the letter once, then again. No smile. No grief. Just a long exhale through his nose. He pressed the parchment against his chest, briefly, then pinned it beside the standard of Alexander—still standing upright in the center of the command tent, stitched with fading gold thread.

He summoned his officers—half of them drunk on frost-wine, the other half waiting to be told how many of them would die.

"The queen walks," he said. "And the boy breathes." A murmur passed through the tent. Not hope. Something older. Guilt, maybe. Memory.

"This is not about east or west," Eumenes continued. "This is not about tribute or spoils or the empire we broke into provinces. This is about what happens when the last blood of Alexander is extinguished, and all that's left is the smoke of men who knew better."

He touched the diadem on the table—Alexander's diadem, frayed now, still bearing traces of the last sweat that soaked it in Babylon.

"You will march with me tomorrow," he said, "not because I command it, but because you are men who once followed a god. Follow his son now, even if you never see his face."

No one applauded. But no one left.

That night, he slept in the royal tent. Alone. No guards. No scribes. Just the wind curling through the flap like an old friend returning to say goodbye.

The letter from Roxana remained beside him, unread a second time. It didn't need repeating.

At some point, he removed his boots, unbuckled his sword, and looked up at the worn tapestry stitched with a lion and thunderbolt—Alexander's old standard, brought from Susa.

"If I fall," he said softly into the dark, "let them tell the boy we remembered him when the rest of the world forgot."

*****

They watched the battlefield from a ridge of dark rock where the frost hadn't melted for days.

Below them, the plain of Gabiene stretched flat and indifferent, a canvas of hoarfrost and kicked-up dust. Soldiers moved like ants in the middle distance—some drilling, some praying, some sharpening blades that would never strike true.

They said the plains of Gabiene had no gods, only mistakes. The land stretched flat as a forgotten scroll, crumpled at the edges by salt wind and cracked with old tracks that led nowhere. The soil was dust over stone, too fine to grip a sandal, too dry to remember a hoofprint by midday. Even the wind had no direction. It came as it pleased, scouring armor and eyes and the inside of your mouth, leaving everything tasting faintly of copper and chalk.

Veterans whispered that sound itself died here—that commands were swallowed before reaching the next line, that a man could scream into the open and hear only the tremble of his own breath.

You could march ten thousand across it and lose them before a single arrow was loosed. Not to the enemy. To the plain.

Some said Alexander had crossed Gabiene once, after Susa. But even he never camped here. He moved quick, like a man walking over a grave he didn't want to admit he felt beneath his boots.

Now Eumenes stood where the others had fled, raising his standard in soil that no longer remembered victory. He wasn't here to win. He was here to prove something could still be carried across silence and survive.

The Silver Shields didn't see it that way. They sharpened their blades without conviction, wrapped their feet in linen, and watched the horizon like it owed them a better death than this.

Behind the lines, someone muttered: "No one buries the dead here. The dust does it for you."

Antigonus stood with a hand resting on his hip, wrapped in a wolf-pelt cloak, his breath fogging like smoke from a dying brazier. Beside him, Demetrius paced like a tethered hawk—eager, restless, still pretending his father couldn't see how young he was behind the armor.

"Why don't we just strike now?" Demetrius asked. "We have more men, more horses. He's boxed in. It's snow or steel."

Antigonus didn't answer right away. He squinted at a distant row of tents flapping hard in the wind. The standard of Alexander—the old lion banner— still rose above Eumenes' command post, barely.

"He's boxed in," Antigonus said, "but not broken. And a man like Eumenes fights differently when he's not just defending himself, but a ghost."

Demetrius kicked gravel down the slope. "Then kill the ghost. End it."

Antigonus smiled, but it wasn't kind. "We don't kill ghosts, boy. We starve them. We deny them oxygen. Then we let their own men decide how long they want to breathe in smoke."

He went to the war table—a map pinned with ivory markers and a goblet half-filled with frozen wine—and tapped a strip of terrain near the river.

"Our cavalry moves here at first light. The train is the real prize—not the line. His Silver Shields are old. Veterans, yes, but they bleed nostalgia. If they lose their women, their coin, their sons..."

"They lose him," Demetrius finished.

Antigonus nodded. "Let them betray him for something they can carry. No one remembers loyalty when they're hungry."

He placed one black tile over a red one and pressed it down. "Eumenes will fall without a sword drawn against him."

A gust of wind scattered chalk pieces from the table.

Antigonus didn't bother to catch them. Demetrius did.

*****

The sky broke late that morning, not with thunder, but with wind—low and constant, driving dust across the Gabiene plain like a veil drawn over the eyes of history.

Eumenes sat horseback near the center, wearing Alexander's old cavalry cloak. The diadem was pinned beneath his gorget, hidden, but felt. Around him, the Silver Shields adjusted their stances, armor groaning like old bones. Some had fought in India. Some in Sogdiana. Some had held the line at Gaugamela. All watched the horizon like it owed them something.

The scouts returned with bad news and dry throats. "Antigonus didn't move for the line," one said. "He took the rear. The baggage. The families."

Silence spread across the ranks. Eumenes closed his eyes. He didn't curse. He didn't shout. He nodded once. "He's not fighting for the field. He's fighting for their hearts."

Behind him, an old shield-bearer whispered: "I've got two sons and a wife in that train."

Another: "So do I."

A third spat into the dust. "I'll trade a hundred kings for one daughter returned breathing."

Eumenes turned in the saddle. "You followed Alexander across the world."

A veteran answered: "Aye. And we buried him at the edge of it."

It didn't happen all at once. No declaration, no mutiny cry. Just movement—small at first. Lines pulling back. A quiet refusal to engage. The Silver Shields turned their spears downward and stood still.

From the ridge, Antigonus watched. No banners raised. Just patience. Just entropy. Exactly as planned. Eumenes dismounted and walked back to his tent alone. He didn't stop anyone. He didn't draw steel. He took the standard down with his own hands, rolled it slowly, and set it in the corner.

That night, they came for him. His own officers. No torches. No words. Just cloaks drawn and guilt sealed into silence.

He didn't resist. He handed them the seal of command.

He gave them his sword, hilt first.

He looked each of them in the eye and said the same thing: "Be sure you get your families back."

They chained him and led him past dying fires, past horses, past old men who couldn't meet his gaze. The wind lifted ash from cookfires and scattered it like snow.

Eumenes didn't ask for rites. He only turned once before the dark and said: "Tell the boy I remembered him."

*****

They did not execute him immediately.

Eumenes was held three days in a tent at the edge of Antigonus' encampment—guarded not by soldiers, but by absence. No food. No torch. Just water in a clay bowl that cracked in the cold.

Outside, Antigonus said nothing to his generals. He gave no speech. He moved tokens across maps, ordered winter supplies, reorganized cavalry ranks. Victory, in his view, required maintenance—not mourning.

On the second night, Demetrius entered.

Eumenes sat cross-legged, sunken-eyed but lucid. His wrists were unbound. There was nowhere to run.

"Why didn't you flee when you had the chance?"

"Because someone had to remember how it ended."

"My father doesn't hate you."

"That's why he hasn't killed me yet." Wind scratched at the canvas like it wanted to listen.

"He says you served a ghost," Demetrius said.

Eumenes smiled faintly. "And he serves what's left after the ghost is gone."

Demetrius left without another word.

*****

At dawn on the third day, Antigonus gave the order.

No spectacle. No blood in the snow. The command passed like a coin: quiet, round, cold in the hand.

They found Eumenes seated as before, already still. Whether he had starved or simply let go, no one could say.

Antigonus entered alone. He looked a long time at the man who had out-maneuvered him at Paraetacene and stitched the east together with parchment and will. At last he removed the signet ring from Eumenes' hand—not to keep, but to be sure no one else would—and dropped it into the cold fire pit.

"He would have made a good king," Antigonus said.

Outside the flap, Demetrius asked: "Will people say he died well?"

"Only if we let them," Antigonus replied.

The wind carried ash across the plain. The war, as always, prepared to continue.

*****

The ship creaked into the harbor of Byzantium at first light, slipping between fishing boats and anchored triremes like a ghost that hadn't decided if it belonged to the living. Fog clung low, rippling like silk drawn backward. The oarsmen didn't speak. The crew tied off without shouting. Everyone seemed to know not to disturb what they were carrying.

Roxana stood near the prow, cloak tight, hands buried in folds. She had not slept since Smyrna. Her eyes had taken on the dry sharpness of someone who no longer expected good news. Behind her, Polyperchon knelt beside the boy, tightening his boots, speaking low about what to expect at the docks.

Thais hovered at the gangplank, barefoot on wet timber, whispering a protection spell against "things that travel on water, but were never born of it."

The city rose—gray terraces, market towers scaffolded, domes capped with green copper. Byzantium. A Greek city by law. A Persian city by memory. A nervous city by trade.

They disembarked without ceremony. No one recognized them. No one bowed. And that, for now, was safety.

They took a rented mule cart north, following the shoreline, silent but alert. The boy dozed against a grain sack. Polyperchon watched intersections. Roxana watched the sky.

In a narrow causeway near the outer wall, a man in a fisherman's cloak stepped from behind a salt barrel and held out a satchel. He said nothing. When Polyperchon moved to draw his knife, the man bowed and vanished into the alley maze.

Roxana unknotted the satchel.

Inside lay a folded strip of purple cloth, burned at the edges as if torn from a royal banner mid-fire. Wrapped inside: a fingerbone, brittle and pale, bound in ash-streaked lambskin. A thin iron ring clung to the joint, blackened but unbroken. At the bottom, the coin from Smyrna—the cavalry drachma—now scorched, its silver blistered, its edges warped as though it had passed through flame and memory both.

She knelt in the street without meaning to. The wind took her veil. The boy stirred but didn't wake. Polyperchon did not look at the items. He didn't need to.

"Eumenes is gone," Roxana said—not with grief, but with the calm of confirmation.

Polyperchon nodded once. "Then we are the last breath of the king."

They said nothing more. The cart lurched forward, wheels squeaking on old stone. Behind them, the Bosphorus gleamed like a blade, and Byzantium returned to its business—unaware that the last general of Alexander had turned to dust, and that somewhere in the north, a boy still dreamed of lions.

CHAPTER 29

CIRCLE OF SMOKE

By the first thaw of 315 BCE, there were no true kings left.

Macedon belonged to Cassander now—at least on paper. He held Pella with a mailed fist and a dead stare, neither crowned nor called king, but moving as if both were already true. He had executed Olympias. Buried her unmarked near the sea, told no one, burned the letters. Let the silence do the work. He ruled not by lineage, but by subtraction. What he couldn't inherit, he erased.

In the east, Antigonus held everything Eumenes had once bled to preserve—Asia Minor, Syria, the satrapies that used to bow to Babylon. He had not crowned himself either—not yet. He didn't need to. He sat like a mountain in the distance, waiting for Cassander to overreach, to declare something untrue, to choke on the name he thought he'd buried.

His son, Demetrius, watched—eager, impatient, and cruel in the way young men get when power is all they've ever seen but never been trusted to hold. He had seen how Eumenes died. He would remember that.

Far south, Ptolemy remained silent. He ruled Egypt like a priest rules a tomb—quietly, deliberately, surrounded by dead gods. He sealed Alexander's body behind another layer of stone, and when asked about the boy, said nothing. Some swore he'd gone blind in one eye; others said he saw too much.

Seleucus, in Babylon, stirred. Not openly. Not yet. He watched Antigonus grow fat on satrapies, and Cassander grow thin with suspicion. He burned letters, but never the ones that mattered. His ambition slept like a coiled lion—not dead, only wintering.

And then there was the woman and the child.

Roxana, widow of a god, moved north beneath false names and wrapped the boy in legends. She no longer prayed. She wrote. She no longer begged. She calculated. She no longer ran. She walked the cracks of empire, carrying the one thing no one else had: the blood that couldn't be replicated.

The boy, Alexander IV, had begun asking questions. Not about war. About stars. About names. About lions. He spoke less. Listened more. He traced constellations in the dirt. He learned the weight of silence. He didn't yet know what it meant to be hunted—but he was learning what it meant to be remembered.

At his side, Polyperchon—the last regent no court still recognized—taught him not how to rule, but how to vanish and remain. He no longer issued commands; he kept fire. He no longer sought thrones; he carried the myth.

In every corner of the fractured empire, someone thought the war was over. But none of them had seen the boy. Not yet.

*****

They arrived in Byzantium with salt still in their cloaks and the child asleep between barrels of grain.

The city was cold and gray-skied, its walls wrapped in mist that never quite lifted. From the quay, Roxana could see the towers of the acropolis rising like broken fingers from an older age—scarred by Persian fires, mended by Athenian stonecutters, ignored now by Macedonian scribes. Even the gods here changed names to survive.

Byzantium in 315 BCE: a modest but strategic hinge on the Bosphorus—Megarian colony, Persian outpost, Athenian dependency, now Hellenistic crossroads. Walls weathered, harbor busy, streets a braid of Greek, Thracian, and Anatolian.

Known for switching allegiances, the city offered both refuge and amnesia—a place built for fugitives, and for forgetting.

They didn't speak as they disembarked. Thais, the wet-nurse turned shadow, handed Roxana the satchel of sealed letters. Most were already out of date.

Polyperchon moved stiffly, joints swollen by sea-damp and silence. He hadn't prayed since Ephesus. He muttered to the boy instead—stories of star-gazers, river lions, and kings who only walked among mortals when drunk. The boy liked those stories. He had started speaking less, but remembering more.

In the forum, sheep grazed beside statues. A priest sold salt in thumb-sized bags, quoting Heraclitus. Two Aetolian mercenaries argued about copper prices beneath a shrine to Apollo whose marble eyes had been long ago gouged out.

Roxana watched the ships come and go for two days without sleeping. She wore saffron wool and paid a Thracian courier three tetradrachms to forget who he saw.

That night they found lodging behind the temple of Hecate, in the quarter once used by Athenian envoys. The house smelled of cedar, parchment, and oil-soaked rope. They boarded the shutters and barred the door.

Polyperchon set three perimeter stones in the courtyard and muttered old invocations—half ritual, half nostalgia.

"He won't remember any of this," Thais said.

"He doesn't have to," Roxana replied. "We will." The boy slept with a lion carving pressed to his chest.

Roxana sat by the fire rereading the last letter from Eumenes. She didn't cry when she burned it—just breathed in the smoke and remembered his closing line:

For the boy. Always.

The fire ebbed. The mist held. Roxana stepped into the courtyard without her cloak, breath snagging in the cold. She gathered what little they carried: a strip of blue linen, a fist of myrrh, and the heel of a honey loaf saved without knowing why.

No priest. No altar. Only stone and sky.

She placed the bread between two bricks and dusted it with salt and date. Broke the myrrh. Lit it. Sweet smoke clung to the throat.

She closed her eyes and remembered a wedding. A coronation. A birth.

Then she dipped the cloth into the coals and drew a sign—not Macedonian, not Persian. A circle: uneven, familiar, remembered from a temple wall in Sogdiana—or a dream.

Polyperchon watched from the doorway. Thais murmured in a language no one else knew. The boy came last. He stepped into the circle and sat, looking up.

The stars were dull through mist; he traced them anyway—connecting shapes no one had taught him. A dog barked. A horse snorted. Both belonged to another life.

The coals cracked. The circle faded. But he kept seeing it—behind his eyes. A circle. Not perfect. Not royal. Just whole.

*****

Cassander lit the torches himself for his Winter Festival of Peace.

The men around him watched like stone cutouts—officers in stiff cloaks, veterans with empty sleeves, priests clutching censers that smoked but gave no scent. Three bonfires rose in the square: one for victory, one for peace, one for the new year.

Not the old calendar. Not the Macedonian lunar reckoning. Not the Olympiads. Not even the ghost-year still dated to Alexander's death.

"This," he declared, voice taut as a drawn string, "is Year One."

He spoke from the high steps of the House of Councilors, where Antipater once issued war orders and long-dead generals learned how to speak without betraying intent. Cassander had never needed to be taught that.

Behind him, the wall where Alexander's likeness once hung was newly scrubbed, the mural white-washed, the Argead star chiseled clean off the stone.

"There is no heir," he continued. "There is only now."

The crowd—staged, selected, starved into obedience—applauded on cue. Coins clattered. Wine spilled. A boy with a broken leg beat a drum he couldn't hear.

Only one man asked aloud where Olympias had gone. He was later found in a latrine trench with his tongue cut out and a papyrus scroll stuffed in his throat. Blank parchment, folded twice.

Cassander's guards called it a warning.

Cassander called it art.

That night, dancers spun in the palace atrium. Foreign envoys toasted him as strategos autokrator. Musicians played old Epirote marches at half-speed, pretending they were hymns to peace. A satrap from Thrace gifted him a map of the known world traced in gold. Cassander burned it before sunrise.

He had already redrawn it in his head.

*****

Two nights later, Cassander married Thessalonike, a half-sister of Alexander the Great.

She was thirty-two—still beautiful, but in the tempered way of survivors. Her cheekbones had sharpened with years—less from age than from discipline. Her hair, once copper-black, was now braided high in the Epirote style, silver beginning to thread through it. She no longer dyed the temples. Let them show. Let the toll speak.

Thessalonike had lived through five wars, three sieges, two betrayals, and the slow erasure of her family name. She had watched her mother, Nicesipolis of Pherae, poisoned; her father stabbed in the theater of Aegae, now modern Vergina, Macedonia's old royal capital during the wedding festivities of his daughter Cleopatra. She had watched as her brother turned into a god before he could become a man.

And now—this indignity. A wedding dressed as policy.

Her body had learned to speak silence. When she stood still, people listened without knowing why. When she moved, she did so with economy, like someone who had counted every step toward ruin and still walked anyway. She rarely raised her voice, but when she did, it came from the chest—not the throat—and left bruises on the air.

She had once loved horses. Now she walked beside them. She had once written letters to cousins in Epirus, folded with lavender. Now she burned her own correspondence after every full moon, just in case.

In the weeks before the wedding, she stopped speaking in public. The palace women said she had taken a vow. The priests called it piety. Cassander called it prudence.

It was none of those. It was grief made sovereign.

At night, she slept with a dagger under her pillow. Not because she feared him.

Because she knew him.

He didn't touch her the first night. Didn't look at her long. Just drank, muttered something about succession, and passed out, limp as usual, with only one boot still on.

She sat at the edge of the bed for hours, fully dressed, watching the brazier burn down to its last ember.

When dawn came, she opened the window herself. The air smelled of smoke and thawing mud. Somewhere, a rooster crowed. It sounded like a funeral dirge.

She had been given titles—Lady of Macedon, Protector of the Line—but none fit. They were scaffolding around a ruin no one dared survey.

She carried the Argead name not as pride, but as weight.

She didn't flinch when strangers bowed. She didn't smile when soldiers offered her wine.

She didn't cry when she walked past the old mural of Alexander—scrubbed now, defaced, overwritten with Cassander's seal.

She only paused once, in a sun-lit hall near the library, and stared at a cracked relief of Philip II hunting lions.

Then she said aloud, to no one: "They've mistaken silence for permission."

And kept walking.

*****

The ceremony was held in the old royal chapel, beneath columns painted with scenes of Heracles slaying monsters whose names no one remembered. The frescoes had faded, but not enough to hide their intentions—violence made sacred, blood turned to dynasty.

She wore silver, not white—not by choice, but decree. Her veil shimmered like fish-skin. Her eyes did not. No hymns were sung.

They stood before the altar once consecrated by Philip II—her father. A brazier burned behind them, fed with cedar from Lebanon and laurel from Olympus. The smoke smelled of memory and rot.

Cassander did not kiss her. He pressed his seal-ring to her palm instead. The gesture was not intimate. It was contractual.

The priests spoke of unity, of securing Macedon's future, of binding old lineages into new. But there were no royal bloodlines left to bind—only this one woman, Alexander's half-sister, the last Argead not buried or hunted.

The witnesses were generals in borrowed cloaks, palace scribes, and a line of mute children dressed as Hours of the Year, each holding a sheaf of barley or a sprig of myrtle. No family attended. No mother. No brother. No son.

As they recited the vows, a thunderclap cracked over Pella's hills. No storm followed—just a sudden wind that scattered petals before they touched the floor.

Later, when the feast was served, Thessalonike did not eat. She sat beside Cassander like a statue, her face unmoving, her hands folded in her lap as if waiting for a different century to arrive.

Cassander drank heavily that night. Not from joy, but from strain. He toasted her once—by name—but not as queen. Never as queen.

The Argead name remained unspoken, as if saying it would summon something too old to kill, too sacred to own.

By morning she was moved to a chamber near the northern watchtower— once Olympias's. The servants changed the linens and repainted the walls, but they could not erase the blood dried beneath the floorboards.

No announcement was made. No coinage struck. No portrait commissioned. Cassander had married the sister of a god.

But he made sure the gods stayed silent about it.

*****

In Susa, far to the east, Antigonus One-Eye held the letter without breaking the seal.

He stood beneath a fluted column in his western court, where Alexander had once walked barefoot on the marble to cool his temper. Those days were dead. The marble had cracked in summer heat. Pigeons nested where satraps once knelt.

Former jewel of the Achaemenid world, now a throne of smoke and marble memory.

Susa had not been built to last—but to remind.

Set on the edge of the Zagros foothills where Mesopotamia yields to Elam, the palace sprawled across a raised platform above the Choaspes River. Once the Apadana, stitched together by Persian kings and artisans from every corner of empire—Lydian, Babylonian, Median, Phoenician, Greek. Its columns still stood, fluted like frozen wind, topped with twin bulls glaring down at every man who dared to rule.

Alexander had walked here, claiming the court as a shared stage for East and West. He had married Roxana here—or so the veterans whispered. He had burned scrolls, planted silk banners, and left no heir on the stone—only footprints. Only ghosts.

Now Antigonus Monophthalmus—the One-Eyed Strategos—occupied the high chamber. He didn't sleep there; he didn't trust stone carved by Macedonian hands. But he held court beneath its eaves like a man waiting for time itself to fracture.

The air stank of age and wax and mildew.

The roof had been patched with timber from ruined cities—Tyre, Gaza, Sidon—each beam a reliquary of conquest. Jackals sometimes howled in the lower courts.

Frescoes faded: lions chasing deer, lotus vines climbing heaven, Darius III at council—his face gouged out with a spearhead.

No one sat upon the lapis throne; even Antigonus walked around it, as if the stone still held heat from Alexander's shadow.

The gardens had withered under bureaucracy. What had been an orchard of pomegranates and cypress was now a corral for horses and scribes. Orders were written on leather, then scraped clean when cities fell too fast for letters to land.

Demetrius trained in the Hall of a Hundred Columns—roofless now, open to starlight. He fought phantoms there, practicing what it meant to be remembered.

Below, barrels of Persian wine and cages that once held rebel kings rusted in the dark. Antigonus never opened them; he only ordered the locks polished.

In a soot-streaked alcove behind the atrium, a mosaic of Ishtar still glimmered faintly. No one dared clean it. The goddess stared out through cracked tiles, amused by men who thought they commanded legacy.

And in a small shrine tended by three silent Median priests, a burnt offering plate remained black with old smoke. On it, scrawled in half-erased ink, one word survived:

Basileus. King.

No one knew which one it meant anymore.

*****

Demetrius sat cross-legged on a sheepskin, shirtless, streaked with sweat and salt. The torchlight traced the lean angles of his shoulders, muscle drawn like bowstring under bronze skin. In his lap, a short cavalry blade hissed against a whetstone in slow, circular strokes. Not for war. For rhythm. For control.

Across the chamber, Antigonus stood beneath a cracked lintel of black marble, one hand braced against the pillar, the other holding a parchment sealed with red wax. His cloak was dusted from travel, boots still crusted with salt from the riverbanks. He hadn't removed his belt. He never did in Susa.

"He's declared a new year," Antigonus said, voice low, worn at the edges. "A world born without a father."

Demetrius didn't look up. "Cassander?"

Antigonus turned the scroll between his fingers, thumb pressing the seal into his skin like a brand. "Who else would name himself god by erasing one?"

He flicked his wrist. The letter dropped into the brazier. Fire caught fast. Ink curled mid-sentence; the Argead lion hissed as it melted.

Demetrius finally glanced up, his brow half-shadowed. "Do we move on him?"

Antigonus stared into the flame as if it owed him prophecy. "Not yet," he said. "Let him fatten on illusion. He believes memory dies as easily as men do."

A servant slipped in—barefoot, pale, breathless. He whispered something. Antigonus's jaw flexed once. Twice. The boy vanished again.

Antigonus exhaled—not quite a sigh, more like history escaping his ribs. "The boy," he muttered. "There are whispers."

Demetrius's whetstone stopped mid-stroke.

"Whispers?"

"They say he lives. Roxana with him. Somewhere north of the Bosphorus."

Demetrius leaned forward, blade forgotten. "What do we do?"

Antigonus didn't answer. He stepped closer to the fire. The brazier's light hollowed his face; his ruined eye gleamed like cooled glass. "We wait," he said. "Let him grow in the dark. Let him gather shadows."

Demetrius frowned. "But he's the heir. If he returns—"

"My quarrel," Antigonus cut in, "is not with boys raised on stars and bedtime prophecy. My quarrel is with men who crown themselves gods without earning thunder."

He let silence settle, heavy and absolute.

Outside, a jackal barked once. Then nothing.

Demetrius leaned back on one elbow. "Not Cassander, then. It's the East that stirs you."

Antigonus said nothing. He moved to the broken colonnade, moonlight slicing pale teeth across the floor. Beyond lay the ruins—courtyards drowned in shadow, columns hollowed by rain, olive trees grown feral in the king's garden.

"You see ghosts out there?" Demetrius asked.

"I see futures," his father said.

He gestured east—not toward Babylon, not even Bactria, but beyond.

"Seleucus," he said at last. "The accountant who became a priest. The clerk who learned patience. He waits in the dust like a buried knife."

Demetrius rose, blade still in hand. "We stripped Babylon bare. He fled. He's nothing."

Antigonus turned, his one eye sharp as obsidian. "He's not nothing," he said. "He's an idea."

Demetrius frowned. "What kind of idea?"

"A quiet one," Antigonus said. "And quiet ideas are the most dangerous. Seleucus doesn't shout. He builds—brick by brick, memory by memory. While Cassander performs and Ptolemy embalms legacy, Seleucus listens. To stars. To omens. To men who still call Alexander Iskander. The East doesn't forget."

He sank onto a rough cedar stool; it creaked like an old ship in heavy sea.

"The Nabateans were first to send him grain," he said. "Not gold. Grain."

Demetrius narrowed his eyes. "So?"

"So grain means hunger. Hunger means vision. They see something. Something neither Macedon nor Egypt—nor even I—can offer."

Demetrius hesitated. "They think they can build a second empire."

"Not a second," Antigonus said. "A different one. One where we're relics. Where the Argead myth is swallowed and rewritten by desert tongues and moon calendars. Seleucus doesn't need to conquer land—he needs to conquer meaning."

The fire cracked inward, the sound of a map folding.

"You believe he'll come west?" Demetrius asked.

"No," Antigonus said, eyes glinting. "He'll wait until we tear each other apart. Then he'll rise—not as general, but as prophet. And they'll call his children gods."

He spat into the fire. It hissed. "Cassander is a symptom," he said. "Seleucus is a system."

Demetrius leaned forward, chilled by the thought. "And the boy?"

Antigonus smiled faintly—an old soldier's grim mercy.

"The boy is a mirror," he said. "What we fear. What we've broken. What we pretend never existed."

He looked into the fire one last time. "When the time comes," he said, "we won't kill him to stop a bloodline. We'll kill him to silence a question."

*****

The tower of Babylon no longer stood, but Seleucus dreamed it anyway.

In the cool silence of the Garden of Books in Memphis's western quarter—where the Nile lapped at shrine steps and ibis stalked among reeds—Seleucus sat cross-legged on the tiles behind Ptolemy's great library. His cloak was tight around him; his sandals lay forgotten. His feet sought something older than comfort—memory, maybe. Or return.

The air smelled of papyrus and incense drifting from the temple of Thoth. But in his mind the air was dust, baked and dry. Babylon again. Not as it was—but as it should have been.

In his dream, the Temple of Marduk still stood, charred but breathing. Fig roots knotted the bricks. The Euphrates crawled below like a dark thought. Oil lamps circled the idol. Babylon had not fallen—it had waited.

He stood barefoot on the highest terrace, cloak tugged by desert wind. The Nabateans called him Sleeper of Lions. The priests called him Regent. He had not yet returned—but he remembered how.

Empires, he believed, were measured not in battles but in eclipses.

War was not force. It was interval.

"Still charting the stars?" a voice asked. Ptolemy—half amusement, half warning.

Seleucus looked up. The ruler of Egypt stood above him, scroll in one hand, lapis belt gleaming. He did not sit; he rarely did with equals. Or threats.

"The stars don't lie," Seleucus said.

"They just refuse to answer," Ptolemy replied.

He circled the garden, papyrus in hand—dispatches from Tyre or Babylon. Seleucus did not ask.

"You dream of it still?" Ptolemy asked. "The city."

"Babylon is not a city," Seleucus said. "It is a silence. The kind that waits."

"You lost it," Ptolemy said. "Antigonus took it."

"I loaned it," Seleucus replied evenly, "to fools who think power comes from naming themselves."

"You think it comes from stars?"

"I think it comes from knowing when the echo dies."

Ptolemy's eyes sharpened. "If you mean to raise banners in my court, don't."

"I raise nothing," Seleucus said. "Not yet." Silence passed between them like a shadow of wings—light, brief, undeniable.

Then Seleucus said, almost gently: "Do you know why Babylon has no king?"

Ptolemy said nothing.

"Because Babylon remembers too many of them."

He stood, brushed dust from his cloak, and moved toward the colonnade. The Nile wind tugged at his hem like a child left waiting.

"I'm not building an empire," Seleucus said. "Let the west burn its memories. Let Cassander choke on peace. Let Antigonus drown in prophecy. Let Ptolemy embalm the past."

Ptolemy folded his arms. "And what are you building, then?"

Seleucus stopped at the edge of shade, hand on the sandstone pillar. He looked east—always east.

"A rhythm," he said. Then, softer: "When gods fall silent and calendars collapse, they'll come to me. Not for orders. Not for blood. For something older than kings."

He unrolled the clay tablet he'd been etching each morning, its surface still soft. Upon it, the symbol he dreamed again and again:

Not a crown. Not a throne.

A circle. Of return.

*****

The sun rose slow and thick over the Bosphorus, casting the city in layers of fire, then brass, then salt.

Roxana stood on the colonnaded roof, sheepskin wrapped at her shoulders, eyes on the western gate.

She had dreamed of a road that never curved, a lion pacing beside her son. The boy had spoken in the dream, but not in words—only constellations, rearranged.

Polyperchon climbed to meet her, a scroll in hand. "From Sestos," he said. "A merchant saw Cassander's torchfires. Claims Olympias is dead."

Roxana nodded. Didn't speak.

"He's declared peace."

"He's declared silence," she replied. "There's a difference."

Polyperchon squinted into the wind. His knuckles were cracked from cold. Inside, the boy painted lions on the stone floor with saffron and spit.

"Then we move before silence swallows us too."

They left Byzantium three days later—no fanfare, no gods. Only a child, a name, and a long road through forgotten kingdoms.

*****

They passed through Perinthos the next day, cloaked and quiet, beneath the crumbling gate that still bore scars from Philip's siege—twenty years old and still bleeding memory.

The town had shrunk since the old wars. Half the homes were shuttered, the harbor half-silted. But the walls still stood, and inside them the people spoke Greek with Thracian vowels and kept their knives visible.

A woman sold dried figs beside a headless shrine of Hermes. A boy chased pigeons in spirals. A man on crutches shouted that the king was dead—though no one asked which one.

Roxana didn't dismount. Neither did Polyperchon.

They stayed long enough to water the mules and trade a bolt of Tyrian linen for barley and salted cheese.

The merchant who took it asked no questions but glanced at the boy's lion carving and kissed his teeth—not in blessing, in superstition.

Thais whispered a prayer outside a burned-out temple. No one answered.

*****

That night they camped in the ruins of an Athenian outpost on the western road. The boy asked if they were still in his father's empire. Roxana didn't answer. Not right away.

The fire had burned low. The mist hadn't lifted. Roxana stepped into the courtyard barefoot, cloak undone, cold unbothered by firelight.

In her hands she carried three things: a twist of myrrh, a scrap of dyed linen, and the crusted edge of a honey loaf gone hard with time.

She placed the bread between two stones, dusted it with ash and date. Broke the myrrh. Lit it. Let the sweetness burn low and slow.

She didn't pray. She remembered.

Not words—those had lost shape—but motion. Pattern. The way a priest in Sogdiana had once turned his hand in a slow arc, drawing a shape on the temple floor with chalk. A circle. Not perfect. Not sacred. Just complete.

She dipped the linen into the embers and drew that same shape now on the worn stone—imperfect, warped at the edge, as if time itself had tried to erase it.

Polyperchon stood nearby, still as one of the columns. Thais watched from the doorway, clutching the satchel of letters as if to keep them from drifting back into the fire.

The boy stepped forward without being called. He moved into the center of the shape and sat cross-legged, one hand resting in the faint warmth left behind. He didn't speak. Just looked upward, toward the hidden stars.

The young Alexander didn't know why the circle mattered. Only that it did. It wasn't a throne. It wasn't a crown. It had no top. No beginning. No edge that said: here the kingdom ends.

It reminded him of the way the stars moved—not in lines, but in returns; the way Polyperchon spoke of seasons; the way his mother's voice looped back to the same phrase when she told the story of his father's death: "He went where stars go."

He had begun to believe that things didn't end. They just turned—disappeared into curve and came back as something else.

He looked down at the faint mark in the stone. Already, the wind was softening its edges. Touching the center with one finger, the boy closed his eyes, and whispered a word he hadn't meant to say:

"Home."

CHAPTER 30

MAP OF FIRE AND BLOOD

THRACIAN HILLS – ONE WEEK WEST OF PERINTHOS, WINTER 315 BCE. She drew her first map that night in dust and memory.

Roxana traced it with a stalk of brittle grass, her fingertip guiding Polyperchon's eyes through a lattice of imagined routes and vanished loyalties. No cities. No roads. Just names spoken in half-whispers around hearths, back when hearths still meant safety. Shrines where Alexander's cloak had once been laid; wells where dying soldiers swore they saw his face in the water; forest glades where horses refused to enter.

Places that remembered.

They sat on a woven reed mat inside a half-ruined watchtower clinging to a ridgeline above the frost-scarred Thracian plains. The tower had once guarded the inland road from Perinthos to Amphipolis—a Macedonian frontier outpost built under Philip, long since abandoned when the satrapal networks collapsed. Stone walls rough with moss, roof collapsed to the stars, hearth cracked but serviceable. It wasn't warm, but it was silent. Forgotten. Perfect.

Outside, the hills rolled east toward the coast, west toward the bones of empire. To the north, smoke from a burned village curled like a warning. To the south, a dry creekbed marked the last place they'd seen hoofprints not their own.

The boy crouched near the hearth—silent, alert. He had taken to sketching lions on clay shards and leaving them in corners, small offerings to gods whose names had gone to ground.

His hair hung longer now, uncut since Babylon. His shadow had started to walk differently.

"This one," Roxana said, pointing with the grass stalk to a blot of loose ash, "was once a temple of fire before the satraps defiled it. They still fear it."

Polyperchon squinted. "And this?"

"Not a place. A woman. Nysa. She nursed Alexander after Issus. They say she walks still, in disguise, with coins sewn into her hem."

Polyperchon grunted. "Ghosts and grandmothers."

Roxana didn't look up. "Ghosts have longer reach than soldiers now." The fire popped. The shadows shifted.

Behind them, the boy rose and wandered toward the coals, where a priest in red robes stirred a copper bowl of ash and pine resin. He'd arrived two nights earlier, a figure from the east wrapped in road dust and silence. His accent braided Persian with something older, and no one asked his name.

"If you trace it in ash," the priest told the boy without turning, "it will burn brighter later."

The boy didn't answer. He picked up a half-charred reed and began drawing over Roxana's dust lines with the priest's ash. Roads became veins. Cities dissolved into signal fires. The map deepened.

Polyperchon watched the lines blacken, then settle.

"They'll say we've lost the world," he muttered.

"We haven't lost it," Roxana said. "We're redrawing it."

*****

In Memphis, the Nile coughed steam into the cold dawn air.

Seleucus stood in the half-built east wing of the palace, a sun-bleached colonnade overlooking the harbor where merchant sails drifted like torn flags. A servant knelt behind him, holding a brass plate and two scrolls.

One bore Cassander's seal—cracked, the wax flaking like old blood. Seleucus didn't unroll it. He had read it once, and once was enough. Promises disguised as decrees; orders steeped in fear. He held it over the brazier. The papyrus curled into itself like a dying snake.

The second scroll was lighter. Thinner. Unofficial. It still smelled faintly of cedar oil.

Ptolemy's hand was deliberate, controlled, almost cold. No greeting. No ornament. Just one line, written like a knife: The boy will rise. That much is certain. The rest depends on where he first casts his shadow.

Seleucus didn't burn this one.

He rolled it tightly and slid it into a hollow bone tube, sealing it with pitch. Then he turned back to the horizon.

Below, the city swayed with motion—priests chanting, hawkers shouting, children chasing smoke between columns.

The empire was breaking, yes. But in every fracture, new edges formed.

He let the wind touch his face, then turned inside.

*****

That night, Roxana's map of fire was finished.

No parchment. No compass. No ruler. Just ash, breath, and the cracked stone floor of a ruined tower. They worked by firelight and memory. The priest said nothing at first—only watched as the boy's finger traced the lines his mother had drawn, now deepened with resin ash and pine soot. Each motion slowed time. Each curve whispered a name.

It was no map of governance. It defied it.

There were no borders. No cities stamped by royal decree. No roads sanctioned by generals or scribes. Only lines of ash—twisting, branching, converging like veins in a living body.

But they didn't lie still. They moved—just barely, but undeniably. Ash flickered under the embers' glow, shifting as if remembering its own heat.

The map didn't mark what was. It summoned what could be.

Each line pulsed like a nerve, a spell still mid-utterance, unfinished. The boy leaned closer. He wasn't reading it. He was listening.

"It moves," he said quietly.

Roxana nodded. "Because it was never meant to stay still."

The priest finally spoke, voice low and cracked with age—but steady, like the last coal refusing to die.

> *"By line of ember and tongue of flame,*
> *What is forgotten shall speak again.*
> *Not by crown, nor by sword, nor by stone—*
> *But by the hand that remembers the way home."*

Polyperchon turned, slowly. "Where did you hear that?" The priest did not answer. He looked only at the boy.

"What god taught you that verse?" Polyperchon demanded.

"The kind we stopped worshipping when kings learned to burn names," the priest said.

Polyperchon smiled faintly—not with hope, but with recognition. History, finally turning back toward the flame.

*****

When it was done, Roxana stood. She stepped back, letting the firelight fall across the full breadth of what they had made.

It sprawled like a nervous system made of myth—from coast to desert, from burned temples to still-beating hearths. A lattice of resistance. A ghost-network. A prophecy drawn in ash.

She crouched and began brushing it into her palm. The lines flaked and broke as they lifted—brittle, but not dead. She poured the ashes into a tight cloth pouch, not to preserve the map, but to seed the next fire. Then she unrolled the oilcloth and handed it to the boy.

"This is your empire," she said.

He looked down at it. "It's not real."

Roxana met his eyes. "It's not supposed to be. Not yet. But it will be—because you've seen it. Now held it in your hands."

He didn't argue. He took it with both hands and tied it shut. The pouch of ash went into his satchel.

Polyperchon stood in the doorway of the ruined tower, one hand resting on the threshold stone. The stars carved there had faded—but they were still visible if you knew where to look: Macedonian constellations, the map of a glory turned ruin.

He reached out, fingers brushing the shallow engraving of Philip's seal-star—the Vergina Sun, weathered by years of wind and rain.

The boy stepped beside him and, without a word, pulled a shard of burnt wood from the fire. He leaned in and scratched something beside the star—a crooked line, then another, slightly angled. A beginning.

Not mimicry. Not homage. Correction.

The priest nodded. Polyperchon said nothing. Roxana smiled, thin and dangerous. Above them, Orion froze mid-hunt. Below, a fox screamed once and went silent. Somewhere in the dark, another cry answered—not beast, not man. A sound like the future catching its breath.

And on the stone floor behind them, though no one touched it, one last thread of ash curled inward—circling the place where the boy had stood.

The map wasn't finished. It had only just begun.

*****

Before dawn, acolytes of Demeter gathered in Pella's temple district in secret, led by a young priest named Thallos, no older than twenty. He held a strip of parchment sealed in wax—the boy's birth record. It had been hidden beneath the hearth of a rural temple, now closed by Cassander's decree.

He read aloud: "Alexander, son of Alexander. Born of Roxana. Recorded in the eighth year after the king's death."

They lit a small flame in the chamber's center and whispered the boy's name—not in mourning, but in vow.

But spies were listening.

Cassander's guard stormed the chamber. No trials. No mercy. Just the sound of boots on stone. The fire was snuffed. The scroll seized. The priest did not scream when they dragged him through the mud.

Later, alone in his private chamber, Cassander held the scroll, read it once, and set it to flame.

But he did not burn the name.

He folded that part away, slipped it into a box of olive wood, locked it, and placed it beside his bed.

Because some part of him still knew: You cannot kill what is already becoming legend.

*****

For three days, they moved westward—silent, careful, marked by ash. The roads were half-frozen and half-watched—not by soldiers, but by strangers who no longer knew which gods to fear.

They made camp at the edge of a collapsed temple once dedicated to Sabazios, the Thracian sky-rider and storm-shaker. His altar had been shattered, his bronze horse's hooves overturned in the snow like forgotten war spoils. Cassander's purges had reached even here.

The temple had no roof left—only four standing columns wrapped in frost and vine. Inside, broken amphorae and twisted iron rings—remnants of a mystery cult—littered the floor like relics of a forgotten devotion.

Roxana walked the perimeter first, marking thresholds with myrrh and soot. Polyperchon took the eastern ridge. The boy wandered the ruins, fingers grazing the altar's cracked surface as if it might still breathe.

Then a sound—not hooves, not voice; a rustle, as if death were testing a whisper. Two guards pulled the rider from his horse: a man in torn satrap robes, blood dried to rust down one leg, the Macedonian sigil on his belt scorched black. He didn't resist. He knelt the moment he saw Roxana.

"A message," he rasped. "From Pella."

She didn't speak. She just nodded once.

He coughed blood. "The oaths have been changed. The name of your son is being struck from the scrolls. Cassander burns the genealogies himself. He's rebuilding the temple walls—narrower, thicker. No windows now."

Polyperchon stepped forward. "And the priests?"

"Some stayed—in silence. Others wait in cellars. They remember. They're waiting for a sign."

The boy said nothing. But he had heard everything. He stepped past them all, into the half-collapsed cella, where Sabazios's cracked visage stared blindly at the winter sky.

He placed his palm flat on the altar stone and whispered: "He doesn't understand. The gods remember."

*****

That night, the fire was small. They dared not build it higher; smoke drew questions. Polyperchon sat on a boulder near the temple steps, cloak drawn tight against the cold. Roxana joined him after the boy had fallen asleep beside the broken amphorae, curled like a lion cub beside the shattered god.

Neither spoke for a long while. Then: "I counted sixteen names on that map," he said. "Places I'd nearly forgotten. People I'd buried."

Roxana didn't look at him. "They aren't buried. They're waiting."

He nodded. "Then we give them something to wait for."

She turned. "I can send a party ahead. Through the grain road east of Lake Prasias. Merchants, not soldiers. Let them reach the city first. Speak to the old quarter. Test the silence."

Roxana hesitated. "And if the gates are sealed?"

"Then we know where the siege begins."

A beat. Then she said: "We don't go to beg for power. We go to let them see he still breathes."

Polyperchon smiled faintly. "That's all he needs to do."

The boy stood in the broken arch, holding the ash map. Behind him, the priest vanished into shadow.

Ahead, over the dark hills, a single torch flickered on the old Pella road— carried by someone who still remembered his name.

CHAPTER 31

THE BURIAL OF NAMES

Cassander entered the archive alone. No torchbearers. No ceremony. Only the draft moving through the stones like a memory trying to escape.

He paused at the threshold—as if waiting for something to rise and stop him. A whisper. A hand. A ghost. But the chamber offered no resistance—only dust, mildew, and the faint tang of rot where history had begun to decay.

Shelves bent under the weight of scrolls spanning three generations—Philip's edicts sealed in black wax, letters from Amyntas III to forgotten satraps, treaty margins where Alexander's boyish hand first traced the bones of empire.

All of it kept here, stacked and sorted, bound by the fragile belief that record could outlast blood.

Cassander walked between the shelves slowly, fingers brushing vellum like an appraiser inspecting relics before a fire sale. He didn't speak. He didn't need to. The order had already been given.

The scribes—men who had once preserved dynasties with ink and twine—now moved with the hollow obedience of undertakers. Scrolls lifted, not read; titles ignored; names discarded. They were tossed into canvas sacks with the indifference of butchers clearing carcasses from a killing floor.

A ledger cracked in two. Another unraveled on the floor like a gutted serpent. No one bent to gather it.

A young assistant wept once, quietly, then stopped. A slap followed from his elder—not for the tears, but for the sound.

Cassander kept walking. At the far wall, he paused before a steel-bound chest etched with the sunburst of Vergina. He placed a hand on it long enough to feel the cold bite of metal beneath his skin. Then he stepped back.

"Start with this one," he said. "Start where they believed the gods would care."

And kept walking.

*****

At the Temple of Apollo, the scrolls were not merely records. They were vows.

Oath rolls sealed by the gods, drawn from temple registries and kept under lock since the days when Alexander was still only a prince shadowing his father through the courts. Names etched in oil and bone-black ink, wrapped in cedar shavings and bound in linen.

These were the declarations of loyalty to the crown—the oaths of allegiance sworn before fires, altars, and witness stones. Each one carried the weight of divine consequence.

The priests trembled as they presented them, unrolling the scrolls with hands too old and too afraid. The ink had faded in places—but not everywhere.

There, again and again, it appeared: Alexander IV — king by blood, sovereign by oath, son of the god. A name that still carried heat.

Cassander took the stylus from the high priest without speaking.

The blade of it was bone, sharpened to a point no wider than a fingernail. He leaned over the first scroll and began to scrape.

Not slash. Not blot. Scrape. Line by line, letter by letter, he wore the boy's name down to the parchment, peeling history from its skin.

It took time. Ink rose in flecks. The stylus hissed with each pass. The parchment thinned beneath his hand.

It was not enough to erase the name.

He needed to wound the page—to make it remember what it had lost. He wanted to feel it resist.

Behind him, one monk stepped back from the gathering. He moved without being seen, a small shadow among many. At the chamber's edge, he knelt beside an open register left untended. One page still bore the child's name—fresh ink, a thumb-smudge no wider than a coin.

He folded it once. Twice. A third time—into a square small enough to hide in a sleeve. Then he pried loose a stone from the eastern alcove—an old repair, easy to dislodge—and slipped the folded parchment beneath it, beside a brittle laurel sprig long forgotten.

The monk's lips parted—not in prayer, but in warning. To no one. To the air. A breath that trembled with treason.

He did not speak. He did not pray.

He only breathed once, shallow and fast, and sealed the stone before anyone noticed he had moved.

*****

The pyre chamber had once been a granary. Now it fed only fire.

The hearth was broad enough for ox-carts to pass through, its vaulted stone arching overhead like the ribs of a dead colossus.

Soot dripped from the ceiling like old blood. Cassander stood beside the rusted grain chute, watching history burn.

Scrolls curled as they caught—dry ones first, their ink blistering into smoke before the parchment blackened. Charters from Susa. Treaty fragments from Tyre. Battle orders from Gaugamela—each stamped with the seal of a king who once believed the world could be contained in a signature.

Now they feathered, cracked, and turned to air.

The fire groaned. Not with hunger, but with resistance—memory refusing to die.

The flames faltered, damp in the bindings. Cassander stepped forward, expression flat. He took a goatskin ledger bound in brass—some ledger of royal muster or sacred oath—and tore it down the spine. Pages clung like wet feathers before he shoved it into the blaze with both hands.

No one behind him spoke. No record was kept. The last historian had been dismissed at dawn, his inkpot shattered on the temple steps.

"There," Cassander muttered as a final scroll unraveled and collapsed into embers. "The last king is ash."

He turned without ceremony. The iron door groaned shut behind him.

It did not open again.

*****

In Memphis, beneath the veiled colonnades of Ptolemy's southern wing, Seleucus sat cross-legged on a reed mat, a map unrolled before him—creased, sun-bleached, and stained with wine and ash.

Babylon sat at the center. Not in ink, but in memory. The gates. The courtyards. The old ziggurat still bearing Alexander's starburst banner—its threads fraying in the desert wind.

He had not spoken the city's name aloud in months.

The scroll from Cassander lay unopened beside him, the wax seal cracked from heat but still unbroken. He tapped it once with his knuckle—then left it.

Ptolemy entered without warning. Sandal straps loose, hands clasped behind his back. "You're not a ghost yet," he said. "But you've learned how to haunt."

Seleucus didn't rise. He only looked up and said, "He's burning the boy's name."

Ptolemy nodded once, slowly. "He's burning all of us."

Seleucus gestured toward the map. His finger traced a line—east through the desert, past Damascus, along the Euphrates. Not a retreat. A return. "I left a key buried beneath the western gate," he said. "Behind the second brick in the arch. It still turns the lock."

Ptolemy studied him, then the map. Then the scroll. "Are you going to read it?"

Seleucus smiled without warmth. "He made the mistake of writing it down."

POLYPERCHON

CHAPTER 32

THE SHADOW AT THE GATE

They reached the last ridge before Pella just before dusk, when the light flattened and the shadows stretched across the pass like a spilled inkpot—thin, dark, and hungry.

The snowmelt had turned the path into a vein of gray mud. The boy's pony stumbled once, catching its hoof on a jagged stone, and Roxana steadied him without speaking.

Ahead, the ruins of an old Argead signal fort clung to the slope—half-swallowed by frost and ivy, its beacon tower cracked down the spine. A chipped mosaic of Zeus still marked the northern face—thunderbolt in hand, eagle on shoulder, eyes that once faced Persia now staring blankly into wind.

They made camp within the broken outer wall, where wild thyme grew between the flagstones and a collapsed hearth still bore the black scorch of forgotten flame. Polyperchon stood with his back to the mosaic, arms crossed, watching the boy draw lines in the dirt with a twig.

"This is as close as we get," he said. "For now."

Roxana didn't answer. She was counting clouds. "You feel it?" she asked. "The pressure in the air? Something's shifting."

Polyperchon nodded. He felt it in the bone, the way old soldiers did.

That night, a courier arrived like a rumor—soaked in sweat, no torch, no guards. Only the wet slap of sandals on stone gave him away. He carried no scroll, only a knotted braid of blue wool worn by temple stewards on feast days.

Inside the braid: a sliver of papyrus, oil-smudged, bearing one hurried line in priestly hand: "The elders will bless the boy publicly. The date is set."

Polyperchon read it twice, the ink catching in the torchlight like dried blood. Then he passed it to Roxana. "It's bait," he said.

"Yes," she replied. "But bait means there's something hungry on the other end." She tucked the braid into her sleeve, next to the knife. "Let them think we're the ones walking into a trap."

*****

At dawn, a scout arrived half-dead.

His horse stumbled into camp foaming at the mouth, nostrils rimed with ice. The man clung to the saddle by a single strap, his head sagging, one boot lost somewhere in the ravines behind him. A younger guard caught him as he fell—more bone than man, glazed in road dust and exhaustion.

"He came from the east," someone whispered. "A Thracian belt. That's Eumenes' mark."

Roxana was already moving. She knelt beside him, tearing her cloak from her shoulders to cradle his head. His face was blistered from wind and fever, lips cracked so badly they had bled into his teeth. He tried to speak, failed, tried again.

Polyperchon crouched beside her—one hand on the scout's arm, the other braced for what was coming.

The man coughed—deep, wet, final confirmation of what they already knew.

Then he forced the words. "Eumenes…" A wheeze. "…gone." Polyperchon stiffened. Roxana blinked once. Hard.

Eumenes was the last spine in the east. The last general who still bled for the boy's name. His death didn't shift the board—it shattered and confirmed it.

Roxana and Polyperchon were prepared. They had guessed. They had feared. But fear is not the same as knowing.

Now they knew.

Antigonus would move. Demetrius would burn the road ahead of him. The eastern gate was open, and the only thing left to hold it shut was a child tracing lions in ash.

Every plan they carried west—every fragile hope sealed with temple vows or whispered in mountain passes—collapsed in the space between two words.

"Cut down with his back to the Taurus Pass," the man croaked. "His last stand. Held for days. Starved. Tortured. Alone."

His body began to seize. Blood at the corner of his mouth bubbled like something fermenting. The air turned metallic.

"He said—tell the boy…"

The words dragged out of him now, scorched and final, the last heat leaving his body through breath.

"Don't become a shadow of his father. Become his fire."

He died with his eyes open.

Roxana closed them with two fingers. Not gently—just enough to keep them from staring back.

For a long moment, no one moved. The wind passed through the broken walls of the fort like a breath the mountain had been holding.

Polyperchon stood first. His knees cracked when he straightened, but his voice came steady. "That's it then," he said. "The east is open. Antigonus has the highlands."

Roxana didn't answer. She kept looking at the body, as if it might rise and say more. As if it hadn't already said everything.

"It wasn't just a death," she murmured. "It was a handoff. Eumenes knew."

Polyperchon frowned. "Knew what?"

"That it was the boy's turn. His war now. His burden. His story."

The general looked eastward, past the ridge and melting snow, toward the deep folds of the Anatolian plateau—the place where the empire once breathed.

"We haven't had a message from him in months," he said quietly. "Not since autumn. I kept telling myself he was fortifying. Holding the rivers. Waiting for the snow to trap Antigonus."

"No," Roxana said. Her voice was flat now. "He was already surrounded. He just wanted to die close enough that word would reach us."

She rose, brushing snow from her knees. "And now Antigonus will ride west," she said. "Not tomorrow. Not next week. He'll move like a crack through glass."

Polyperchon nodded, still watching the horizon.

"And Demetrius will ride ahead of him. Bright. Fast. Loud. Like a torch."

"And Cassander behind us," Roxana added, "smiling through his teeth. Playing host."

The silence between them thickened. The map was no longer a board of pieces and frontlines. It was a closing hand. A pressure rising, not with battles, but with inevitability—the kind that breaks bloodlines, not walls.

Polyperchon turned to look at the boy, still asleep beside the fire's pale embers. He hadn't stirred once.

"They'll come for him soon," the old general said, almost to himself. "As gods. Or as executioners."

Roxana tightened her cloak, the knot at her collarbone drawn close. "No," she said. "They'll come as liars. And if we're lucky, only one at a time."

She looked again to the east, where the sky was just beginning to bleed with light. "There's no one left to write to," she continued. "Only to carry the letters into fire."

✳✳✳✳✳

The news of Eumenes' death reached Cassander by whisper—through a Rhodian merchant who'd heard it from a grain inspector who'd been bribed by a cavalry quartermaster in Sardis.

Cassander didn't ask for confirmation. He only raised an eyebrow when the name reached him—like a candle guttering out in another room.

"Eumenes. Slain at the Taurus."

He looked down at the map spread before him. It was not a battle map—no banners, no troop markers. Just a merchant's chart of grain flows and port tolls across the Aegean.

"Cut down with his back to the mountain," the advisor added, unsure whether to sound solemn or satisfied.

Cassander let his gaze drift to the edge of the parchment, where Babylon had already been blotted out in red wax.

"He held on too long," Cassander muttered. "That was always his mistake."

He rolled the chart slowly, tying it with a green cord. "Good," he said after a pause. "One fewer priest at the altar."

The advisor shifted, unsure whether to laugh.

Cassander stood, brushing invisible dust from his sleeve. "Antigonus will push now. That's his nature. Forward, forward, always forward."

He turned toward the window, where smoke from the temple quarter rose in straight black lines. "So we won't," he said quietly. "Let him move. Let them all move. I'll be the only one who's still standing."

He rested his hand on the sill. The stone was warm from the rising sun.

Below, the city moved in silence—merchants unloading grain, priests sweeping ash from the steps, soldiers drilling with wooden swords. To Cassander, it looked like order. To everyone else, it smelled like fear.

*****

They left the ridge behind in silence.

Roxana led. The boy rode behind her, lion toy tucked into his cloak, the cracked paw poking out like a wounded talisman. Polyperchon and the loyalists flanked them—no banners, no greetings, only the dull grind of hooves and the soft creak of leather stiff from cold.

As they descended toward the city, a shadow darted across their path.

A fox. Thin. Ragged. Familiar.

The boy leaned down from the saddle and whispered, "Not alone." The animal paused, turned once—eyes glinting gold in the pale light—then vanished into the underbrush.

The farmlands outside Pella were gray with frost and grief. Orchards stood like skeletons. Fields of winter wheat bent under the weight of the wind. Families watched from thresholds but did not step forward. The road that once bore Alexander's triumph still remembered his boots—but the flags lining it had forgotten.

New banners rose along the stone markers: crimson and bronze, stitched with Cassander's sigil—a closed sun, its rays folded inward like a wound that refused to bleed.

At the gate, soldiers waited. Not an honor guard. Not a welcome. Just men told not to smile.

Cassander did not greet them. He sent a magistrate in lacquered armor, pale-faced and stiff. "You are guests," he said flatly.

Roxana studied his stance—the way he avoided the boy's eyes, how his gloved fingers crushed the scroll he never offered.

"Guests," she repeated. "Like prisoners with clean sheets."

The old Argead watchtower still stood at the city's heart, hunched against the skyline like something too proud to fall completely. Its spiral groaned underfoot with each step; lichen crept from the cracks. The wooden railing had rotted in half a dozen places. It wasn't a vantage—it was a theater.

The boy was told to climb alone. Two guards followed him—not beside, not ahead—just behind, close enough to catch him if he fell, but never to reach. Shadows trained not to exist.

Roxana stood at the base, watching until he vanished into the tower's upper chamber. She did not follow. That, too, had been the arrangement.

At the top, the wind hit him first. Bitter. Dry. Reeking faintly of lime mortar and burnt myrrh.

Below, the square spread open like a wound.

Hundreds had gathered. Not in celebration. Not in mourning. Just watching, as if to see whether the ghost they'd heard about could cast a shadow.

The boy stepped forward, pausing. He could see their eyes. Mothers.

Merchants. Children clutching shawls. Temple priests. A scattering of old soldiers with faces like collapsed walls. No one called his name.

He raised his hand. A half-wave. Half-dare.

A ripple moved through the square. Small. Ugly. Human. "He has the look."

"No. He's too soft."

"Still. The eyes…"

"Gods save us, the eyes."

A woman pulled her daughter behind her. A baker turned his back. The old women on the temple steps made the sign of warding—thumb to tongue, palm to sky, three fingers raised.

The boy held the wave a moment longer, then lowered his hand. Slowly. Behind him, one of the guards cleared his throat. A signal.

The show was over.

The boy stood another heartbeat longer. Then let it drop.

*****

That night, they were installed in the old summer palace—Philip's retreat from heat and politics, now reclaimed as a prison with better curtains.

The stone floors sweated with damp. The gardens had turned to rot beneath the ropes. The windows had been nailed partway shut—not for draft, but for control. Even the moonlight was rationed.

Guards posted at every threshold. Their eyes didn't wander. Their hands didn't move. They had been told one thing: watch.

Polyperchon walked the perimeter once. Didn't speak. But when he passed Roxana in the corridor, he gave the faintest shake of his head.

The silence between them now was not tension. It was agreement.

Inside the antechamber, Roxana paced—tight steps, hands knotted behind her back. She didn't look at the boy. Not yet.

He sat on a stone bench before the cold hearth, cloak drawn around him, lion still tucked inside. He hadn't spoken since the tower. But his shoulders weren't hunched. He looked straight ahead, into the unlit fire.

Finally, Roxana stopped. "This city," she said, "remembers too much to love you." The boy didn't flinch. His voice came soft but steady. "But enough to fear me," he said. "That means I'm not gone yet."

He turned toward the window, where the iron crossbar cut half the view. "They still see me," he said. "And that's enough."

She opened her mouth. Closed it. Sat beside him. For the first time that day, she reached for his hand—and let it rest there.

*****

Far to the south, in Alexandria, Ptolemy stood alone on the roof of the unfinished tomb. The stars had come out over the harbor. Sailcloth snapped in the wind below. He looked at the uncarved marble faceplate, then down at the urn in his hand—dust that had once been Alexander's cloak, its fibers glimmering with god-touched thread.

"The bones are mine," he muttered. "But the spirit… still unburied."

Later that night, when the guards had returned to their dice and the oil lamps guttered low, the boy climbed the narrow stair of the tower's northern wing.

The stone steps were chipped from frost and time. At the top waited a room no wider than a chariot wheel—a place once used by scribes to watch for fire.

There was only an arrow-slit now, cut eastward, toward the hills he would never see again. He sat on the ledge until his legs ached. The lion toy rested in his lap, one paw crumbling at the seam.

Below him, the city breathed like something sedated.

The wind shifted—from north to west—carrying the scent of olivewood smoke and the salt kiss of the sea.

He opened his eyes.

A shadow moved at the edge of the square. Too fast to follow. Too real to ignore. The fox again—or something older, wearing its shape.

The boy didn't call out. He touched the lion's head, smoothed its mane with one finger, then turned back to the slit in the wall and watched the horizon for a spark.

EPILOGUE

THE GHOST EMPEROR

They would say later that an Empire ended in Babylon. Or in Macedon. Or perhaps it never ended at all.

Empires fracture, yes. Maps are redrawn. Names are struck from oaths, burned from scrolls, carved from stone.

But something remains—not in the palaces or the tombs, not even in the regents who crown themselves heirs. It lingers in the spaces in between, where stories refuse to die.

A boy once traced stars into dust with a fingertip. An old general called them constellations; the boy saw lions. A mother spoke not of what the world had taken from her, but of what might still be made from ash. A voice sealed in stone echoed laughter when no one was near.

Across mountains and deltas, cities and deserts, something kept moving— quiet, patient, unclaimed. It passed from the mouths of priests to the ears of spies. It bled into songs sung by those too young to remember conquest, but too proud to forget the name that birthed it.

A name whispered like a curse. Or a blessing. Or a question. They built new kingdoms and crowned new kings and queens. They always do, and they always will.

They called the past a shadow—then flinched when it flickered. But for those who listened—in the dust, in the dark, beneath stars long dead—there was always a voice. A Ghost Emperor.

And he did not speak of land.

He spoke of inheritance.

And he waited. And waits still.

*****

Now, two thousand years and more beyond the last Argead breath, the fractures have returned— not of marble, but of meaning. The world no longer splits by sword, but by signal.

Nations unravel not from war, but from forgetting. Maps, imperial and corporate, continue to be redrawn.

We witness not only the fall of cities, but of families and friends—the slow corrosion of myth, of courage, of shared belief. The rituals we once believed in—community, decency, sacrifice—are treated as artifacts. Curiosities. Ghosts. Memes.

But history never needed emperors to survive. It was the unnamed mason who hoisted the stone.

The midwife who whispered warnings. The caravaner who carried gossip across dunes.

The old woman who remembered a name and passed it to her grandson.

It was the ones who did not inherit the world—but sustained it anyway. Call them what you will—commoners, workers, civilians, citizens.

But they are the ones who bear the ember of myth, long after crowns have fallen to rust. And so it matters still.

Because inheritance is not about land. It's not about bloodlines or monuments or laws inked in gold.

Inheritance is the memory we carry forward despite what power tries so hard to forget.

It is the myth of hope that we refuse to bury—the voice we hear in the quiet between headlines, in the courage that rises when the world says it's too late. Or too hard.

The Ghost Emperor does not ask to be remembered.

He asks only that we listen—and decide what we will carry.

—The Author

APPENDIX

Ashes of Empire: Ghost Emperor is rooted in real events—but it is not bound by them. While this novel draws heavily from the historical record, archaeology, and ancient sources, it is first and foremost a work of fiction. It aims to illuminate emotional truths, psychological tensions, and geopolitical consequences that often exceed the constraints of recorded fact.

Alexander's death in 323 BCE is one of the most consequential moments in world history. His empire stretched from Greece to India, yet he died in Babylon without naming a clear successor. The resulting power vacuum led to the Wars of the Diadochi, a generation-long series of brutal conflicts between his former generals—each vying not just for territory, but for legitimacy through his mythic corpse.

Primary sources referenced: Arrian, Diodorus Siculus (Book 18), Plutarch (Life of Alexander), Curtius Rufus, and fragments from Babylonian astronomical diaries.

This appendix serves as a boundary stone marking where record dissolves into vision.

HISTORICAL FOUNDATIONS

THE DEATH OF ALEXANDER (323 BCE). The novel begins at the historical inflection point: the sudden and mysterious death of Alexander the Great in Babylon. The cause—fever, poisoning, or divine retribution—remains unknown and contested. This enduring ambiguity is preserved in the novel as a thematic cornerstone, inviting the reader to inhabit the uncertainty that haunted his successors.

THE PARTITION OF BABYLON AND THE WARS OF THE DIADOCHI. The Babylonian partition, which divided Alexander's empire among his generals, is a documented historical event. Perdiccas was appointed regent for the unborn child of Roxana and Alexander, though others pushed for the elevation of Philip Arrhidaeus. The novel renders this period with close attention to known facts while infusing the rivalries between Perdiccas, Ptolemy, Antipater, Seleucus, and Antigonus with psychological realism. The succession crisis was not merely political—it was spiritual, ritualistic, and drenched in foreboding.

ROXANA AND ALEXANDER IV. Roxana, Alexander's Sogdian wife, and her posthumous son, Alexander IV, became central to dynastic legitimacy. Her assassination of Stateira is widely accepted by historians, and the novel follows this account, while also dramatizing the emotional and political weight of her decisions. Her portrayal reflects both what we know and what we can infer: a woman navigating survival, prophecy, and ambition in a collapsing world.

THE FUNERAL CART AND THE HIJACKING OF THE BODY. Alexander's funeral cart was a real and opulent construction, reportedly taking two years to complete. Described by Diodorus Siculus in lavish detail—with gilded lions, golden chariots, and a canopied bier—it was meant to carry the dead king to Macedon. Ptolemy's interception of the cart and redirection to Egypt is historically attested. In the novel, the cart functions not only as a vehicle but as a relic, altar, and contested object of mythic legitimacy.

CASSANDER'S RETURN AND THE MACEDONIAN POWER STRUGGLE. Cassander, son of Antipater, returns to Babylon in the shadow of Alexander's cult and resentment. His eventual rise as King of Macedon—and his historical role in executing Olympias, Roxana, and Alexander IV—is foreshadowed in the novel through his psychological arc: watching, waiting, loathing. Though the details of his early moves are sparse in the record, his presence is constructed with fidelity to his known ruthlessness.

EUMENES AND POLYPERCHON. Both men played pivotal roles in the wars that followed Alexander's death. Eumenes, once Alexander's secretary, became a loyalist general who waged war for the survival of the royal line. Polyperchon, a more obscure figure, emerged as a mountain-savvy tactician and one of the few to remain aligned with the infant heir. Their arcs in the novel are grounded in the record, with speculative texture where history runs thin.

THE LANDSCAPE AND CULTURES OF BABYLON, EGYPT, AND CAPPADOCIA. The novel's geography—Babylon's palatial sprawl, the ritualized topography of Egypt, the rugged highlands of Cappadocia—is drawn from archaeological evidence, ancient sources, and modern travelogues. These settings are not mere backgrounds. They are active characters in the story: carriers of omen, witnesses of grief, and agents of resistance.

EMBALMING DISPUTES AND RITUAL CONFLICT. Though the exact procedures surrounding Alexander's embalming remain uncertain, the novel extrapolates from the ritual norms of Babylonian, Persian, and Egyptian mortuary traditions. Conflicting practices and theological claims likely collided. The depiction of ritual tensions, omens, and embalming horror is speculative but grounded in plausible cross-cultural friction.

RELIGIOUS SYMBOLISM AND PROPHECY. Omens such as hawk sightings, liver divination, and dream prophecy were central to Mesopotamian and Egyptian worldviews. The gods invoked—Marduk, Ea, Ishtar, Nergal, Ereshkigal—are drawn from documented cult practices. The novel dramatizes these rites to mirror the period's obsession with divine favor, death as passage, and the collapse of cosmological order.

CREATIVE LIBERTIES

INNER LIVES AND DIALOGUE. The private thoughts, personal traumas, and conversations between characters are necessarily invented. Ancient texts offer us outlines—this novel fills in the silences. The voices are crafted to feel plausible within the emotional and psychological registers of the era, filtered through a contemporary lens.

THAIS OF ECBATANA AND OTHER ORIGINAL CHARACTERS. Figures like Thais of Ecbatana (a priestess turned wetnurse) and several camp followers, aides, and minor generals are fictional. They exist to show how imperial politics ripple through everyday lives—and to give voice to those the ancient historians ignored.

THE SCROLL WAR AND OMENS. The mystical and symbolic dimensions of this novel, including recurring omens, protective verses, and the so-called "Scroll War," are part of its mythopoetic frame. These moments reflect ancient ways of understanding fate, legitimacy, and divine will—not modern rationalism.

COMPRESSION OF EVENTS AND CHRONOLOGY. In some cases, timelines are occasionally compressed for narrative cohesion or travel speeds accelerated to maintain narrative tension. The core sequence of events— funeral, partition, wars of succession—remains historically sound, though some timelines are tightened for story logic.

CHARACTER AGES AND INTERACTIONS. The age of Alexander IV is historically accurate within the context of this volume (~2 years old), but his precocious presence and symbolic function are slightly heightened. Likewise, interactions between major players—while plausible—are often dramatized to reveal power shifts and philosophical contrasts.

MOUNT ARGAEUS AND THE ARGAEUM. The mountain temple and the sacred myths surrounding it are grounded in ancient regional cults but rendered with artistic license. The spiritual geography of the Hellenistic world was richly layered, and the novel leans into this interpretive space to evoke ancestral memory and dynastic myth. A place where gods sleep beneath stone, mountains bleed, and memory echoes louder than law.

CHARACTER BY CHARACTER:

THE BABYLON PARTITION AND THE MEN WHO DISMEMBERED THE EMPIRE

The map they drew was not a vision. It was a vivisection. The empire was not passed on—it was pried open. Each name etched into the ledger was also etched into the corpse of Alexander's dream. These were the inheritors, not of ideals, but of logistics. Geography over glory. Proximity over purpose. What follows is both a brief historical grounding and an insight into how each figure is portrayed in Ashes of Empire—as both man and myth.

PERDICCAS

Historical Role: Imperial Regent and bearer of the signet ring.

Territory: None—he ruled over the court and the child.

In the Novel: Perdiccas is the man who tried to hold the center. Trusted by Alexander, feared by none, he wagered that stewardship would outlast ambition. He was wrong. His belief in protocol, in ritual, in cosmic alignment—all of it rendered him vulnerable in a world now ruled by appetite. His authority was abstract, his enemies physical. He became a ghost before he died.

PTOLEMY

Historical Role: Satrap of Egypt, future founder of the Ptolemaic Dynasty.

Territory: Egypt, along with Cyprus and adjacent lands.

In the Novel: Ptolemy is both embalmer and opportunist. He does not mourn Alexander—he repurposes him. His theft of the funeral cart is no mere rebellion; it is an act of symbolic conquest. Egypt suits him: a land where kings become gods, and gods require guardianship. His genius is not military, but narrative. He makes death a pageant. He inherits by desecrating reverently.

ANTIPATER

Historical Role: Regent of Macedon and Greece.

Territory: Macedon and Hellenic territories west of the Aegean.

In the Novel: He is the old mastiff in the courtyard. Too tired to fight, too shrewd to lose. Antipater does not chase power—he waits for it to rot and drift toward him. He sees the rest as boys with daggers playing gods. His loyalty is to the bones of Philip, not the blaze of Alexander. But even bones grow brittle.

SELEUCUS

Historical Role: Appointed satrap of Babylon, future founder of the Seleucid Empire.

Territory: Babylonia.

In the Novel: Seleucus understands infrastructure. Temples, roads, scribes, ledgers—he sees the empire as a ledger waiting to be audited. Babylon, with its priestly archives and decaying grandeur, becomes both crucible and crown. He is patient. He is watching. If Ptolemy wins by spectacle, Seleucus wins by scaffolding—quiet, slow, inevitable.

ANTIGONUS

Historical Role: Satrap of Phrygia, future architect of the Antigonid dynasty, later titled Monophthalmus ("the One-Eyed").

Territory: Phrygia, Lycia, and Pamphylia.

In the Novel: Antigonus is the last of the old war-beasts—scarred, cynical, and vastly underestimated. He did not attend the Babylon conference, but he did not need to. While others bartered over provinces and prophecy, he fortified supply lines and made his son into a spear. Antigonus has no illusions. He does not believe in omens, only in opportunity. He watches the cart, the corpse, the child—and waits. If Ptolemy is mythmaker and Seleucus is engineer, Antigonus is the executor: blunt, methodical, and unsentimental. One eye on the past. One on the throne.

DEMETRIUS

Historical Role: Son of Antigonus, later called Poliorcetes ("the Besieger"). Not yet a major actor at this stage but destined to become king and founder of the Antigonid royal line.

Territory: None at this time, but raised for rule.

In the Novel: Demetrius is war born in human form—a beautiful ruin in the making. Still young in Ashes of Empire, he haunts the margins of the campaign tents like a half-finished prophecy. His father sharpens him daily, not in love, but in legacy. He learns to read maps before myths, to distrust every oath but blood, and to smile while setting sieges. While others dream of empires past, Demetrius dreams of machines to break their walls. He is a future problem made flesh: too charming, too clever, too doomed. A myth being assembled in real time, brick by brick, betrayal by betrayal.

PEITHON

Historical Role: Satrap of Media.
Territory: Media and the Upper Satrapies.
In the Novel: Peithon is the coin tossed into the mountain wind. Young, mostly loyal, mostly unused. His appointment is a litmus test in obscurity. He stands on the eastern lip of empire with too many tribes behind him and not enough messengers ahead. He dreams of clarity but finds only smoke. History might forget him. The land will not.

EUMENES

Historical Role: Appointed to govern Cappadocia and Paphlagonia (though these territories were not yet under control).
Territory: Cappadocia (in name only).
In the Novel: The Greek among Macedonians. The secretary turned general. Eumenes believes in oaths, not outcomes. He is fighting not just for land but for memory—for the right of Alexander's bloodline to continue. His war is metaphysical. His loyalty: absolute. His downfall: likely. But he will not break first. He will be broken.

ROXANA

Historical Role: Bactrian wife of Alexander, mother of Alexander IV.

Territory: None. But she carries the future in her arms.

In the Novel: Roxana is not a pawn. She is a priestess of survival. Her Bactrian blood marks her as outsider; her womb marks her as regent. She sees more than she says. In the highlands and the hush of exile, she begins to sculpt her own myth—one that cannot be erased by men's treaties or their swords.

ALEXANDER IV

Historical Role: Son of Alexander and Roxana, posthumous heir to the empire.

Territory: All of it, in theory. None of it, in practice.

In the Novel: He is not just a boy. He is a relic, a symbol, a threat. A child born into prophecy, protected by wolves and betrayed by cousins. His silence is loaded. His every breath contested. History will kill him, but the novel lets him live—for now—as the last ember of legitimacy.

CASSANDER

Historical Role: Son of Antipater, future king of Macedon, executioner of the royal bloodline.

Territory: Initially none. Later Macedon and Greece.

In the Novel: Cassander is not haunted by Alexander. He is infuriated by him. His whole life has been lived in the shadows of statues. He was sent to study under Aristotle, not to shine. But memory is a poor substitute for victory, and Cassander wants legacy, not lectures. He is slow to rise, but when he does, he carves names off tombs.

PHILIP III ARRHIDAEUS

Historical Role: Half-brother of Alexander, made king in name only.
Territory: None—used as a puppet monarch.
In the Novel: Philip is the body without a mind, the crown without a will. A man yoked to a throne he cannot wield. But in his lucid moments, flickers of sorrow, resistance, even defiance slip through. He is the most tragic figure in the ensemble—born royal, used ritualistically, and doomed to be forgotten.

STATEIRA II (BARSINE)

Historical Role: Daughter of Darius III of Persia, wed to Alexander at Susa in a gesture of empire unification. Her marriage symbolized reconciliation between conqueror and conquered—a merging of dynasties meant to sanctify Alexander's rule across East and West.

Territory: None of her own; her dowry was symbolic—the legitimacy of Persia itself.

In the Novel: Stateira is the bride of empire rather than of a man. A quiet presence wrapped in ceremony and expectation, she embodies the dream of fusion that Alexander proclaimed but never lived to realize. Beneath her composure lies the tragic awareness that her life—and lineage—exist only as instruments of conquest. Her beauty is described not as sensual but ceremonial, a mirror for ambition. When Roxana sends for her under the guise of sisterhood, Stateira comes dressed for reconciliation, not execution. Her death is swift, nearly soundless, a disappearance rather than a murder. In that silence, the myth of unity dies with her.

WORLDBUILDING THE AFTERMATH OF EMPIRE

This was not simply a world without an emperor. It was a world without a center. The death of Alexander did not merely end a reign—it destabilized the very architecture of belief that held the ancient world together. Ashes of Empire builds upon this historical moment by imagining how memory, ritual, geography, and power interact in a fractured cosmos.

THE PSYCHIC RUIN OF THE EMPIRE. While the map may have been redrawn by generals, the psychic map—the one in the minds of soldiers, mothers, oracles, and servants—was left in ashes. The novel approaches empire not as a machine, but as a dream disrupted. Grief, disorientation, hallucination, and prophecy fill the vacuum where command structures once ruled. This is not post-apocalyptic fiction, but post-mythic fiction: a world where the gods may still be speaking, but no one agrees on what they said.

RITUAL AS GEOPOLITICS. Ritual in this novel is not decorative—it is strategic. Embalming becomes a form of propaganda. Temple access denotes sovereignty. An omen seen by one camp but not another can shift the course of war. Worldbuilding here reflects ancient realities: that the metaphysical was political, and that to control a corpse was to control a kingdom.

THE NON-HUMAN CHARACTERS: LANDSCAPE, WEATHER, SILENCE. The Euphrates stinks of memory. The mountain of Argaeus broods with ancestral presence. Silence becomes a weapon in diplomatic scenes. Throughout Ashes of Empire, non-human elements function as emotional vectors, echoing the beliefs of ancient peoples who saw gods in stars, ancestors in hills, and destiny in birds. The world is not just described—it conspires.

LANGUAGES, SCRIPTS, AND FORGOTTEN TONGUES. The novel features whispers in Aramaic, prophecies in Old Persian, and allusions to Sumerian hymns. While rendered in English for clarity, these linguistic echoes hint at a world teetering between translation and transformation. Names are incantations. Seals and scrolls are magic as much as bureaucracy. And the confusion of tongues is not just a Tower of Babel cliché—it is a narrative pressure point in the struggle for legacy.

MYTHOPOEIA IN ACTION

Though grounded in fact, *Ashes of Empire* embraces the idea that history is authored by power, and myth is authored by grief. The novel seeks not to reconstruct what happened, but to channel what it must have felt like to live at the edge of the known world, in the shadow of a dead god, clutching a fragment of memory and daring to call it truth.

Babylonian / Mesopotamian Symbolism

Liver divination (Hepatoscopy) – Already dramatized; Babylonian priests reading omens in sheep livers.

Astronomical Omens / Sky Signs – Babylonian astronomical diaries are cited and serve as both record and prophecy.

Dream Interpretation – Woven into several characters' decision-making.

Silence as Prophecy – Beautifully used as a leitmotif (e.g., silent infants, unread scrolls).

Invocation of Gods – Marduk, Ea, Ishtar, Nergal, and Ereshkigal mentioned appropriately.

Protective Verses and Incantations – Used by Thais of Ecbatana and in Scroll War elements.

Egyptian Symbolism

Embalming Rituals – Accurately dramatized as contested and political.

Funerary Processions as Religious Theater – The cart is treated as relic and altar.

Gods of Death – Anubis, Osiris not named directly but culturally implied in Ptolemy's treatment of the body.

Greek / Macedonian / Hellenic Symbolism

Omens from Birds (e.g., hawks) – Recurring throughout; evokes Aristotelian natural philosophy and Homeric precedent.

Sacrificial Rites – Alluded to in various camp scenes.

Apotropaic Gestures and Charms – Especially among women, guards, and nurses.

Chthonic Myths / Mountain Deities (e.g., Argaeus) – Original but plausible, evoking syncretic Hellenistic mystery cults.

Dynastic Naming / Cult of Personality – Reflected in Alexander IV's symbolic role and Cassander's desecration of memory.

Delphic or Sibylline Oracles (Greek) – Adds pan-Hellenic spiritual frames beyond Babylon/Egypt.

Nabataean or Pre-Islamic Desert Rituals

These will especially appear in later volumes as the Antigonids move further toward Petra, Wadi Rum, and the southern trade routes, and will include incense rituals, blood markings, and moon-based divination.

Zoroastrian Fire Rituals (Media / Persia)

Peithon's satrapy would have been steeped in this. Includes fire temple ruins, eternal flames, and priesthood factions that still honor Ahura Mazda.

Chaldean Astrology

Often overlaps with Babylonian astronomy but more mystical and priest-driven, integrating themes of astrological counsel.

Necromancy or Spirit Rites (Cross-Cultural)

A more speculative or horror-inflected element—someone (perhaps Philip III?) seeking answers from the dead via ritual. Documented in Greek, Persian, and Egyptian sources.

The Ritual of Naming

Especially with royal infants like Alexander IV: this was often ceremonial, involving stars, bloodlines, and divine invocation.

Reading the Dead

To read a corpse is to read a kingdom. *Ashes of Empire: Ghost Emperor* is also a story about interpretation—of signs, bodies, rituals, dreams, and histories. The ancient world did not separate meaning from matter. A liver could foretell defeat. A silence could mark a king. A scroll could kill.

This novel invites the reader to become an ancient interpreter: to read between myths and monuments, between embalmed bodies and vanished heirs. The war for Alexander's empire is also a war over his memory—and the reader is not a bystander.

You, too, are a Diadochus now. Choose wisely.

POSTSCRIPT FOR SCHOLARLY READERS

While this appendix outlines a clear framework of historical foundations and creative liberties, readers familiar with ancient historiography will recognize that many aspects of Alexander's death and its aftermath remain subject to intense debate. The surviving sources—often fragmentary, partisan, or written centuries after the events—leave ample space for both interpretation and contradiction.

A few points of historical contention worth acknowledging:

THE FATE OF MELEAGER. While some accounts suggest Perdiccas ordered his execution after a failed power-sharing arrangement, others imply the decision arose from a broader military consensus—or a chaotic collapse of command. The novel preserves this ambiguity, exploring Perdiccas's authority as both tenuous and haunted.

THE BABYLONIAN ASTRONOMICAL DIARIES. These records provide invaluable glimpses into the period's chronology and celestial interpretations, but their authorship and intent remain debated. Some scholars question their retrospective insertion of political narratives. In the novel, these diaries are treated as both factual records and cosmological symbols—half ledger, half prophecy.

THE DIVISION OF TERRITORIES AT BABYLON. While often depicted as a clear partition, some historians argue the boundaries were more fluid and contested than later records suggest. The novel renders the map as both ledger and battlefield.

THE TOMB OF ALEXANDER. Though classical writers describe its construction in Alexandria, no definitive archaeological evidence has surfaced. The tomb's location—if it survives at all—remains one of the greatest unsolved mysteries of antiquity. Ashes of Empire leans into this absence, treating the body not as buried, but as fought over, reimagined, and endlessly rescripted.

THE ROLE OF OLYMPIAS IN STATEIRA'S DEATH. Roxana is often credited with orchestrating the murder of Stateira (and possibly Drypetis), but some traditions hint at Olympias's involvement. The novel centers Roxana while acknowledging the murky web of alliances and maternal agendas surrounding the royal harem.

THE AUTHENTICITY OF ALEXANDER'S FINAL WORDS. Ancient sources vary: some claim he whispered "to the strongest," others suggest he gave no final instruction. The novel preserves this ambiguity not by choosing a version, but by dramatizing the consequences of uncertainty itself.

THE STATUS OF ALEXANDER IV'S REGENCY. While Perdiccas and later Polyperchon are described as regents for the infant king, it is unclear how much authority was truly exercised on his behalf. The novel imagines a world where the child is both shield and spark—protected by ritual, manipulated by generals, and bearing a name too dangerous to survive.

These uncertainties are not obstacles—they are invitations. Gaps in the historical record offer spaces where narrative can re-enter. Ashes of Empire does not claim to settle these debates; rather, it seeks to stand among them, torch in hand, listening to the ghosts.

FINAL THOUGHTS

History is not a fixed script but a contested archive. The ancient sources themselves contradict one another, shaped by propaganda, personal loyalty, and retrospective bias. Ashes of Empire embraces this ambiguity. It aims not to reconstruct the past with sterile precision but to enter its emotional weather—its grief, its ambition, its belief in omens, and its hunger for power and permanence.

Readers curious to learn more are encouraged to explore primary sources (Plutarch's *Life of Alexander*, Arrian's *Anabasis*, Diodorus Siculus, Justin's *Epitome*) as well as modern histories such as Robin Lane Fox's *Alexander the Great*, Peter Green's *Alexander of Macedon,* and Mary Renault's *The Nature of Alexander.*

What lies ahead in *Ashes of Empire* will carry us further from the known into the mists of dynastic memory. But the foundations remain: stone, blood, and ambition.

BIBLIOGRAPHY

Have you ever written a historical fiction novel with a full bibliography and an appendix detailing all historical foundations and creative liberites? I have. Here's why.

History is not a museum. It's a crime scene. And sometimes, it takes fiction to dust for fingerprints.

When I set out to write Ashes of Empire: Ghost Emperor, coming this fall from Premium Pulp Fiction, I wasn't interested in draping old statues in new robes. I wanted to stand in the wreckage of Alexander the Great's world and ask the uncomfortable questions: What survives when empire collapses? Who decides which names are carved into stone—and which are burned from the record?

This wasn't casual reenactment. This was excavation.

Every chapter stands on a bedrock of ancient sources, cross-referenced accounts, and archaeological debate. And at the end? A full bibliography. And an appendix that openly outlines where creative liberties were taken—why they mattered, and what they allowed us to see more clearly.

Why go to that length?

Because in a world collapsing under bad faith and shallow narrative, it matters to show your work.

Fiction can wound. But it can also heal.

When it's rooted. When it's transparent. When it dares to both honor the record and challenge the silences it keeps.

And because nonfiction, in some quarters—mine included—is being muzzled.

Too many stories are filtered through committees, legal redlines, or paranoid brand optics.

There's a deep, quiet fear—of naming things as they were. Of being honest. Of saying too much while claiming to innovate. Of remembering too well.

But fiction is still dangerous in the right hands. It doesn't need clearance. It only needs courage.

History deserves more than curated narrative. It deserves memory with teeth. And sometimes, the most honest way to do that is through storytelling.

—Douglas Stuart McDaniel
Author. Futurist. Myth excavator.

CLASSICAL SOURCES AND TRANSLATIONS

Arrian. *Anabasis of Alexander*. Translated by P. A. Brunt. Loeb Classical Library. Cambridge: Harvard University Press, 1976.

Curtius Rufus, Quintus. *The History of Alexander*. Translated by John Yardley. London: Penguin Books, 2001.

Diodorus Siculus. *Library of History*, Book 18. Translated by C. H. Oldfather. Loeb Classical Library. Cambridge: Harvard University Press, 1933.

Plutarch. *Life of Alexander*. In The Parallel Lives. Translated by Bernadotte Perrin. Loeb Classical Library. Cambridge: Harvard University Press, 1919.

Justin (Marcus Junianus Justinus). *Epitome of the Philippic History of Pompeius Trogus*. Translated by J. C. Yardley. Oxford: Clarendon Press, 1994.

Babylonian Astronomical Diaries. *In Astronomical Diaries and Related Texts from Babylonia*, edited by Hermann Hunger. Vienna: Austrian Academy of Sciences Press, 1996–2001.

DIADOCHI AND SUCCESSOR KINGDOMS

Anson, Edward M. *Alexander's Heirs: The Age of the Successors*. Oxford: Wiley-Blackwell, 2014.

Billows, Richard A. *Antigonos the One-Eyed and the Creation of the Hellenistic State*. Berkeley: University of California Press, 1990.

Bosworth, A. B. *Conquest and Empire: The Reign of Alexander the Great*. Cambridge: Cambridge University Press, 1988.

Grainger, John D. *The Wars of the Diadochi: 323–281 BC*. Barnsley, UK: Pen & Sword Military, 2018.

Goukowsky, Paul. *The Rise of the Successors of Alexander: 323–281 BC*. Paris: Les Belles Lettres, 2019.

Heckel, Waldemar. *Who's Who in the Age of Alexander the Great: A Prosopography of Alexander's Empire*. Oxford: Wiley-Blackwell, 2006.

HELLENISTIC WOMEN, DYNASTIC MARRIAGES, AND LEGITIMACY

Carney, Elizabeth Donnelly. *Women and Monarchy in Macedonia*. Norman: University of Oklahoma Press, 2000.

Ogden, Daniel. *Polygamy, Prostitutes and Death: The Hellenistic Dynasties*. London: Duckworth, 1999.

Ogden, Daniel. *The Legend of Seleucus: Romance, History and the Founding of the Seleucid Empire*. Cambridge: Cambridge University Press, 2017.

Brosius, Maria. *Women in Ancient Persia: 559–331 BC*. Oxford: Clarendon Press, 1996.

Pomeroy, Sarah B. *Goddesses, Whores, Wives, and Slaves: Women in Classical Antiquity*. New York: Schocken Books, 1995.

RELIGION, RITUAL, PROPHECY, AND DEATH

Assmann, Jan. *Death and Salvation in Ancient Egypt.* Ithaca: Cornell University Press, 2005.

Bremmer, Jan N. "The Rise and Fall of the Afterlife." *The 1995 Read-Tuckwell Lectures at the University of Bristol.* London: Routledge, 2002.

Burkert, Walter. *Greek Religion.* Translated by John Raffan. Cambridge: Harvard University Press, 1985.

Chaniotis, Angelos. *Age of Conquests: The Greek World from Alexander to Hadrian.* Cambridge: Harvard University Press, 2018.

Koch, John, ed. *Celtic Culture: A Historical Encyclopedia* (for distant or comparative rites—e.g., bird omens, silent funerals).

Noegel, Scott B. *Dreams and Dream Interpretation in the Ancient Near East: A Sourcebook.* Münster: Ugarit-Verlag, 2007.

Rochberg, Francesca. *The Heavenly Writing: Divination, Horoscopy, and Astronomy in Mesopotamian Culture.* Cambridge: Cambridge University Press, 2004.

Rollinger, Robert, et al., eds. *The World of Berossos.* Wiesbaden: Harrassowitz Verlag, 2010.

Van der Toorn, Karel. "From Her Cradle to Her Grave: The Role of Religion in the Life of the Babylonian Woman." *In Women in the Ancient Near East,* edited by Mark Chavalas, 209–228. London: Routledge, 2006.

GEOGRAPHY, INFRASTRUCTURE, AND EMPIRE ADMINISTRATION

Alcock, Susan E., John F. Cherry, and John Elsner, eds. *Pausanias: Travel and Memory in Roman Greece.* Oxford: Oxford University Press, 2001.

Ando, Clifford. *Imperial Ideology and Provincial Loyalty in the Roman Empire.* Berkeley: University of California Press, 2000. *While post-Alexandrian, Ando provides useful frameworks for interpreting loyalty and symbolic geography.*

Cohen, Getzel M. *The Hellenistic Settlements in Europe, the Islands, and Asia Minor.* Berkeley: University of California Press, 1995.

Engels, Donald W. *Alexander the Great and the Logistics of the Macedonian Army.* Berkeley: University of California Press, 1978.

Sherwin-White, Susan, and Amélie Kuhrt. *From Samarkhand to Sardis: A New Approach to the Seleucid Empire.* Berkeley: University of California Press, 1993.

Talbert, Richard J. A., ed. *Barrington Atlas of the Greek and Roman World.* Princeton: Princeton University Press, 2000.

MODERN NARRATIVE INTERPRETATIONS

Fraser, P. M. *Ptolemaic Alexandria.* Oxford: Clarendon Press, 1972.

Green, Peter. *Alexander of Macedon, 356–323 B.C.: A Historical Biography.* Berkeley: University of California Press, 1991.

Lane Fox, Robin. *Alexander the Great.* New York: Penguin, 1973.

Renault, Mary. *The Nature of Alexander.* New York: Pantheon, 1975.

ABOUT

PREMIUM PULP FICTION

WHERE TRUTH GETS ITS HANDS DIRTY.

Premium Pulp Fiction is an independent literary imprint dedicated to forensic storytelling — the art of reclaiming what history tried to forget. We publish works that live between literature and reportage, between fiction and the public record. Each story digs through archives, rumors, and memory to uncover the buried moral codes of a place and time.

We believe pulp isn't a genre — it's a promise. It means writing that bleeds, breathes, and refuses to look away. Our books trade nostalgia for evidence, sentiment for clarity, and myth for the difficult grace of the real.

Premium Pulp Fiction champion voices that:

- Confront the tension between truth and narrative.
- Explore regional histories, forgotten women, moral crimes, and civic amnesia.
- Treat landscape and class as living evidence, not setting.
- Balance literary craft with investigative grit.
- We publish anthologies, short fiction, and hybrid works that refuse to separate art from conscience.

Our house voice blends Southern Gothic restraint, journalistic precision, and cinematic moral tension. The prose can be lyrical or lean, but it must always reveal something human, hard-earned, and true.

Premium Pulp Fiction sits where literary craft meets cultural excavation. Think Capote's In Cold Blood edited by Joan Didion, printed on Southern soil. We aren't chasing bestsellers — we're building an archive of the stories that outlast local memory.

FICTION IS HOW WE TELL THE TRUTH WHEN RECORDS LIE.

DOUGLAS STUART MCDANIEL

ABOUT

THE AUTHOR

DOUGLAS STUART MCDANIEL, THE FOUNDER OF PREMIUM PULP FICTION, doesn't write to escape the world—he writes to expose what festers beneath its surface. His stories move through the fault lines of American identity: the haunted towns of the South, the sterile corridors of techno-feudal power, and the digital mirages of our near future.

Born in the shadow of the Appalachian Mountains and raised on fire-and-brimstone sermons, Cold War dread, and dog-eared pulp paperbacks from roadside swap meets, McDaniel came of age between two Americas—our spectral past and our engineered tomorrow. For three decades he's lived in the liminal spaces between them: narrative architect of megacities and the global industries of nuclear, space and civil infrastructure, chronicler of civilization's edge, and now, the voice behind a new canon of forensic, morally charged fiction.

From consulting on smart-city infrastructure in the Middle East to excavating ancient archives in Rome, Cairo, Tangier, Barcelona, and Bahrain, McDaniel's career has been anything but conventional. But the stories never left him—tales of vengeance and revelation, betrayal and reckoning, born in the rot of old Southern ghosts and lit by the hard glow of speculative futures.

With Premium Pulp Fiction, McDaniel tears off the mask. No pseudonyms. No pretense. This is where all of his worlds converge—Southern Gothic epics, prophetic science fiction, and genre-defiant thrillers written not for mass approval but for readers who crave something unflinching.

His debut novel in the Premium Pulp library, *Ashes of Empire: Ghost Emperor,* sets the tone: a prestige historical epic of blood, betrayal, and dynastic collapse in the brutal decades after the death of Alexander the Great—when the body of a god becomes the crown itself.

McDaniel builds worlds with consequence—places that remember you long after you leave. Places where memory is a weapon, and forgetting is fatal.

**WELCOME TO PREMIUM PULP FICTION.
SOME STORIES STAY WITH YOU.
OTHERS COME FOR YOU.**